For my Danish friends,
Luise, Karen, and Steen.
And, as always,
for Michael.

With thanks to Jane Evers who unknow-
ingly gave me the idea, and to Doctor
John Gaynor for his help with the physical
details of Bo.

'Sophie was just fastening my veil to my hair... 'Look at yourself in the mirror.' So I turned to the door: I saw a robed and veiled figure, so unlike my usual self that it seemed almost the image of a stranger.'

Jane Eyre
Charlotte Brontë

DEADLY REFLECTION

'She was a plain woman, and she was
thirty-seven years old. That's all.'

Jenitha Wren wants a husband. Someone
who'll come home every night and still
be there in the morning. When a friend
introduces her to Thomas, a handsome
Dane, she dares to hope she's found him.

Thomas is not free to marry her, but
wants Jen to make a serious commitment
to him. Desperate for affection, she agrees,
blinding herself to growing misgivings
about her enigmatic lover. Together they
travel to Thomas's remote birthplace where
Jen is forced to confront the bleak truth that
her blindness may have led her into mortal
danger.

All characters in this publication are fictitious and any resemblance to real persons, living or dead, is purely coincidental.

DEADLY REFLECTION

by

Maureen O'Brien

Magna Large Print Books
Long Preston, North Yorkshire,
England.

British Library Cataloguing in Publication Data.

O'Brien, Maureen
  Deadly reflection.

A catalogue record for this book is
available from the British Library

ISBN 0-7505-0704-7

First published in Great Britain by Headline Book Publishing
plc, 1993

Copyright © 1993 by Maureen O'Brien

The right of Maureen O'Brien to be identified as the author
of this work has been asserted by her in accordance with
the Copyrights, Designs and Patents Act, 1988.

Published in Large Print 1994 by arrangement with Headline
Book Publishing plc and the copyright holder.

Magna Large Print is an imprint of
Library Magna Books Ltd.
Printed and bound in Great Britain by
T.J. Press (Padstow) Ltd., Cornwall, PL28 8RW.

Chapter One

What I saw shook me.

She was a plain woman, and she was thirty-seven years old. That's all.

I was thirty when I met Jean-Pierre, thirty-four when he left. I hadn't looked properly into a mirror for three years.

'Jenitha Wren was born, grew up, worked in Kentish Town Public Library, retired and died.' My epitaph.

You can't have more of time, only less. It piles up behind you, in dunes. Three of my years had gone by without my noticing, without my living them. That couldn't go on. There were things I wanted, things I needed, things I must do before it was too late.

What I really wanted I was too shy to tell anyone. But...

'What I want,' I said to Ben in the staff room next day, 'is someone who won't just walk out one day without notice. I want someone who'll come home every night and still be there in the morning. I want someone to cook for in the evening—all my lovely cooking going to waste—I want—'

'What you want is a husband,' Ben said.

'Yes!'

'Don't look at me, love. I'm spoken for.'

'Not you,' I said. 'I can't stand the smell of yak.' Ben wore furry sweaters in untreated natural wool.

'Who then?'

'I don't know any husbands. That's the problem.'

'Put a card on the noticeboard,' Ben said.

I went round to James and Margot's after work. 'What I want is a husband,' I said.

'They have their uses, I suppose.' Margot was watching James. 'Mine wields a mean corkscrew, for instance,' she said.

'Husbands?' James sniffed the cork. 'Well, Jen, there are plenty of them about.'

'But they all belong to someone else. I don't want to steal one. I want one all of my own.'

'What's the best way for her to find one, James?'

'What's the best way to find a plumber?' James poured the wine. 'Advertise.'

'That's what I'm doing.' I lifted my glass. 'Cheers.'

Later these larky exchanges gained an ironic significance. At the time they were tumbled in events and forgotten.

Margot dashed into the library. It was eleven o'clock. My break. We went to the café across the road. Luke-warm coffee, ice-cold croissants. Margot didn't notice. She had news.

'Remember Thomas Peterson?' she said.

'Yes.'

'Quiet chap, blond, smokes a pipe would you believe?'

'Yes.'

'You've met him a few times at our parties.'

'Yes.'

'Remember his wife?'

'Yes.'

'Younger than him, rather childlike, big eyes.'

'Elizabeth,' I said.

'Oh, you remember!'

'Yes.'

'Well, she's left him. She's gone.'

'Just like that?'

'Night before last. Wasn't there when he got home. No sign of her. No note. Nothing.'

'They seemed so happy.'

'All married couples seem happy to you.'

9

'Yes.'

'Even me and James.'

'Even you and James.'

'Anyway, I told Thomas to come round tonight. Will you come and help us out?'

'He won't want me there,' I said.

He stood in the kitchen white-faced, holding his pipe, not smoking it.

'How do you know she's left you?' Margot slapped supermarket cheddar on to a thick slice of bread.

'She wasn't happy with me,' he said.

'But people don't just walk out.'

'Oh, don't they?' I said.

'At least Jean-Pierre left you a note.'

'Yes.'

'What's she doing for money?' She clapped another slice of bread on top of the cheese.

'She has money of her own.'

'A lot?'

'Enough.'

'Has she made a withdrawal lately?'

'I don't know.'

'You must find out.'

'Why?'

'I mean, anything could have happened to her.' His white face lifted. 'Thomas, people disappear every day.' She plonked down the cheese sandwich. He looked at it. 'You've got to tell the police.'

10

'She has left me. She has a right to her happiness. I should not prevent her having what she wants.'

James came in.

'Hello, old chap.' He patted Thomas. 'Sorry to hear about— Dreadful thing. Very sorry.'

Margot wouldn't let the subject drop. But Thomas was obdurate. He refused to shop his wife. About nine-thirty I stood up to go. Thomas stood up too.

'If you don't mind I'll walk down the road with you?' he said.

I was horrified. What would I find to say to him?

It was dark. The days had suddenly shortened. There was just a suspicion the summer was past its height, a hint of crispness in the air. Thomas lit his pipe. I was awkward. The silence went on and on, right to the corner of my little street.

'This is where I live,' I said.

'Oh.'

We stood looking at the pretty little houses curving away.

'Would you like a—drink or a—coffee or—?'

I didn't expect him to say yes.

'Oh yes!' he said.

Next-door's dog sat on the step waiting to be let in. Thomas patted him. The dog wagged and fawned. I was surprised. He

11

was a suspicious little wretch as a rule.

'Good old chap,' Thomas said, then something I couldn't understand.

'Is that dog language?' I said.

'Danish.'

'Danish?'

'Yes.'

'Why Danish?'

'I am Danish,' he said.

'But you speak just like an English person.'

'Not quite.'

It was true. He used language carefully, with few shortened forms. It explained his deliberateness. His silences perhaps too.

'How do you speak the language so perfectly?'

'I came here at sixteen. I ran away to sea.'

'How romantic.'

'Not at the time.'

'No, I'm sure.'

'I was poor. I had to survive. The young adapt well.'

'Protective colouring,' I said.

'Just that.'

'So how are you spelt?'

'I'm sorry?'

'Well, I had supposed you Peter*son*, but perhaps—?'

'Ah. Yes. I am. I changed from Peter*sen*. To be more English.'

'More protective colouring.'

'Yes.'

He asked for cocoa as though it were wicked and indeed I was a little shocked. I also gave him my fish pâté on thin slices of wholemeal bread. He ate it easily unlike Margot's cheese sandwich which he had left untouched. Afterwards he said, 'Do you mind if I smoke a pipe?'

'No, of course,' I said though I was dropping on my feet. We didn't say another word until he stood up and thanked me. It was not a conventional thank you. He meant it.

'I hope you'll be all right,' I said.

'Oh...' He shrugged.

On the doorstep he paused. 'I have thought. I will tell the police. Margot is right. They must find out if she is safe.'

'He's told the police!' Margot, next evening on the phone.

'Oh good, I'm glad.'

'What on earth did you say to him, Jen?'

'Not me. You.'

'They asked if any of her clothes were missing. Thomas hadn't thought to look!'

'And were they?'

'A few. He thinks! And a sort of weekend bag. And a pair of shoes. Maybe!'

'So, Margot, she's really left.'

13

'Looks like it.'

'How awful. I wonder where she's gone.'

'Another man. Bound to be.'

'Dreadful not to know.'

'Gruesome enough when you do know.'

'Indeed,' I said.

She got the point. 'Do you ever hear from Jean-Pierre?'

'I get a Christmas card. *Joyeux Noel*. From them both.'

'Oh, lovely. What do you send him? Pretty little jars of salmonella pâté?'

'Too expensive,' I said.

'Darling, you have to forgive and forget.'

'Never happened to you, Margot.'

'No.'

Elizabeth's photo was in the papers: beautiful. Thomas's was a blurred snapshot that could have been anyone. On TV a policeman made an appeal. Could she please ring up to say she was safe? No one would force her to come back. I squirmed. Such an embarrassing position she had put Thomas in.

Margot and James went to Epping to see Thomas. I gave her a chicken in aspic to take to him.

'He won't be eating properly, Margot.'

'You're the limit,' she said.

They dropped in for a drink on their way back.

14

'Well, it's sort of normal there.' Margot was perplexed.

'But very quiet,' said James.

'That's it. As though the whole neighbourhood is waiting. And watching. You can feel all the eyes.'

'It's a depressing part of the world,' said James.

Margot shuddered. 'Sinister,' she said. 'We've told him to come and stay for a bit. He can't stop there.'

'For Christsake, Jen, where've you been? You've got to come and help me out! I can't stand it any more. He doesn't speak. He just sits. He has no social responsibility at all.'

'I should think he's a bit shattered, isn't he?'

'Oh I know. I'm such a monster, not being able to put up with it but I really can't. I can't work. I can't concentrate. I'm going mad.'

I laughed.

'It's not funny,' Margot said. 'Come round tonight.'

Before dinner I sat in the conservatory with Thomas. He said, 'You were away for the weekend?'

'Yes, I went to see my aunt.'

'Where?'

'A little place near Bristol. By the sea. Well, the Severn really but it looks and smells like the sea. I do the heavy gardening for her now.'

'Family is important,' he said.

'She's all I've got.'

His eyes were so compassionate I had to look away. 'This is a nice garden,' I said.

He took the pipe from his mouth, and deliberated. 'Overcrowded. Chaotic.'

'Like Margot,' I said.

He turned and looked at me. After a time he said, 'Yes...like Margot!' as though I had said something really interesting. I felt a fool. To cover my confusion I picked up the book he had been leafing through when I came in. It was a *Felix*.

'Very good, aren't they?' I said. 'And James's illustrations are so clever. They're among the most popular books in the Children's Library, you know. That's how I met Margot. She always comes in to read bits from the latest one to the children, and answer questions. Did you read the last one?'

He said slowly, 'I was just reading this one.'

'*Felix Fights the Foe*. Weren't you engrossed?'

He removed his pipe. 'No.'

'No? Oh.' I was pink with embarrassment. After all, we were guests in the

16

authors' house. 'You—didn't like it?'

I saw that he would have liked to be able to say yes. He tried, then, puzzled, he shook his head. 'It is a children's book, simply.'

I looked at his honest blue eyes and all at once I apprehended that, unlike most of us, he was almost physically incapable of telling a lie, even to flatter, even to be polite.

'You are looking—accusing?' he said.

'Oh, no! Far from it, I assure you.'

He turned away and sighed, thinking of the police, perhaps.

'How are the police getting on?' I said.

'They have found out little. They ask me all my movements in detail before she left. Whether we had quarrelled. Where she might have gone.'

'And where might she have gone?'

'Do you know, I have no idea. You see, her parents died before we married. She has no aunt even, as you have. I thought she had no friends.'

'No friends!'

'No, but there is a girl who worked in the local hairdresser's. The police tell me they met for coffee and so on. She didn't tell me about this girl. I never knew.'

'Did the hairdresser know where she might go?'

'Receptionist, it appears.'

'Oh.'

'She knows nothing. Except, she says, that Elizabeth was unhappy. That she cried sometimes and said—how terrible life was with me.'

'Oh no!'

'She complained to this girl that I was away too much, she was alone. When I was there, she was—still alone.'

'Still alone?'

'Because I didn't speak to her, she said. I ignored her.'

'And did you?'

My boldness surprised me.

'She wanted all my attention. She wanted me to give up my job and spend all my time with her, live on her money. I couldn't do that.'

'Oh, no.'

'We could travel, she said. She had such dreams.'

'Oh dear.'

'Yes. Oh dear. And now she's gone.'

'Do you think the hairdresser girl is lying, to give her time to—escape?'

His blue eyes opened wide.

'Good heavens. It's possible, I suppose. But I don't think so. The police believe what she said. The police are not stupid after all.'

'You think not?' Margot sped in with olives.

18

'The man in charge struck me as quite shrewd,' Thomas said.

'Such touching faith, darling.'

'I have to trust them, Margot.'

'Oh Thomas, I'm sorry. I'm an insensitive bitch, crashing on. Take no notice. Can I get you another drink?'

Margot had been knocking back the wine herself. I went to the kitchen to the make the spaghetti sauce. If I didn't we might not eat that night.

'That's what I need, a truly domesticated woman.' James made me jump. He'd been working in his studio on the top floor.

'All going to waste,' I said cheerfully.

'It's tragic, Jen. Got to find you somebody.'

'I don't think you've been putting your minds to it.'

'How about——?' He gestured towards the conservatory where Margot could be heard entertaining a silent audience. 'Lively chap,' he said.

We laughed quietly.

'You're terrible,' I said.

'I know.'

It was a silent meal. Margot had run out of steam. James was lost in thought. Thomas and I, in the presence of the others, had nothing to say to each other.

Chapter Two

'Have they really found no trace of her?' James said.

We sat round the detritus of a meal a week later on a blowy night. Thomas shook his head.

'They have asked every neighbour, every station and bus person, shopkeepers in Epping. Nothing.'

'It's as though she's been spirited away.' James shivered. 'Almost supernatural. Shows how easy it is.'

'Easy?' Thomas looked at him.

'Yes, if you wanted to disappear—'

'No, James, I think not easy. I think she must have planned. For weeks. To get away without being seen. It's not so easy. The neighbours are retired busybodies without much to do. They spend much time at their net curtains. She had to find, she must have found, the perfect moment to go.'

It was a long speech, for Thomas. The picture he evoked, of that pretty young girl sitting alone day after day, plotting her flight, watching the neighbours watching her, was both creepy and pathetic. We were quiet.

'What do the police think?' James said.

'The police suspect me of doing away with Elizabeth.'

The statement dropped like a stone. Ripples of silence circled it.

'Christ,' Margot said at last.

'They question me every day. Even at the office now. They question my colleagues, everybody. It will soon be you.'

Margot scowled. 'What shall we say?'

'Say the truth.'

'The truth about what? What will they ask?'

'How long you've known me, my character, was I happy with Elizabeth. Oh, I don't know.'

'Christ.'

'Do they "take you in for questioning"?' James said.

'I have been taken to the station once. Mostly they drop in to the house. Now to the office too.'

'Ugh!' Margot shuddered.

'It's okay,' Thomas said. 'They have to do this, I suppose. Such a sudden disappearance.'

'I'm sorry now I told you to tell them.'

'Oh no, Margot, you were right. If I had left it longer to report her missing, this would be worse.'

'But, darling,' Margot voiced her thoughts,

'are they looking for— What are they looking for?'

'They did a forensic examination of my car.' Thomas's voice ran out.

Margot recovered first. 'Well, they didn't find anything horrid, did they, darling?'

'No, of course not.'

'Well then that's okay.'

'*It's not okay!*' Thomas's anger made him paler. Margot almost shrank back.

'It's not okay,' he said, quieter. 'It has made me feel...ohh...' He rubbed his forehead, rested his head on his hand. Then he looked up. 'All I wanted was to find out if she was all right. I'm sorry. I did not know I would shout.'

It was time to leave. Late, even. I didn't like the jagged feeling in the room.

It had become a habit for Thomas to walk me back to Kelly Street: 'To keep you safe and to get some air.' His monumental lack of need for speech was impressive. We didn't speak at all, that night. Eventually awkwardness fell away, even for me. We just stood at my corner, like two horses in a field. At last he said, 'Well...'

'You won't come in?' I was dead tired, being polite.

'No thanks, it's late. And not fair on you.'

'How?'

'You might be questioned too.'

'Oh. You mean...?' I looked over my shoulder at the dark between the street lights.

'I feel—always watched,' he said. He sounded tired and looked it.

'I wish I could help,' I said.

'You do.'

He put out his hand. It was a warm hand. It swallowed mine, a minnow in the belly of a whale. He waited till I had got into my house, gave more a salute than a wave, then plodded off back to Margot and James. I had just locked my door when the policeman phoned.

James rang a few minutes later.

'When are they coming to you?' I said.

'Ten-thirty.'

'I'm first then.'

'Nothing to be afraid of.'

'Why didn't the silly girl just leave, like a civilised person?' I said, 'Get a separation or something? Tell somebody?'

There was a small silence.

'Yes,' James said.

'James— What are you—?'

'Nothing. But...'

'James, you know the man.'

'No one knows anyone.'

'James!'

'I don't mean I think he—did anything to her. It's just that one really doesn't know.'

'I profoundly disagree.'

'You can't disagree with a fact, Jen.'

'I don't think he's capable of deceit.'

There was a pause. James considered.

'No, I think you're right,' he said.

I woke at two, at four, at five-thirty; and at six I got up. I cleared leaves, cut back dead wood. I tied up the tentacles of climbing roses loosing their petals like snow flakes. I heard the doorbell ring.

He was a tall man with a long sad face, dressed in a suit. The blonde girl with him was in uniform. They filled my little hall.

'Grant, Epping CID. Sorry to disturb you at this hour. Just a few routine questions,' he said.

I took them into my living room which suddenly seemed smaller too.

'You've known Mr Peterson long?'

'A few years. I suppose three or four.'

'Would you say you knew him well?'

'Well, no. Not until these last few weeks, since... No, not really, no.'

'How did you meet?'

'Oh, at James and Margot's parties. I often found myself talking to Thomas and Elizabeth. Sometimes for hours. In the conservatory usually.'

'In the conservatory, hmm?'

He was teasing me. I felt better. I smiled.

24

'What did you talk about?' he smiled back.

'I don't know. Living in London, the advantages of the suburbs and vice versa. It's so hard to remember what one talked about. Yes! Travel! Elizabeth said how much she wanted to "take off" as she put it, travel the world.'

'Oh yes?'

I blushed. I could feel it, burning my neck and face. 'You think I'm lying!' I said.

'I'm meant to think that everyone's lying. It's what they pay me for. Calm down. As a matter of fact, I believe you. Can't think why.' He leaned forward and grimaced at me as at a fractious child. His face was like one of those sponge rubber masks. You put your fingers inside from behind and twist it into any expression you want. 'If you can bear it,' he said, 'please carry on.'

'We talked about gardening once. Thomas is keen on gardening.'

'And so are you.'

'Yes. Oh.' I took off my gardening gloves.

'And Elizabeth? She keen on gardening too?'

'No. Thomas and I were persuading her to try it. Everyone thinks it's boring till they try it.'

25

'Some of us think so *after* we've tried it.'

The policewoman smiled.

'Elizabeth would have agreed with you,' I said.

'So where did Elizabeth want to travel to?'

'I don't think she mentioned anywhere specific. She might have said something about Kashmiri house boats. Or maybe that was me. It's so hard to recall who said what.'

'And what was Mr Peterson's reaction to these notions of travel?'

'Well...he would just look fondly at her. I think he said. "If only one didn't have to work", or something like that. And she said, "One doesn't", and he said, "Man cannot live by bread alone", and she said to me, "You see, he's a terrible old stick in the mud. I can barely get him to go to Brighton for the day, let alone Katmandu." She may not have said Katmandu, but somewhere like that.'

'It was a quarrel then?'

'Oh no! It wasn't. She was smiling up at him. She was sitting on the floor. Her hands were on his knees. He touched her hands. They were both smiling. They seemed happy, to me. It wasn't a quarrel. Really not.'

'When was this?'

'About Easter, I think it was. James and Margot's last party. Yes, about four months ago.'

'Have you ever been to Mr Peterson's house in Epping Forest?'

'Yes. Once. A long time ago. Years. Their house-warming party.'

'How did it strike you?'

'How did what strike me?'

The rubbery face twisted itself into a grin. 'The house, the place, the party...'

'I didn't like the place. I couldn't live surrounded by trees. Elizabeth had made the house nice though. Pretty cushions and things. But nothing was quite finished. Well, they hadn't been there long. There were lots of flowers everywhere. Thomas said she'd stripped the garden bare.'

'Had she?'

'I couldn't see the garden, it was dark.'

'He was angry with her?'

'Angry? No! He had his arm around her. He was tender to her. Terribly. Always.'

'Okay okay. Was it a good party?'

'I don't know. I think it was all right.'

'Nice people there?'

'Yes, I think so. Margot and James and some people I see at their parties. Some computer people from Thomas's firm.'

'What were Elizabeth's friends like?'

I stared. 'I don't think I met any of Elizabeth's friends.'

'No friends of Elizabeth's?'

'I don't think she had many friends. Thomas said recently she didn't. It worried him.'

'Ye-es,' he groaned. 'Anything else?'

'I suppose I'm rather unobservant, but I thought they were really in love. Very happy.'

He got to his feet with a grunt. The girl had been perched on a chair arm. She smiled at me. He handed me a card.

'If anything else springs to mind, that's my number. Nice talking to you.'

He walked like a rubber man, loose and bouncy. Before he opened the front door he said, 'You've been seeing a lot of Mr Peterson in the last few weeks.'

'Well, yes. James and Margot have sort of been—looking after him. And I've been—sort of helping out.'

'A friend in need, hmm?'

I just looked at him. I didn't know what to say.

Margot came at lunchtime. We went to the café opposite the library.

'What a gorgeous man,' she said. 'Those mournful brown eyes, that subtle face.'

'Rubbery,' I said.

'You didn't like him!'

'What did he ask you?'

'How Thomas met Elizabeth. Don't

28

know. How they got on. Don't know. Were there signs of her wanting to leave. Don't know. Did they quarrel. Don't know.'

'Was there anything you did know?'

'Yes! What sort of person was Thomas. Boring! Thomas could bore for England.'

'Denmark.'

'What?'

'He's Danish,' I said, just to see the look on her face.

On Saturday Margot asked me to a celebration lunch.

'Celebrating what?'

'Find out when you get here.'

It must be the publication of their latest book. I took champagne. Thomas was there. We stood in the kitchen.

'Now,' Margot said. 'To Thomas.'

We raised our glasses.

'Why to Thomas?' I said.

'He's become inactive, darling! Isn't it wonderful?'

Thomas explained: 'The file of some missing persons is called active. That is, the police are looking hard suspecting people etcetera and so on.'

His English had slipped, the only sign of excitement, or champagne.

'Yes!' Margot said. 'And now Elizabeth's file has become inactive. They're letting her and Thomas get on with their lives in peace. I knew my charm must have been working on that policeman. They're just trained not to show it.'

'Oh Thomas, I—Congratulations—I suppose. It's...' I petered out. After all, it meant Elizabeth might never be found. Thomas was just where he had been, after a month of being suspected of—who knew what? He looked at me. I saw he was thinking the same. But playing the game for Margot's sake. And after all, it must be a relief to be returned to the ranks of ordinary human beings, unquestioned, un-spied on, un-followed. Unhappy.

We all laughed a lot for a short time as one does with champagne. I've never really liked champagne, the taste of death in it, the false joy before the bubbles fade.

James and Thomas melted into the conservatory as men tend to do when women start to prepare food.

'Know what I'm celebrating?' Margot pulled a lettuce apart in reckless handfuls. She spoke in a hoarse whisper.

'What?'

'Getting Thomas off our backs! I hope my gladness doth not show too much.'

'I don't think he'd suspect.'

'He's nicer than me, you mean.'

'I didn't say that,' I smiled.

'No, but you meant it, you tactful cow, and you're right. But, oh God, I'll be glad not to see him for a week or two.'

But his life could be even emptier with the police off his back. I imagined him going back to that house in Epping Forest every night, the woods closing in.

'We're off to Wales on Wednesday!' she said at dinner, making sure.

'For a fortnight,' James said.

They had a cottage in Pembrokeshire.

On impulse that night at the corner of my street I suggested an outing to Kew Gardens next Sunday.

Thomas nodded thoughtfully, took out his pipe, nodded again with decision and said, 'Yes. Thank you. That would be very nice.'

Chapter Three

The streets were Sunday morning silent, silver with dew and ankle-deep in litter. There was hardly a soul at Kentish Town West but at Hampstead the little train began to fill. Voices rose in pitch with the holiday mood. At Kew, children and dogs fell over each other in their eagerness to be off. In the wide sunny street outside the station people ate breakfast at café tables. A waitress flapped a tablecloth and sparrows scattered like leaves.

Thomas was sitting in his car. He stared ahead, unseeing, naked without his pipe, defenceless, as some people are without their spectacles. He was handsome, his mouth firm in sorrow. He turned his head. He saw me, first without expression, then with a slow smile. He got out of the car. I felt shy.

'It was nice on the train,' I said.

'Yes?'

'Holiday atmosphere. Just Sunday, I expect. And the lovely day.'

'Ah. Yes.'

'Shall we walk to the gardens?'

He locked the car, checking all the doors and the boot. There was something curled on the back seat. It was just a coat. But I thought of the forensic men, the fingerprint dust, every hair removed for examination. I looked away.

'Was there much traffic?' I said it for something to say.

'When?'

'On your way here.'

'Oh no, I drove here in record time.'

I felt panic. I had invited a stranger out for the day. We had nothing in common, nothing to say.

We passed large Victorian rooms with marble fireplaces, white bookshelves, bowls of roses on gleaming pianos, glimpses of gardens beyond.

'Handsome houses,' I said.

'I'm sorry?'

'These houses. Lovely, don't you think?'

'Oh.' He looked about. 'Yes, they are nice.'

'The palm house is closed,' I said.

'Palm house?'

'The lacy thing that looks as though it dropped from the sky.'

'Oh.'

There was no sign of the recent hurricane, apart from the little black figures that crawled over the palm house roof, mending its airy shapes.

A man at the lake threw bread in the air. A seagull caught it on the wing, not halting in flight. I laughed.

'Why do you laugh?'

'I don't know, Thomas. Sun, sky, seagulls. I don't know.'

'You regret you asked me today.'

'No!'

'I think so, yes. I am slow and sadness makes me slower.'

Shame slapped me.

'Come on.' I even took his arm. 'We'll eat lunch in the grass garden. You'll like it there.'

We sat on a bench where the pampas fronds waved over us. Concorde zoomed above.

33

'Beautiful,' Thomas said.

'But such a noise,' I shouted.

'I'd like to see it every day.'

'Move to Kew then.'

When the roar had ceased, I said, 'Seriously, will you move?'

'Move?'

'House.'

'Oh no. I can't. If Elizabeth wants to come back, where will she come?'

'Do you like it there? In your house?'

I thought of the dark forest, looming.

'I like the forest,' he said.

'Not lonely?'

'Lonely, yes, but I am waiting, of course.'

I opened the basket, took out the sandwiches, my mother's damask napkins, the silver salt and pepper pots, the blue paper plates. Thomas ate.

'You had no breakfast, Thomas!'

He looked sheepish.

'That's naughty,' I said.

'Yes.'

We finished with my lightest Victoria sponge, to which he said, 'Excellent.'

'I seldom bake cakes,' I said.

'But you knew I was coming.'

I stared. A joke. 'Thomas!'

He almost smiled.

He stretched out his legs and started to light his pipe. I wandered along the little oblongs of grass, reading their names. 'Sheep's fescue'. 'Bored creeping red fescue'. I laughed. 'Look, Thomas, "Danish smooth stalk meadow grass"! Now you should feel at home.'

He came to my side. He looked for a long time at the green oblong.

'She won't come back,' he said.

'Oh Thomas.'

'But I have to wait in case she does. You see.'

'Yes, I do see that.'

He straightened his back, braced his shoulders.

'Also,' he said, 'I have to harvest the last of the summer vegetables.'

I managed not to laugh.

In the Duke's Garden the blue border was a haze of colour, butterflies in the michaelmas daisies, bees in the salvia. Thomas walked quietly at my side.

'Don't you find it lovely?' I said.

'Flowers.' He stood still. 'They are so strange to me.'

For some reason I thought of Elizabeth who was like a flower: fragile, decorative, colourful.

'Strange?' I said.

'Yes.' He stooped. 'They are too—' he fingered an autumn crocus, '—too delicate. They frighten me.' A petal fell from the flower. He pulled his hand away. The other petals fell. 'Their lives are so short,' he said.

'They're strong too, in their way. It wasn't flowers uprooted by the hurricane, it was trees, big trees.'

'They bruise, the flowers. They blemish. They bleed.

'Bleed?'

He covered his eyes.

'She is not coming back,' he said. He was on his haunches. I stooped next to him. I touched his back. I, who never dare to touch. He was so vulnerable. He was desolate. There was nothing to say.

Another silver bird roared over us, shattering the garden silences. I led him by the hand to a bench. We'd been sitting some time before I noticed that my hand was still holding his. How was I to free us without embarrassment?

'Thank you,' he said.

'Oh heavens for what?'

He removed his hand from mine and rubbed his face.

'Have the police quite gone now?' I asked,

'Yes. Police, newspapers, television, everything. All gone.'

'It must have been—'

'Terrible. Yes, it has been terrible. And now it only just begins. The finding how to live afterwards.'

'Yes,' I said, 'I know all about that.'

'How do you know about it, Jen?'

And I found myself telling him about Jean-Pierre.

'He was younger than me,' I said. 'Only four years but it seemed a lot. I adored him so. I used to wake up in the morning and see his head on the pillow and I could hardly believe how lucky I was. The feeling was so—I don't know—acute, it actually hurt. He loved me too. I know he did, I know.' I started to cry. I couldn't stop. Thomas pushed a big white handkerchief into my hands. I covered my face with it. 'So embarrassing. So sorry,' I said.

'I'm not embarrassed.' He waited for me to subside. 'And why had he left?' he said.

'He'd known this girl all his life. They were at school together. She had married young. To a man older than she was. When her marriage broke up she started writing to Jean-Pierre. Each of his holidays to Paris to see his parents he was meeting her. It was going on for three of the four years we were together. And I didn't know.'

'He didn't tell you of this girl?'

'Not a word. Not a hint. Nothing. They had planned the date of their wedding before he left me.'

'You mean he left you without telling you?'

'I came home one evening from work. He didn't come in. It got later and later. No phone call. Nothing. In the end, very late, I went up to bed. There was a note on my pillow.' I blew my nose again. 'It said he was getting married in Paris next week.' I laughed.

Thomas's eyes were unbelieving.

'Oh yes, it's true. He sent me a fuller letter later, sort of explaining it. Do you know, he had never told his parents about me? In four years. For some reason that was what hurt me most of all.' My voice shook. 'I don't know why.'

'Poor Jen.'

'Yes, a pathetic tale. Almost Victorian really. Like me. I should have been took with the green sickness and wasted away, but I survived.'

'This man was a monster,' Thomas said.

'Oh no, just weak. I knew that all the time really. I didn't mind. It was the having lived a lie I couldn't bear. It gave my world such shaky foundations. Chasms opened everywhere.'

'Oh yes,' he spoke with feeling. 'A person living two lives and one of them a secret from you. That is a cruel thing.'

'Yes.'

I looked around. The sun was still shining. The sky was still blue.

'The world didn't end,' I said. 'Though at the time I wished it would. It doesn't end. It just goes on and on. And after a while you're glad it didn't end. Really you are. Patience is what you need. One day at a time.'

'If she were dead, at least I could mourn.'

'Yes. Betrayal is in some ways harder to accept than death. After all, people can't help dying.'

I had been folding his hankie carefully in four then eight then sixteen. It was an inch-thick wet cube now, clenched in my fist. I felt shaky.

'Sorry,' I said. 'I don't know why I told you all that.'

'You said it to help me.'

'No such thing.'

'Oh yes, I think.'

'Oh. And does it? Help you?'

'No. Not yet.'

'Well, it helps *me*. It's the first time I've talked of it. In quite that way.'

'And to be kind to me you talked of it.'

'Not kind!'

We were tired. Long shadows stretched along the grass. People still poured through the gate. A queue a hundred yards long. I felt we had been there more than a day. I refused a lift: 'I have my return ticket.'

My nerves were scratched. I felt a little bruised, like Thomas's autumn crocus, as he drove away.

He rang on Thursday night.

'Thank you for Sunday,' he said.

'Not at all. Thank *you*. What have you been doing?'

'Nothing much.'

Silence.

'Are you back at work?' I tried.

'Oh yes.'

Longer silence.

'Are you still there, Thomas?'

'Yes, I—I was ringing to ask if you would like to go—somewhere—at the weekend.'

'Oh Thomas, I'm sorry, I'm going to my aunt's. I'm setting off after work tomorrow.'

'Oh, if you have already made arrangements of course—'

After I put the phone down, remorse struck me. I rang Aunt Jess.

'Oh, poor man. We must cheer him up!' she said.

So I called him back. He was touched, which had the effect of making him more silent than before.

'You can drive us,' I said, to comfort him.

Aunt Jess lived in a small Georgian house,

its back to the cliff, its face to the sea. A canopy on fine iron legs protected the ground floor window and front door from the glare and the wind.

She was a tiny woman, my aunt, but because she brought me up and had therefore been for the first part of my life much bigger than me, her tiny proportions were now, each time I saw her, a surprise. She enfolded me in the doorway, a sparrow hugging a pigeon.

'Darling Jen. Thomas, I'm delighted. Come in.'

The garden was narrow, like the house, and long. I walked down to the apple tree, laden now, apples in the grass and on the path. I bit into one. It was a Worcester Permain, not quite ready but good. I sniffed the air. How entrancing it was, the falling dark, the rising moon. Home. Happiness...I jumped. Thomas had arrived at my side without a sound.

'You gave me a fright.'

'You were absorbed.'

'Yes. Enchanting, isn't it?'

'You like it here.'

'I'd live here if I could.'

'Why can't you?'

'Library jobs are hard to come by these days. I'm lucky to have mine. Even harder outside London. Libraries everywhere are closing down. But one day...'

41

'Perhaps it is just a comforting dream, living here.'

'What do you mean?'

'You just want to dream about it, not live it.'

'Yes, perhaps,' I said.

I threw the apple away.

Outside the French windows he stopped me. 'I have said something wrong?'

'I don't know.'

'I have made you desolate.'

I suddenly laughed.

'Why do you laugh?'

'You're so—accurate.'

'Why is that funny?'

'I don't know. It's a word an Englishman would never use.'

'But the right word?'

'Yes.'

'I am so sorry.'

'I'm not desolate any more.'

'Oh. That's good!'

Supper was roast lamb, roast potatoes, runner beans from the garden, peas from the garden with the garden mint.

'You and Jen are equally excellent cooks,' Thomas said to my aunt.

She blushed and almost wriggled. I smiled at her.

'I taught Jenitha the basics,' she said. 'But she's better than me now.'

'I'm not better.'

'Oh yes, Thomas. She's gone beyond me.'

'You—brought her up?'

'Oh yes! Hasn't Jen told you?'

She left the room, a little flustered, to take the plates and fetch the pudding.

'My parents died when I was seven,' I said.

'How did they die?'

'In a car crash.'

'This must have been terrible.'

'Don't make me desolate again,' I smiled. 'It was thirty years ago.'

'Oh. Yes.'

My aunt came back. Thomas took the tray from her, pulled out her chair. After the perfect apple pie he sighed, stretched his legs and took out his pipe. Aunt Jess's eyes became round with dismay. She had a horror of smoking. The smell made her sick. But she hated to be impolite.

I said, 'Shall we have a stroll in the garden, Thomas? Or down on the seafront perhaps?'

'Oh.'

Though perplexed and reluctant, he agreed. My aunt grew larger with relief.

'Put on a jacket, Jen. The nights are cooler than they seem.'

'Oh, deceptive nights,' I said.

We went down the sloping street, the sea on our right. How good it smelled.

I liked the smell of Thomas's tobacco, too, drifting across the foreground of my senses.

'Why did we have to come out?' His silence had lasted a good five minutes.

'I'm sorry, I should have warned you. Aunt Jess doesn't like smoking in the house.'

'But why did she not say?' His voice was horrified.

'She's too polite.'

'And you also were too polite.'

'I suppose so, yes.'

'I should have asked permission.'

'Now *you* are desolate.'

'Yes, I am.'

He leaned his elbows on a railing, put his head in his hands. His hands covered his ears.

'Thomas, it's not as bad as that.'

'Oh God. Oh God.' He sounded as though he might weep.

'Thomas, it's a tiny breach of etiquette, that in any case is my fault! How can it matter this much?'

'I loathe this, I loathe this.' His body squirmed.

'What do you loathe?'

'To get things wrong. Not to do the right thing. The right thing.'

I began to feel distressed.

'Thomas, please.' I touched his arm.

44

Suddenly he stood straight.

'Oh,' he breathed out, 'you must think...I don't know why I am so affected by this. But your aunt seemed so kind. Has been so kind.' He gave a gasp or laugh. 'I hate to get things wrong.'

'You've been through a lot of strain recently. Your nerves must still be bad, I should think.'

'Yes. Yes.' He pushed a hand through his hair. The moon was behind him, its light outlining him. He seemed a true Viking, standing there. Tall, strong, blond, straight.

'Let's go back.' I smiled at him. 'If you've smoked enough, that is.'

He was not amused.

'And you?' He was abject. 'You hate tobacco too? I never even thought to ask.'

'I love it,' I said.

'I wish people were not polite,' he said. We were halfway back up the steep street. I still saw him as a Viking: strong, simple, too straightforward to cope with the complicated commonplaces of ordinary English life.

He carefully emptied his pipe outside the gate and put it away.

He offered to wash up. My aunt normally refused guests' offers of help. She accepted his.

'Why?' I asked her in the dining room.

45

'He wanted to make amends, poor man.'

He made amends the whole weekend. He carried her shopping bag, he fixed a washer on the bath tap, he washed up, it seemed, continuously. He even on Sunday organised a bonfire in the garden. We had fun. Aunt Jess most of all. At the door on Sunday evening she put both her tiny hands in his.

'I have so enjoyed this weekend.' She look up into his face. 'Do come again, Thomas.'

I got into the car. We waved goodbye. My aunt looked so small in her pretty doorway. So alone.

We were on the M4 before Thomas spoke.

'How old is your aunt?'

'Seventy. Oh dear.'

'Seventy is not so old.'

'No, but she's all I have. And one thinks how little time there is left.'

'It is good you think this.'

'Why?'

'It makes you cherish her while she is here.'

'She liked you very much,' I said. 'She is usually rather reserved with people she doesn't know. Doesn't know well.'

'She liked your—French man?'

'Jean-Pierre? Afraid not. It was depressing. She wasn't rude, you know. She could

46

never be that. In fact, Jean-Pierre had no idea. But I knew.'

'But with me?' he said. 'Perhaps you are deceived? Perhaps again she is merely being polite?'

'No no, Thomas, I'm not deceived. How could I be? She likes you exceptionally much. But why does it matter so much to you? She's only my little Aunt Jess.'

'She is a good woman. She is your aunt. And I made this stupid error.'

'Oh, I see.'

But I didn't properly understand.

Chapter Four

'We're back! Couldn't stand the country another minute. Filthy place. Wellies and log-chopping. James saw a snake under the terrace. It was the last straw. Isn't London wonderful? All this lovely brown air and exhaust fumes, I feel quite renewed. Come and eat on Saturday.'

'Thomas is coming here,' I said. 'You and James come too.'

'My, how dutiful you are. Can't.'

'Why not?'

'James has invited someone else.'

'Oh drat.'

'Strong language! Bring Thomas here.'

When I got there Margot was still in the bath. James gave me a drink and took me through to the conservatory. Standing at the window looking out was a small wiry man with a neat dark head. He wore a waist-length leather jacket. There was something about him I immediately disliked. He turned his head. His eyes were small and brown with a hard humorous glitter, as meaningless, I guessed, as a nervous tic.

'John Bright,' James said.

We shook hands. His hand was small, warm, dry, and surprisingly strong. He had a face my aunt would describe as common: narrow, dark, with a wide tense mouth.

'Must get a lot of trouble with your name.' His voice had a horrible nasal London twang.

'Yes, I do.'

'Jenny Wren. Parents had a sense of humour, did they?'

'I'm afraid not. No.'

'A-ha.' The eyes glinted at me. I thought I detected a slight squint. His back was to the light so I couldn't be sure.

'Do you live nearby?' I said, for something to say.

'Bit upmarket for me round here. I rent an armpit in Crouch End.'

He obviously intended to amuse. Indeed, James laughed.

I said, 'Oh.'

'Staying with my ma in South Norwood at the moment, just until I—' His voice petered out. He rubbed a hand over his face and turned to the window again. He downed his drink in one gulp and held out the glass to James. 'Like to top this up, old lad?'

'Going at it a bit, John, aren't you?'

'Certainly am. The elixir of life. Don't you think so, *Miss* Wren?'

Objectionably, he put the Miss, as it were in quotes. Why the 'Miss' at all? I wondered.

'Jen,' I said.

'A-ha.' He raised an eyebrow. What was so funny?

'No, I don't think so,' I said. 'I prefer wine.'

'Wine's okay but the hit is slower, don't you find?'

'What do you do, Mr Bright?'

'John,' he said.

'What do you do? John.'

'I'm a policeman. Jen.'

I felt a stirring behind me. John Bright's eyes shifted, swift, like an animal's. I turned my head. Thomas was standing there, large, calm, pipe in hand. I hadn't heard him come in. I introduced them.

They shook hands. Silence had entered with Thomas. It settled like a large dog in the middle of the room. No one could step over it or squeeze round it. The policeman stood jingling the change in his pocket. Thomas sat on the wicker sofa and contentedly puffed. Minutes passed.

'What's your tobacco?' Bright said.

Thomas took out his pipe, paused, said an incomprehensible word and put the pipe back in his mouth.

'Eh?'

'Thomas is Danish,' I said.

'A-ha?'

'But this is a Dutch tobacco,' Thomas said.

'Very cosmopolitan.' Bright took the drink from James. 'Thanks, lad.'

'How did you two meet?' I asked James.

'I went to his police station to ask advice about uniforms and gear for one of the books.'

Felix and the Force,' Bright said. 'Good book.'

'He gave me a lot of help. Beyond the call of duty. I decided for a bobby he wasn't half bad.'

James liked this man. Why? I loathed him. And I loathed his being there. His presence set my teeth on edge. I felt the room to be full of jagged shapes, as though a mirror had broken and scattered in shards. Then I caught Thomas's eye. He smiled at me. A long slow smile. And suddenly I felt better. Light-hearted even. I turned to James and caught Bright's sharp little eyes on me. Again I felt the spears of broken mirror in the room.

Margot breezed in, kaftan billowing. She was the only woman I knew who could still wear the clothes she bought in the seventies and get away with it.

'Oh, I've heard a lot about you. Imagine, the second policeman I've met in a fortnight. Oh God, I'm sorry, Thomas. Oh dear. Well, Thomas has had a spot of trouble. But it's over now.'

Was I mistaken or did Bright look amused? He had a way of smiling, or almost smiling, without moving his face.

'A-ha?' he said.

'Oh for heaven's sake,' I butted in. 'Don't let's talk about all that. Thomas has had enough of it for a lifetime, I should think.' And enough of policemen, I wanted to add but didn't.

Thomas sighed and nobody else made a sound. The big dog silence was settling again so I said, 'Thomas's wife ran away without leaving any clue to her whereabouts. He had to report it of course so there has been a fuss.'

Bright nodded, still with that look of concealed amusement. I felt I might be

51

going to blush. Why? I felt so angry with Margot, inviting a policeman to dinner. She might as well have served Thomas himself as the main course. Then Bright turned to him and said, 'You must be having a pretty bad time.'

Thomas looked up with slow surprise. 'Yes.' His voice cracked and he coughed. 'Yes.'

'Sorry, mate,' Bright said. 'I haven't been following the news lately. I should have known. Is her file still active?'

Thomas shook his head. 'They said not.'

'How long did they give it?'

'Oh...about a month, I think.'

Bright let out a short harsh breath between his teeth. 'You can't mourn, that's the—well...' He gulped his drink.

Thomas said uncertainly. 'No. That's it.'

The men were deep in computers when we brought in the coq au vin. Thomas, the expert, talked least.

'We feed all this stuff in.' Bright was attacking him. 'Tons of data. Weeks go by. Months of man-hours, day and night monitoring, miles of print-outs, data sifted and compared by these machines and then the villain is found. By accident. By the bobby on the beat!' Thomas made to demur but Bright went on, 'That guy who was found round here somewhere, axe murderer bloke. The computers had been at him for months. And how was he found? A local fuzzy recognised his car outside a house.'

'Big coup for Kentish Town police,' James said.

'Big coup for human observation,' Bright said.

'The coq au vin's delicious, Margot,' I said.

'Darling, I've always excelled at any dish involving lots of wine.'

'Computers are our tools,' Thomas said.

'Easier to deal with than human beings?' Bright's little eyes glinted at him. Thomas went still, or did I imagine that?

'They are logical,' he said. 'Without emotions. They don't deceive.'

'Unlike women.' Bright gazed into his glass of red wine.

'In my experience,' I said, 'men are more deceptive than women.'

They all looked at me, James with a rueful crinkle of his nose, Thomas sharply, then down at his plate. Bright stared, serious and slow, without that hint in his eyes of light on steel. His eyes had retractable blades, like flick knives, I thought. I must be drunk.

Then Margot entered bearing aloft the

most beautiful of pies, shining golden with a decoration of pastry leaves on top. Steam rose from it, and the smell of apples and cinnamon. And I looked at Thomas and there was a desk lamp behind him and light all round him, especially round his head and I realised I was in love.

The voices receded, the light grew dim, I didn't know where to look. Margot was asking me something.

'Sorry?' I said.

'Are you all right, darling?'

I caught Bright's eye. He seemed to know my thoughts. But when you are in love, I remembered, you feel shell-less, transparent, a peeled prawn.

'The wine,' I laughed, 'seems to have had an extraordinary effect on me tonight.'

'You said that very well,' James said. 'All the esses in the right place.'

'Thank you.'

'I think we need some coffee, love,' Margot said. James got up. So did I. I wanted a calm moment alone.

What a face. Eyes neither big nor small, brighter than usual tonight. Lips neither full or thin, trembling a bit tonight. Skin chapped a little from the days by the sea, reddish across the wide cheeks. Could a woman with such a face be made to look beautiful? With make up perhaps, and her hair swept up? I saw this lovely woman, décolleté in candlelight, with diamonds round her neck. Then I remembered my bony shoulderblades and the freckles on my back. The spell was broken. I felt extraordinarily sad, the feeling you have at fourteen when you want so much to be beautiful and know you will never be. Then I grinned. The funny face grinned back.

Margot called, 'Jen?'

'Yes?'

'Are you okay?'

I unlocked the door.

She crept into the bathroom and said in a low voice, 'He's just lost a girl he was crazy about.'— Thomas? But I knew that!—'You must have heard about it. An actress who was suspected of killing her best friend.'

Oh, it was Bright she was talking about. The policeman. I recalled the case.

'That's him?' A shiver ran over me. 'Good heavens.'

'James is fond of him. Been looking after him a bit lately.'

'Margot, do you know anyone who doesn't need looking after?'

'Nobody at all.' She smiled at me wickedly and swept down the stairs.

They were wandering towards the conservatory when I came down. I tried to avoid Thomas but somehow he was by my side. He even put a hand on my shoulder.

'You are okay, Jen?'

'Yes. Fine. Why?'

'Oh, I don't know, you seem—I don't know.'

'I'm all right. The wine went to my head for some reason, that's all.'

'I am concerned for you.'

'Oh, ridiculous.' I managed to escape from his arm. 'You have enough on your mind.'

Determined to keep my head above water and not to succumb to my cowardly dread of John Bright, I sat next to him on the sofa.

'Are you working on an interesting case at the moment?' I asked.

He gave a sort of groan.

'John's on extended leave for a bit,' James said.

'Oh.'

'He was a bit too much in the public eye.'

'I was a scandal and a shame.'

'He was highly commended.'

Bright's face became sharper, his mouth a narrower line.

'So now he's having a break,' James said.

'From which I may never return. To policemanship.'

'What would you do instead?' James was sceptical.

'Grow roses, read Proust. Who knows?'

'And what are you actually doing?'

'Drinking Scotch.' He downed half a glass of whisky. 'That answer your question, Miss Wren?'

Embarrassed and cross, I said nothing.

'Oh, sorry, Jen, isn't it? Got any decent music, James?'

He was unbelievably rude. But drunker than I was, I realised.

'What's decent? Mozart? Scarlatti?'

'Procul Harem, I was thinking of.'

James laughed. 'Margot! Your department!'

Terrible sounds began to issue from the dining room. John Bright turned and stared at me, sharp. He did have a squint. Or perhaps he only had it sometimes. Are there squints that come and go? I wondered.

'Do you like to dance, Miss Wren?'

My mouth opened and closed. James looked amused, Thomas alert. Margot said, 'I do.' She handed me the coffee tray and pulled John Bright to his feet. I poured the coffee. It gave me something to do. The music was powerful, actually not unlike Bach. I wanted Thomas to dance with me, so much it was almost a physical pain. This was terrible. It would have to

57

stop. I gave James his coffee.

'You don't like my policeman friend, do you, Jen?'

'He's horrible,' I hissed.

James laughed. 'He's okay.'

'How can you like him?'

'Can't explain.'

I drank my coffee so hot it burned my tongue and said I had to go. Thomas, as always, offered to walk me home.

'It's early,' I said. 'I don't want to drag you away.'

'But you know I would be glad, I am always glad—'

'Absolutely not, I won't hear of it. Stay where you are.' I didn't look at him.

I went to the kitchen to say goodnight to Margot. She was the same height as John Bright, about five foot eight, but she looked taller. His head was resting on her shoulder. Over his head she winked at me. His eyes were closed. It made me shudder, seeing him cling round Margot like that, but she didn't seem to mind, and nor did James. I went out into the night.

A wind had risen. Newspapers wrapped my ankles. My eyes watered. The orphan of the storm.

In the art shop window at the corner of Angler's Lane someone had put a wonderful painting: a room full of light and shadow, dappled, woolly. Miles away from the foreground, over acres of Persian carpet, a lace curtain blew at a window. And there on a chaise longue a woman lay, almost invisible in the moving light. Now you see her, now you don't. The painting was by Vuillard. It expressed all the uncertainty I felt: suspended, nothing beneath my feet, yet the suggestion of air and light and beauty somewhere, not far away.

'Oh Lord.' I put my hand on the window, just to touch something real. The glass was cold. I put my face against it. I saw that there was a little dog in the painting, just there at the woman's feet. I was glad she wasn't alone. I moved on.

I sat on my sofa in the dark and said, 'I think I got drunk. I haven't really fallen in love.' I closed my eyes.

I woke, still on the sofa but without a hangover. The sun shone. Leaves swirled. I took a bus to Parliament Hill and walked up to where they fly the kites. Last night seemed a dream. I remembered falling in love with Thomas with the halo round his head. The memory abashed me. Falling in love with a married man, a man still besotted with a wife who had run away. What could I have been thinking of? Watching a magenta kite hop, then hover, then soar into the sky, I suddenly knew what had happened: 'I didn't fall in love last night; I fell out! I fell out of love with Jean-Pierre. That's why I feel so good this morning. As high as that tiny magenta punctuation mark up there in the sky.'

I walked on. I was receptive today, blotting paper. My mind was full of silly images, the kite and the sunshine and swirling leaves. There was no time to be wasted, or simply to be lost, as I had lost the last three years, grieving for Jean-Pierre. I had no idea where these thoughts were leading, but a shaky stealthy happiness crept into me and, as I watched a small girl feed the ducks on Highgate Pond, a sudden resolve. Since I was not in love with Thomas, I was free of a burden. I needn't feel constrained any more: I would ring him as soon as I got back. This afternoon.

'Where have you been? It's like the *Marie Celeste!*' James was ringing my doorbell, the Sunday papers under his arm. He often dropped in on Sunday morning. I had utterly forgotten him.

'I went on the Heath early, it was such a lovely day.'

'And I came to see if you were all right.'

'Oh, I'm fine. No freshly baked bread though, I'm afraid.'

'Disgraceful woman.'

'Yes, I know.'

I served the coffee in my dark green cups with the gold rim, a legacy of my years with Jean-Pierre. James put down the colour supplement.

'So you didn't exactly take to my friend, John Bright.'

I shuddered.

'He's like a—he's like a—an electric screwdriver,' I said.

James's eyes opened wide. 'He seems to have made something of an impression.'

'What do you see in him?'

'I don't know, I just like the guy. He gave me a lot of help over the book. I was grateful. We just started having a drink now and again. Then of course he had this terrible business of losing his girl in that way. Couldn't have been much fun. A pretty nasty way for it to end.'

'He drove her to it, didn't he? That's what I read. He tricked her into telling him everything by pretending to be in love with her, didn't he?'

'Well, Jen, I got the impression it wasn't quite like that.'

'I wouldn't be at all surprised if it were true. He seems just the type.'

'Well, that's it, you see. I don't think he's quite what he seems.'

'Humph.'

'Humph? What sort of noise is that for a well-bred girl like you? Humph?'

I laughed.

'James?' I said. I was fiddling with a coffee spoon.

'Yes?'

'You didn't invite him in connection with—in connection with—Thomas—at all, did you?'

'What?' James was astonished. I blushed.

'Oh, I don't know. I thought—I wondered—completely silly I know—'

'You thought I'd invited John Bright to give Thomas the once over? A sort of professional opinion, you mean? My God, Jen, what do you take me for? And anyway, for heaven's sake, we hadn't even invited Thomas. You invited him.'

'I'm sorry I even mentioned it. I'm an absolute fool.'

'What if he *had* done away with Elizabeth? Don't look like that. A mere hypothesis. What if he had? Wouldn't you want him to get caught?'

'Oh no!' The words shot out of me.

'Jen!'

I was as surprised as James.

'Oh I don't like people to get caught,' I said.

'Why ever not?'

'I killed my parents, you see.'

'Your parents died in a car crash, you said.'

'Yes, but because I wasn't there.'

'You were a little girl. How could you have prevented it?'

'My father was a terrible driver. Absent-minded, you know, always pointing things out and talking about things. My mother's heart was always in her mouth, and since it's impolite to speak with your mouth full she'd sit silent, clutching her vocal cords with one hand and her little leather handbag with the other. So I used to tell him, "Daddy, look where you're going. Daddy, there's a car coming towards us. Daddy, someone's overtaking us." He normally worked on Saturdays, but that Saturday he had the day off. He suggested we went for an outing in the car. But I had a piano lesson that afternoon. And I stubbornly refused to cancel it. He drove me to my lesson. I stood on the pavement with my music case, and watched him drive off. I thought at the time, "What will he do without me? I should have gone with him." Well, I was right, you see. So that's why I don't like people to get caught. I got away with it, as it were. No one accused me, ever.'

'But, Jen, your dad must have driven his car—'

'It was a Morris Minor. Grey.'

'He must have driven it a thousand times without you.'

'Yes, but those times he hadn't asked me to go with him. I hadn't refused. You see the difference?'

James shook his head and laughed. 'Yes.' He touched my hand. 'I suppose I do. And this has given you a sympathy with all criminals for ever more.'

'Yes. And my punishment was to lose my driving licence for life. I've never been able to learn to drive.'

'You're crazy.'

'I do seem to be, the last few days. I don't know what's the matter with me.'

'You're in love,' James said.

I gasped. 'Who with?' I held my breath.

'John Bright,' he said.

I gasped again, then laughed.

In spite of my resolve on the Heath, it was much later in the day before I had the courage to phone Thomas.

'Are you in the dark?' I said.

He was cautious. 'What do you mean?'

'I imagined you standing in the dark.'

'Sitting.'

'In the dark?'

'Yes.'

'There, then.'

'Yes?'

This was an odd conversation. I must

try to sound more normal. 'Thomas?'

'Yes?'

'Are you all right?'

'Yes.' Silence. 'I am quite—I am a little bit—how would one say it? Sorry, when I am alone I think in Danish. I am a little bit—at a loss?'

'Yes, I'm sure. What have you been doing today?'

'Oh, gardening. I had a bonfire such as at your aunt's last week.'

'Oh yes?'

'But people came to watch.'

'The bonfire?'

'No. Me. So I had to go indoors.'

'How awful, Thomas.'

'Not so many as there were the last weeks. They—diminish.'

'Thomas, put the light on, draw the curtains and eat something. Please.'

'Yes, I will.'

'Good.'

Silence.

I plunged: 'Meet me—for tea, next—Wednesday?'

'Oh. Yes. Thank you,' he said. 'Wednesday would be fine.'

He looked as big as Gulliver sitting in Valerie's with his pipe. He towered over the dancers and actors at the rickety little tables. I did not blush when I saw him, as

I had half expected to. I simply thought, Oh, there's Thomas. Now I'm safe. It was an odd thought. He stood up to greet me, so correct, a difficult operation in that crowded place. He did not return my smile. That was one of the things, I thought, that made me trust him so. He never answered a smile automatically with a smile. He managed to pull out a chair for me. I squeezed into it and gushed into nervous chatter.

'Oh thanks, sorry I'm late, the traffic's awful, the crowds are terrible, of course it started to rain and I left my brolly at home and just before I left Aunt Jess rang up to say she's not very well and—'

'Oh?'

'Yes. Feels sick all the time. Thinks it might be a bug. It's strange. She's never sick, darling Jess. I've told her to get the doctor. I wish I could be there.'

'I am sorry.'

'Oh, well.'

The tea came.

'Did you stay long at James and Margot's the other night?' I was pouring. The teapot leaked. The teapots always leaked at Valerie's. Thomas mopped up.

'Quite long.'

'How was it?'

'I talked with James. Margot danced.'

'With that awful policeman,' I said.

'Why awful?'

'Didn't you think so?'

'No.' Thomas was puzzled. 'He was just a chap. What did you find wrong with him?'

'Oh,' I mumbled. I wished I hadn't started this. 'I just didn't like him being there, that's all.'

Thomas's face cleared. 'You mean on my account? But this was nothing to do with me.'

'No, I know.'

'Oh, Jen. Was this what was wrong with you? Why you did not want my company to your house?'

'Well, partly, yes—'

'Jen.'

Both his hands took hold of my left hand. I stared at these three hands. My heart beat fast. My eyes didn't see very well. I was rather cut off from the experience. My hand noticed by itself that the palms of his hands were slightly moist. It was hard to know what to do next. We were both staring at the three hands. Then I made a little movement with mine and Thomas seemed to wake up. He let go in order to do something to his pipe. My hand felt a little forlorn, left to itself. I put it in my lap and clasped it tight.

'You are a person of unusual loyalty,' Thomas said. His voice was muffled.

'Not unusual. But my friends are my friends. That's normal, I think.'

'No, not normal at all.'

'Surely.'

'No. Many people have changed towards me since this business. Some, out of curiosity, want to know me. Some, out of fear, want no longer to know me. Some of those I had thought were friends.'

'Oh, Thomas.'

'Yes.'

We sipped the tea. He put down his cup.

'I thought Margot was a friend,' he said.

'Margot?'

'She invites me now from duty.' How truthful he was.

'No, Thomas.' How easily I lied.

Conversation In Another Place

1

'Hi, Reg.'

'John Bright!'

'How did you know?'

'I'd know that horrible voice anywhere.'

'A-ha. Listen. You had a missing person file, now inactive, an Elizabeth Peterson, that right?'

'That's right. Why? You found her, John?'

'No.'

'Wouldn't put it past you.'

'What's the score, Reg?'

'You mean what do I think?'

'Yeah.'

'I think he killed her.'

'The husband? Peterson?'

'Yeah. But no evidence, not a crumb.'

'I met him.'

'Christ.'

'Yeah. A bloke who illustrates kids' books. His wife writes them. Met him at their place.'

'The circles you move in.'

'A-ha.'

'So you see what I mean about him, John?'

'I dunno. A bit too good to be true, p'raps?'

'That's it.'

'He's already kind of involved with another woman.'

'You're kidding.'

'I'm not, mate. Trusting soul. No beauty but nice. Know what I mean?'

'I met her. Jenny Wren.'

'Jen, apparently.'

'You falling in love again, John?'

'Don't joke, Reg.'

'Sorry, mate.'

'No, there's just something about her. Likes to look after people. Needs looking after herself. Sees no evil, you know?'

'So what do you want? Come and join the Epping CID?'

'Funny you should say that... No, it's just I'm in a position to keep an eye out. But I don't want to tread on any toes.'

'I'll keep mine under the table. Everyone else's toes round here dance to my tune. You'd be doing me a favour. Haven't the manpower to reopen the file.'

'A-ha. That's what I thought.'

'Come and have a jar one of these days, John.'

'I will, Reg. I will.'

Chapter Five

Aunt Jess, on the phone, sounded feeble, rambling almost. She still felt sick, wasn't eating now.

'What does your doctor say?'

'A virus, of course.'

'Flu?'

'Gastric flu. There's a lot of it about.'

70

'When did he see you?'

'Mmm?'

'Aunt Jess?'

'Mmm?'

'I'll come at the weekend.'

Ben gave up his free Saturday to double for me at the library. 'Greater love hath no man,' he said.

Thomas couldn't drive me to Clevedon. He was at a conference. But the conference was in Bristol and finished on Friday night. 'I'll meet you at the station,' he said. 'It's only a twenty-minute drive.'

'Aunt Jess! We're here!'

No sound.

'Aunt Jess?'

Nothing.

I ran upstairs—'Aunt Jess?'—and opened her bedroom door.

The smell shocked me: not quite cleared up vomit. The room was orangey dark from the closed curtains, the bed a hummocky mess. The eiderdown had half slipped to the floor. She lay with her head off the pillow, hair matted. I pulled the curtains open so fast that one came off some of its hooks. Her mouth was open. Her face was the colour of ivory, and wet. She breathed with effort, long spaces between the breaths. One arm hung out of the bed as though trying to reach the phone. Why had she placed it on the floor and so far away?

I rang nine nine nine for an ambulance. I flipped through her little address book and called her doctor. He was out but could be bleeped.

I turned round. Thomas was at the door, staring. I pushed past him to the bathroom. I wetted a face cloth, picked up a towel, came back, pushed past him again. He had not moved. I touched Jess's hand. It was pale, like her face, and cold. I rubbed it with both of mine, put it back under the covers, fixed the covers, lifted her head carefully, moved the pillows, placed her head more comfortably on them, wiped her face with the damp face cloth. The moisture stayed on her skin, a shiny slime. Was it grease, perhaps? It would not go.

'Jess? Jess, darling, my darling Jess.'

A deep shivering breath in, a long pause, a weak rattling breath out. Her eyes were closed.

'Jess, it's Jen. Can you look at me? Darling, will you look at me?'

The eyelids fluttered. She could hear then. An effort was being made.

'It's Jen, darling. Please. Open your eyes, precious. Can you, my love?' I lapsed into the Somerset speech of my childhood: my lover, my love, my little love. 'Jess!' I had to make her open her eyes. I had to keep her with me. I had to fight. I gripped her shoulders. I would hurt her if I must. She was trying. Her eyes opened once. I mopped her face continuously.

'I'm here now, darling. I'll take care of you. You'll be all right now. You will. You will.'

'What's been happening here?'

The doctor was a flabby man with ash on his jacket. I hadn't heard him arrive. He thrust me away from Jess, opened her eyes with his fingers, closed them again, felt her pulse.

'Cancel the ambulance,' he said.

'You mean she's going to be all right?'

'She's gone.'

'What do you mean?'

'She's dead.'

He went to the phone.

'When did you get here? How did she get like this? I saw her on Thursday. She was on the mend. She was weak, she'd been bad, but she was on the mend. What's been going on?'

He spoke into the phone and put it down.

Thomas said, 'Jen was working until yesterday, she couldn't get away.'

The doctor calmed down.

'Come here.' He took me to the window. 'You've had a shock. Sit down.'

I sat in the pink Lloyd Loom chair. It had been there all my life. Like Jess.

'Why?' I said.

'I don't know. It's a weird virus, this one. It's taken people some funny ways, different for each one. It's attacked the old the worst, like everything. This is the third death in two days. All elderly. All from this flu.' He moved his shoulders uneasily as though he felt a draught. 'But I'd have sworn she was on the mend.'

'Perhaps she tried to do too much too soon,' Thomas said.

'Yes. She would. I warned her but of course they don't listen. Not women like her. Got to be doing, haven't they? Now look, I'm making out a prescription. You take four of these a day, one after each meal, one at night. For the shock. They'll ease you over it.' He gave the piece of paper to Thomas. 'Get this at the chemist for her. Make sure she takes them. Don't let her blame herself. Nobody's fault.'

'You are certain it was this flu?' Thomas said.

'Oh yes, it's been a real epidemic round here. Frankly there's not much we can do. It's a case of viruses rule okay. I'd have said Miss Wren was healthy enough to withstand it, but there you are. You never know. It's become pneumonia, you see. But it's happened so fast. Same with the other two.' He snapped his fingers. 'Just like that. In their sleep.'

He and Thomas went downstairs. There was no sound at all in the room. I felt too tired to live my life. I hadn't the strength. And anyway what was the point without Jess? I was still in the chair when Thomas came back. He gave me pills to swallow.

I said, 'It was just the same with my parents. I wasn't there. I knew I ought to have been there, but I wasn't. Thomas, will you ring the library? Tell them I shan't be in next week.'

And then I didn't speak again. I was silent when they took the body away. I was silent with the undertaker and the vicar. Thomas spoke for me. I was glad to let him.

Margot and James arrived on the day of the funeral. I stood at the door and watched them get out of the car. I'd never seen Margot in black before. James was in jeans but with a black jacket. He even wore a tie. Margot took me in her arms. And over her shoulder I saw John Bright get out of the back of the car.

'I'm sorry, darling, I know you're not keen on him. He stayed at our place last night and as we were leaving I said, "Why don't you come too?" I never dreamed he'd say yes. You don't mind too much, do you? Yes, you do, Oh hell.'

But I didn't speak. I walked into the house and they followed me.

The church was right up on the cliffs over the sea, the graves sloping down by the cliff path they call Poets' Walk. Gulls wheeled above. Jess would hear their cries as she had all her life. Her neighbours were there, wiping their eyes. Thomas was there, strong and stern. When we came out into the wind to put Jess into the ground, the doctor was just outside the porch smoking a cigarette. John Bright was with him.

They all shook my hand when it was over, and Thomas said, 'Please come back and have a cup of tea.' He took my arm to lead me to the car but I shook him off and walked away to the cliff path. I heard Margot say, 'Let her go, Thomas.'

I walked between the high bank and the low, the yellowing leaves and the shrivelling brambles, smelling the mouth of the river that only looked like the sea.

Thomas was waiting at the bottom of the path to drive me back. I handed out tea and sherry, sandwiches and cakes. People spoke to me about Jess but I didn't reply. The doctor asked for whisky. When I brought it, he was again talking with John Bright. I heard John Bright say 'Inquest?' The doctor shook his head. 'Third in a week, all the same,' he said. John Bright asked for whisky too.

'Sorry for intruding,' he said. 'Wanted to pay my respects.'

The people didn't stay long. Mrs Bowyer who lived next door hovered till last.

'Jen,' she whispered. 'Jen.' Her pale eyes watered. She dabbed with the wet ball of cotton in her dimpled hand. 'I should have been here,' she said. 'But I saw her on Thursday morning. She was out in the garden, Jen. She seemed all right. She was planting bulbs. I always go to my daughter in Portishead on Friday as you know, but I could have popped in first. I'll never forgive myself. I'd have done anything for poor old Jess.'

I wanted to answer but I couldn't. I watched as Margot led her to the door. John Bright was on the path outside. Mrs Bowyer spoke to him, dabbing her eyes. He put a hand between her shoulder blades and steered her to the house next door.

I looked round at the debris of glasses, cups, plates and crumbs. The French windows were open. I went out to the garden. I stood on the terrace. I looked at the apple tree. The apples wouldn't be picked this year. Under the apple tree a small woman stood. She bent down. She was burying something or planting something. She patted the earth as though

77

it were a dog. She stood up and looked at me. It was Jess.

I walked backwards to the house. I put my hands on the warm bricks behind me. They had been there a long time, the bricks. They might give me some of their strength, some wisdom, some acceptance.

Why wasn't I there? Why didn't I know? My mind repeated questions, dully rhetorical.

'Jen? Jen?'

I did not move because I could not move.

'Jen!'

James came out of the French windows. 'What is it?' he said. 'Jen?'

He touched my arm. I could see his hand and follow what it did. That's all. I couldn't feel. He tried to move me but found it impossible. I had to keep my hands against the bricks. I was safe there. He tried to get his arms around me but couldn't manage it. I stood pressed against the wall.

Then Thomas said, 'Jen! This is where you are!'

And she was gone. Where there had been Jess, there was now not Jess. Always and everywhere there was now Not-Jess. I catapulted off the house and into Thomas's arms. He held me. I shook.

'Brandy,' he said.

78

Someone gave him the brandy. He manoeuvred me somehow into one arm and put the glass against my teeth. My teeth were clenched.

'Come, Jen, drink. Come, Jen, come.'

My teeth opened a crack. The brandy burned my mouth, my throat, my heart, my head. My eyes watered. He made me swallow the glassful. I still shook. He led me in and up the stairs and into my room. He pulled back the duvet and sat me on the bed. He pulled off my shoes. He lifted my legs onto the bed, pushed me down and covered me. Then he sat on the bed and took my hand.

It was dark when I woke. Thomas sat in the chair by the window, reading a computer journal. I sat upright. Then I remembered. He came and sat by me. I slept again, I woke, I slept again, and each time I woke he was there. I woke five times, but sleep was like a hammer: one bang and I was gone. The sixth time I woke, the room was empty. I went to the bathroom.

On the way back to bed I stopped at the landing window to look at the garden under the moon. By the apple tree there was a movement. Stupidly I thought, Aunt Jess, she'll get cold. Then Thomas moved out from behind the tree. He stood in the moonlight on the path.

Suddenly he raised his arms straight up. Two large white hands faced me. They rose against the sky. They closed on the lowest branch of the tree. He hung there swaying, then dropped. He folded his arms. He seemed to gaze up at the house. Was he looking at me? He didn't move. He just stood there, arms folded, staring.

I shivered suddenly in the night chill. I moved from the window, back to my warm bed. The hammer hit me again. A man hung from the apple tree in my dreams all night. Faceless, he put up his hands. The hands, large, white, disembodied, followed me low in the sky like two white birds on silent wings. I didn't dream of Jess.

Thomas wasn't in the room in the morning when I woke. Margot brought me breakfast. I drank the orange juice and the coffee but couldn't eat.

I got out of bed. My legs shook, boneless, when my feet touched the floor. I went to the window and pulled the curtains back. I recalled my dream of Thomas under the tree. It must have been a dream?

'I think we'll just wash up breakfast and get off. We don't want to hang about. That all right, Jen? That's if we can wake Thomas. He was up most of the night

80

with you. We offered to relieve him but he would not be moved. Touching devotion. Shall I run you a bath?'

The streaming water smelled of Margot's expensive bath oil. 'Take your time, love. No one's rushing you.'

I looked down at the garden again. No one stood under the apple tree. Not Thomas. And not Aunt Jess. A few apples had fallen in the night.

A shadow stepped suddenly onto the terrace. John Bright followed it down the path, his feet bisecting the diagonals of brick. He stood under the tree. He picked up an apple and bit into it. He looked up at the back of the house.

'He stayed in a hotel last night,' Margot said. 'He thought you wouldn't want him in the house.'

I watched them eat lunch and still Thomas did not wake. James ate with one hand, held me with the other. After lunch Margot went upstairs. She came down with my bag.

'We'll go without him,' she said.

I looked into the little drawing room. They should bury their things with people, as they did with the pharaohs. Or make their houses their tombs, locked upon everything within. I wanted never to go there again.

They left a note for Thomas and we

got into the car. John Bright sat next to Margot in the front, I in the back with James. Margot chattered. James answered her. John Bright was almost as silent as I. They dropped him off in Crouch End. He turned and shook my hand. My hand drew back as if stung.

'Hell,' he said. 'Sorry. Okay?'

He walked off, saying goodbye over his shoulder to Margot and James. They took me back to their house.

'She can't go home on her own, can she, James?'

'No, she can't, darling. Can you, Jen?'

Margot put me on the sofa under a duvet. James filled a hot water bottle. I held it on my stomach. The hot rubbery smell was Aunt Jess and my childhood ailments, her cool hand on my brow. James put Satie's *Gymnopédies* on the record player and sat at his desk. Margot sat at hers. The small sounds of industry and contentment. I floated, a mind without a body, a body without a mind. Was this what they meant by coming apart?

'She's all right, Thomas! She's here with us!' Margot was on the phone. The curtains were drawn. It must be night. Later, I believe Margot tried to feed me some soup. Then I was alone. They must have gone to bed. The sounds of nothing and nobody, and Not-Jess. They had left a little light on by my bed. I looked at my hands. I could see the skeleton inside them, pinkish, outlined against the light. What does it mean to be a living thing? The hammer struck me again.

The next week I was a land after a hurricane. I was a devastation. Awake or asleep? I hardly knew the difference. Nor did my friends. I heard a conversation from the kitchen I wouldn't have heard had they thought me awake.

'I can't stand it, James. I love her dearly, you know I do, but if she stays much longer I'll go out of my mind.'

'Sshh,' James said.

Perhaps the pills the doctor had given me perpetuated my inertia. I neither knew nor cared.

Ben from the library came. He talked to me. They looked at each other and raised helpless hands and kissed me.

'I'll tell Grahame,' Ben said. 'He must see her. He'll have to give her leave of absence for a bit.'

My job. Yes, I recalled it. People. Books. But that was in another country and besides...

'I'll move into her house with her!' Thomas stood up. 'Just until she is able to manage. I'll take care of her.'

Margot and James looked at each other. My body got up and walked to Thomas. He held me by the shoulders.

'Well!' Margot said. 'That seems to be all right by Jen.'

So Thomas and I went home.

Conversation In Another Place

2

'Her aunt died.'

'Christ, John. What of?'

'How does gastric flu grab you?'

'That the verdict of the inquest?'

'No inquest. Doctor had seen her a few days before. Other old people have been snuffing it from the same bug. So he just signed the death certificate.'

'Well, he wasn't to know, I guess.'

'Bumbling old creep. Covered in ash. Hands shaking till after the second scotch. A salutary example.'

'Eh?'

'What I'll be like in a few years' time if I carry on like this.'

'Well, you won't, will you, John?'

'How do you know?'

'Call it one of my hunches.'

'Can't have her dug up, can we, Reg?'

'Any evidence against our Danish friend?'

'No chance. Woman next door saw a bloke at the aunt's front door Friday morning. Thought it was the doctor. That's why she didn't drop in. Only it wasn't the doctor, natch.'

'Can she give us a description?'

'Nah. Could have been anyone. She only saw his back. Our guy was meant to be at a conference on Friday. Guess where. Bristol. A few miles up the road.'

'We can check his alibi.'

'It'll check. The guy plans ahead.'

'Still. Never know. Nutcases get careless.'

'He might not be a nutcase. Might just be money. Elizabeth got dough from her parents. Jenny Wren inherits from the aunt.'

'The aunt let him in, this bloke, Friday morning?'

'Neighbour didn't even see that. Natch again.'

Reg Grant and John Bright stared into their drinks.

'And now he's moved into Jenny Wren's house,' Bright said.

'Christ, John.'

'A-ha.'

Chapter Six

It was strange to see a man's things in my bathroom again. And not just in the bathroom. Thomas's tobacco jar sat on the mantelpiece, his pipe on the little table by the armchair, his computer on the desk in the front window. I diminished in size, becoming smaller as Thomas's things filled up my little house, while Thomas padded about on large white feet in his dressing gown.

And he was happy. He hummed. He fed me in the morning: soft-boiled eggs and tea. He ran baths for me, modestly turning his back and closing the door on my naked skin. He brushed my hair. He put his big arms round me and carried me sometimes, upstairs or down. He looked after me night and day. But he never spoke. He dealt with my continued silence by not speaking to me. I did not find this odd. He stayed with me each night until I slept.

Grahame, my boss, came to see me. He spoke. He said how sorry he was and how did I feel and did I think I would be ready to come back to work soon. He waited. I sat. His words seemed nothing to do with me. He asked if my doctor had seen me. He said to Thomas, 'I'll need a doctor's certificate for leave of absence. I'll have to hire short-term staff in Jen's place. In your place, Jen. Just till you come back. No rush.'

Thomas said, 'I will see to that.'

'Thank you.'

Grahame was tall and gangling like a puppet. He dangled above me from his strings.

'Well, Jen, I'll drop in again. I'm sure you'll be better soon.'

One of his loosely jointed arms came up and pushed his glasses higher on his nose. I smiled at him. His smile was radiant with surprise. He looked at Thomas as if to say, 'She smiled!' But Thomas was looking at me.

Ben came and brought me books. Thomas said, 'She does not read.'

'Good lord, what does she do?'

'Nothing at all.'

'Poor Jen. Nothing at all?'

I smiled at him.

Ben said, 'Don't smile at me, Jen. It's awful, love.'

So I stopped.

'Shall I read to you, Jen? Thomas, shall I read to her?'

'Well...'

'What harm could it do?'

Thomas said slowly, 'Yes. It's a good idea perhaps.'

'I'll read something she knows. Jane Austen, that's what she loves best.' Ben pushed past Thomas to my bookshelves. 'Here. *Sense and Sensibility*. That'll do.'

Ben's Northern accent added to the humour of Jane Austen in a way she would have enjoyed. He disobeyed every rule in her lecture in *Mansfield Park* on reading aloud, but despite that, he read well, acting all the characters with gusto. I was much comforted. To savour it, I closed my eyes. Thomas immediately said, 'She's tired, now, I think that's enough.' I opened my eyes quickly, but Ben had closed the book.

'Oh, yes, right,' he said. 'Okay. All right if I drop in now and then and read to her some more?'

I clutched both his hands.

'Oh hey, Jen!' Excited, he turned to Thomas. 'Look at that! She's all there, you see. It's just the speaking, isn't it?'

Thomas shook his head. 'No.'

'Oh.' Ben gazed at my face. 'No. You're right. The shock, you see. Just too much. Aunt Jess was everything, wasn't she, Jen?'

He was the first person since my silence to mention Aunt Jess's name. I held on to his hands.

The doctor came, a young man I hadn't

met before. He felt my pulse, shone a light in my eyes. He was in a hurry. 'Nothing physically wrong,' he told Thomas. 'Just shock. Give her these three times a day.'

'What are they, Doctor?'

'A mild anti-depressant. To get her over the hump. Make an appointment in a couple of weeks, see how she's getting on.'

Then he went.

Thomas sat at his computer a lot. It made digestive noises: gurgles and hiccups. Margot said, 'Can't that horrible thing be switched off?'

'What horrible thing?'

'That!'

Thomas looked shocked. 'It has not completed its program yet!'

'That frightful noise can't be good for Jen in her condition. Going on all the time like that.'

'Noise?' Thomas said.

'The hum. And those sinister squeaks and gobblings. Can't you hear it, Thomas?'

Thomas listened hard. 'Oh, I see,' he said.

'Can't it go upstairs or something?'

'Well...' He was torn.

'I can't stand it for five minutes. It's just the sort of noise to drive Jen round the bend. Not that you're not already round the bend, isn't that so, my darling?'

I smiled at her.

'Like hell!' she said.

Thomas didn't move the computer. I could quite see why. Upstairs, he could not be near it and, at the same time, me. And soon its gulpings and gurglings became a sort of comfort. I'd have missed them had they stopped.

After Ben's visit with the books, Thomas began to read to me. When he read he became intensely Danish. He garbled the words, went back over crumbled sentences, compounding the ruin. Punctuation, meaning, he trod underfoot. He tried hard, wanting to please me. That made it torture. I tried to look pleased, to save his feelings, dreading each time the moment when he picked up poor Jane Austen and opened her.

One sunny afternoon, ears abused beyond endurance, I clenched my hands and my eyelids tight. When my eyes opened, his face was red: enflamed, engraged, engorged. He threw *Sense and Sensibility* across the room. Threw it. A book. I got out of bed and ran. I picked it up. The flyleaf said 'To my dear niece on her fifteenth birthday. Love from Aunt Jess'. And the date. I examined the book. It was unharmed. I hugged it.

Thomas stood at the window, fists clenched, shaking, like the time he had made the faux pas at Jess's. I put the book down, went to him and placed my hand on his back. He banged the window sill, made muffled cries. I wasn't afraid. I understood now. I spoke. I said, 'There, there.'

He stopped. I stopped. We stared. His face opened. He stood straight. He lifted me and ran to the bed with me. He threw me down, and himself next to me. He held me and rocked me and said, 'Jen Jen Jen' over and over. 'Oh Jen.' He kissed me. He had not kissed me before. Not in a state of extreme excitement like this. His eyes had a blinded look. Then all at once he leaned away from me, holding both my upper arms in a hard grip. He breathed deeply, gulped, breathed and gulped. He squeezed his eyes shut. After this immense effort his breathing quieted. Gradually his grip relaxed. And at last his eyes fluttered open. The danger was over. A triumph of self control. I smiled at him. His face reddened. He turned on his back, his face away from me. I found his clenched hand and loosened its clutch, got my fingers inside so that his hand enclosed mine. We lay holding hands. Later he turned his face to me, white.

'Forgive me, Jen.'

'For—what?' I was a stranger to speech.

There was hardly any voice. The words came slow.

'My terrible behaviour,' he said.

I couldn't tell if he meant his sexual arousal or the throwing of the book. My whispery voice laughed.

'But I love you, Thomas,' I said.

'Jen.'

He rested his forehead against mine. Then he swung round, and sat on the edge of the bed with his back to me.

I woke alone in the dusky room. Evening? Morning? I couldn't tell. I tried out my voice. I said, 'Thomas.' No sound came but I had formed the word. It was something. I looked at the ceiling. I had given up my membership; did I want to join again? Speaking would mean that. Silence had been an oddly comforting, or at least comfortable, state. And all at once, I remembered. How could I have forgotten.

At the end of my music lesson no one came for me. The music teacher sat me in a cold room from where I heard other children bang out *Für Elise* on the other side of the wall. I looked at an encyclopaedia while dark crept in at the window. The music teacher brought me some tea. She was tall. She had dark hair in a bun low on her neck. I loved her. We talked about the Arctic Wastes, where I had reached in the A's. Then the phone rang.

When she came back she said, 'Jenitha, dear, your mummy and daddy have been—delayed. They won't be coming back today.'

And I knew. I had always known they would die if I wasn't there to look after them. If I kept absolutely still, absolutely quiet ('Jen. Quiet, dear. Daddy's working, sshh.'), they would not really be dead. They would come back. If they came back it would no longer be my fault.

And so I entered the Arctic Wastes of my silence.

Jess came to fetch me. It was late. Later than I had ever been allowed to stay up. She took me home with her to Clevedon. My clothes were in a suitcase. I carried two dolls, Jess one. We went in a taxi.

There was a cat at Clevedon. A big tabby with yellow eyes called Oliver. The way he looked at me, with affectionate amusement, and the way he patted me sometimes in a friendly way, reminded me of my father. I remained in the silence a long time, possibly months. Then Oliver died. We found him in the street, Jess and I, on our way to the little school where I sat silent every day. We picked him up and carried him indoors. We put him in a cardboard box lined with his blanket and his cushion and containing his milk bowl and his food dish. All his worldly possessions, like a pharaoh. We buried him in the garden, Jess and I. Under the apple tree. As she dug the hole, she cried. Jess never made a fuss; the tears rolled down quietly. I didn't cry. I watched. I was thinking it out. We finished burying Oliver. Aunt Jess and I stood looking down at the earth that covered him. And I spoke. I said, 'Are Mummy and Daddy dead, Aunt Jess?'

And she, with no surprise at my speaking after so long a silence, said, 'Yes, my darling, they are.'

'Were they perfect, like Oliver? Not broken up? Or cut?'

'Yes, my darling, they were perfect,' she lied and I believed her. I always believed Jess. I turned and pressed my face against her stomach. She was not a demonstrative woman. She seldom touched except to fix one's pigtails or hold one's hand. She never hugged or kissed. But at that moment she put her arms around me right out in the garden in full view of everyone and we both cried out loud for a wild ten minutes. And whether we mourned Oliver or my parents I'm sure neither of us knew. Perhaps Oliver's last kindness to me was to enable me to grieve for my father and my mother, breaking my silence at last.

How long had I stayed becalmed in that harbour of silence? Several months. Odd to have forgotten I had put in there before. Odder to remember now. This time my grief would not cry out, I thought. As Ben had said, there was too much of it. It had worn me out. I was an old coat with no one inside it. Grief had made a scarecrow of me. For the first time I understood Eliot. I was hollow, my head stuffed with straw. I was a waste land.

So I returned to the silence. When Thomas came in with tea he looked close at my face, searching.

'Jen?' he said.

I simply looked back at him. He understood. He seemed unperturbed. Glad, even? He kept staring into my eyes, however. He wanted to know if he had heard aright last night. Had I said, 'I love you, Thomas?' Was it true? I was the living equivalent of dead. How could I love anyone? What did it mean? I got tired of his silent questioning. I closed my eyes. The eyelid is a powerful prison door. It shuts you in. It shuts them out.

But next day the sounds in the street were different. It must be Saturday. I swung out of bed. The sun shone. I opened the wardrobe and saw my dead clothes hanging. Then I looked at the garden. Neglected. Autumnal. A few ragged fuchsias showed little globs of colour, their branches awkwardly poking up through mounds of next-door's rusted sycamore leaves. There was mildew on the roses. Sorrow was grinding in my chest. I would not be able to bear this. Thomas knocked and came in. I turned and walked into his arms. Long groans came out of me. I heard them, though I did not cry.

Later he sat me on the bed. He took from the wardrobe cord trousers and a big sweater. He took from the chest of drawers a pair of knickers and a pair of socks. They looked odd in his hands. Like crushed flowers. He knelt. I watched my feet disappear inside the socks. Then my stockinged feet slide through the holes in the knickers. He put his hands under my armpits and stood me up. He pulled the knickers up into place under my nightdress. He hardly touched my flesh and didn't look at me. The same with the green cords. He wouldn't be able to get the sweater onto me without removing the nightdress. What on earth would he do? He turned me to face away from him. He swept the nightie up and off in one swift movement. We were reflected in the mirror. I wanted to meet his eye in the mirror. I wanted to read his thoughts there. But his eyes were lowered; I could read nothing. Then his eyes did meet mine. A deep colour flushed his neck and his face. He looked away. Then he pulled the sweater down over my body, and went out of the room.

I was angry. Angry, angry. I was wrapped now, parcelled. My poor body, the shameful thing, was hidden. Well, what did it matter?

The storm passed. I put on my boots, straightened the bed, screwed up the nightie and put it into the laundry basket. I closed the lid.

When I came downstairs he was holding my jacket. I took it from him; the parcel was capable of wrapping itself. He opened the door. I walked ahead to his car, waited for him. There was no traffic. He drove quite fast. I knew where he was taking me.

Chapter Seven

It was a squat house, door in the middle, a window either side, two windows above. Trees squeezed close to it and straggled around, an unruly crowd. The roof of another house could be seen amongst them fifty yards away. He opened the gate and I followed him up the path.

All the interior walls had gone. The windows on all sides showed trees which seemed in the house, or getting in, or waiting. The room had pale carpet, few items of furniture, two wood carvings of tree-like forms. It ought to have been a pleasant space. Elizabeth gone, it was bleak, hardly lived in. You wanted to run and hide but there was nowhere to hide. Thomas touched a switch and some lamps came on, defining the space, reducing it. He strode to the far end of the room and disappeared. I half remembered from my previous visit a smart white kitchen.

I sat down on a tweed couch. It was comfortable. Elizabeth came up to me and said, 'Jen, isn't it? We've met at James and Margot's many times. I'm so glad you could come. Thomas specially wanted to ask you. He likes you very much. So do I, of course!' She laughed, covering her mouth. She had a child's voice, high and breathy, sweet. 'Have you got a drink? Oh, good. I'm not a very experienced hostess, I'm afraid. I've never given a party before. But Thomas is so well organised I didn't have to do much really. You've always been so good to Thomas. Oh yes, you have. You see, he's so shy and—withdrawn, isn't he?—that most people sort of give up. They don't persevere with him. He's really so nice and gentle, and so clever too, but people don't often stick around to find that out. Well, you do, that's all. So I've always felt—well—that you must be—awfully nice—' She ended on a breathy blushing charming laugh, and hid her face. What had happened to make her desperate enough to run away?

Thomas appeared with steaming cups.

'How long is it since Elizabeth went?' I said.

'Only three months.'

'I was remembering her.'

He stared at me, his cup clasped between big strong hands. I stared back. I was speaking again. So what?

'Don't go on living here, Thomas.'

'Why?'

'I don't like it here.'

'I thought we had made it beautiful.'

'You have of course, yes. But it makes me shiver.' I paused. 'And she must come into your thoughts all the time.'

'Yes. She does,' he said.

'Do you want her to come back, then?'

'No.'

The long silence after that, I had no desire to break. I drank the coffee, a rich dark Italian roast, as though it were the only thing in the world.

I had spoken twice now, but that was no guarantee that I would speak again. I had the sensation of one who has been swimming underwater many miles. I had put up my head a couple of times and taken air. But I could gently sink down again if I wished, into the comforting liquid dark.

Then Thomas was speaking, his words muffled and slow, his head hanging.

'I'm sorry, Thomas, what did you say?'

'I want to marry you.'

'Oh.'

It was an odd thing for me to say: 'Oh'.

'Why?' 'Why say it here?' 'But you can't so why mention it?' 'Why should you want to marry a person whose body you're ashamed to look at or touch?' These were questions it was impossible to ask. So I just said 'Oh'.

'You don't wish it?' His voice whispered and shook, like the trees outside.

I shrugged and sighed, meaning: 'What's the point?'

'If it were possible?' he said.

'It's not.'

'It is.'

'How? You have to wait—seven years, isn't it?—if a person has disappeared.'

'We could have a—private marriage. A

secret wedding. No one would know. Just us. No witnesses.'

'What would be the point?'

'To—solemnise. To—celebrate. To be able to say, "You are my wife. You are my husband".'

'You are my husband.' I heard my voice whisper it.

Thomas and I were facing each other, knees almost touching.

'How can you have a ceremony without witnesses?' I said.

'We must imagine our chosen witnesses.'

'Who would you imagine?'

'My mother. In Denmark, you know. And you?'

'Margot. James. Aunt Jess.'

I had said her name. And as I said it, into my mind came a vision of John Bright at her funeral, hands in his pockets, sharp eyes stabbing. I shivered.

'Are you cold, darling?' Thomas's voice stirred like the trees, a cold breath. I did not reply. 'What do you think of what I say?'

'You said darling.'

'Will you?'

'Why not?'

'You mean you will?'

'I mean I will.' I was without emotion, saying it. 'Why not?' I said again.

His light blue eyes looked blinded, as

101

they had yesterday afternoon on my bed. I waited, passive, I was tired, lying on a wave that lulled me, carried me forward on the tide. The sensation was not unpleasant, existence without will.

Thomas covered his face with his hands. Then he dropped his hands. He leaned close to me. He said, 'Here?' His breathing was fast and light. He said, 'Now?'

I must have looked bewildered.

He said again, 'Now, Jen? Here?'

I waited, perhaps for guidance. None came. I was still afloat on the tide. I said again, 'Why not?' I heard myself saying it, and thought, Why not?

He said, 'Come.'

I took his hand. The stairs were opposite the kitchen. We went up. The wall was hung with photographs, abstracts in black and yellow: stripes, arrows, circles. Signs without soul. He led me to a room with a modern brass bed, ornate snaky shapes at its head and foot. Branches pressed on the window, a few dry leaves hanging by a thread. The carpet was thick. I stood, left there, while he closed the curtains nineteen-eighties tapestry, heavy and dimly colourful.

At the window he turned. He tried to say 'Wait', but could not. He put up his hands, palms towards me, in a gesture meaning, 'Stay there'. His hands quivered a little. He

102

left the room. I stayed. I waited. The thick tapestry curtains cut out the little light that might have filtered through the trees. The room was drenched in the half light that permeates some dreams.

There was a slight sound, a swishing, a rustling. I turned to face the door. He stood there, holding a wedding dress. It was long, it was full-skirted, it was white. He held it with reverence. Tulle veiling clouded about it like ectoplasm. It was ravishing. My eyes must have asked what my mouth could not—Was it Elizabeth's—for Thomas said,

'I had it made for you. In your shape.'

'In my image and likeness.'

I was walking towards him. My hand reached out to touch the heavy gleaming white stuff, to stroke it. It felt cool and smooth, like skin. I shut my eyes. I was swaying a bit. His strong hand held my arm. We went to the bed. He laid the dress out on it with care, gently. He gripped my upper arms.

'I'll be your strength,' he whispered. 'I'll be your support.'

He reached behind him and switched on a lamp. 'Like a good deed in a naughty world.' Wasn't it Portia who said that, returning from the cruelty of Venice, to Belmont, 'on such a night as this'? I felt the same sudden shocking gladness to be coming home. Was I, then, coming home?

He said, 'I have to run a bath.'

He led me past the head of the stairs to a room full of steam and golden light, smelling of chestnuts and rosemary. He closed the door. I was alone.

Silken water lapped me, licked me. White foam shifted, subsided, with faint plopping sounds like lips on skin, kissing me as I sank down. I don't know how much time passed before Thomas tapped and said, 'May I dress you, Jen?'

I rose from the waves into warm air, stepped on soft carpet, wrapped myself in a hot towel. I touched the misted mirror with the palm of my hand, cleared a halo for my face. There I was, flushed, damp hair curling, eyes big. I hadn't seen myself for weeks. I didn't look the same. I dried myself and put on a thick white towelling robe that looked new. Thomas was outside the door. We went back to the bedroom. He closed the door softly. He stood me by the bed. He took off the robe and laid it over a chair. He came back to me. He lifted the dress, lowered it to the floor, spread it at my feet. I lifted one foot and stepped into the dress. Then the other foot. He pulled the soft white stuff upwards. I put my arms into the sleeves, the cool shining second skin. He turned me and fastened the back. He turned me again and placed on my head the white cloud, held by a wreath of Botticelli flowers. I didn't want to see myself. It would be better to imagine, surely? But he led me to the mirror. The veil covered my face and through the veil I was lovely. I was young and flushed. He, beside me, was big and blond and dressed in bridegroom black. We were the bride and groom on top of the wedding cake. I had a sudden sharp longing for Aunt Jess to be there. Thomas turned away to the bedside table, then came back. He held out his hand. In it was a plain gold band. He showed me some lettering etched inside.

'This was my father's ring,' he said.

He turned to face the mirror. I, at his side, did so too. The mirror was to be our witness then. All our witnesses.

'Do you, Jen, take me, Thomas, to be your lawful wedded husband, in sickness and in health, from this day forward, until death do us part?'

It was like a children's play of a wedding, with the solemnity that children's games can have.

'I do,' I said.

He waited. He stared at me in the mirror.

'And do you, Thomas, take me, Jen,

to be your lawful wedded wife in sickness and in health,' my reflection said, 'from this day forward until death us do part?'

'I do.'

His reflection looked at me. My reflection looked at him.

'With this ring I thee wed.' He slid the ring onto my finger. 'With this body I thee worship,' he said to my reflection. 'I declare us man and wife.' He turned to me: 'Now I may kiss my bride.'

He lifted my veil and carefully arranged it behind my head. He brought his lips to mine. He lifted me to the bed and laid me down. I lay and watched him take off his clothes. His chest and shoulders were broad. His legs were strong. He walked to me. He lay on me. He kissed all the flesh of me he could see: face, neck, hands, the upper part of my breasts. I wanted him to take off the heavy white dress. But he did not. Our lovemaking was soon over. We needed no more time, this first time. I cried out in pain as well as pleasure. The pain was at the breaking of the dam. The dam of silence, the dam of loneliness, the dam of grief. Thomas cried out too.

I opened my eyes and looked at him. He was pale, his expression serious. He searched my face. I felt naked though I was still clothed in the crumpled wedding dress. It was Thomas who was naked. I waited for him to speak. He said, 'Now you are really my wife.'

'Oh Thomas. Put your arms round me please.'

The heat his body gave out surprised me. He burned. But he did not sweat. Jean-Pierre after making love would be flushed and damp. He would wrap his arms and legs around me and drop into a short sleep, whoosh, like a stone into a pond. Thomas stretched out stiff and strong, all the length of me. His arms held me like iron gates. I felt safe. Thomas protected me. A great joy surged through me from the soles of my feet to the crown of flowers on my head.

'Oh, Thomas,' I said. 'You have married me!' I kissed his face all over. 'I have a husband!' I said.

Conversation In
Another Place

3

'I'm sorry, sir, we don't do men.'
'I haven't come for a haircut, love.'
'Oh? Well, how can I help you, sir?'

'You could have a coffee with me.'

'Oh no, I couldn't! We don't—'

'When's your break?'

'We're not allowed, we—'

'It's about your friend, Elizabeth.'

'Oh God.'

'Yup.'

'Have they found her then?'

'No.'

'Oh...so—?'

'I wish they had.'

'Are you a policeman then?'

'Do I look like a policeman?'

'I thought they'd finished with her, dropped the case.'

'They have. I don't think they should have.'

'Oh...So?'

What was his interest, she wanted to ask; and didn't know how.

'I'm a—friend of a—friend.'

'Oh...' She wasn't satisfied. He could be anyone. 'Good morning Madam. Luigi's just combing out, he'll be with you in a jiff.'

'What time's your break?' He gave her no time to think.

'I can't. Truly! Honestly, I can't!'

'Don't you want Elizabeth to be found?'

'Ohh... All right. I'll see you in the Wimpy. Should be safe enough in there, I suppose. Ten forty-five.'

Chapter Eight

I got up off the bed and looked in the mirror. I was an odd sight. The crown of flowers hung to one side, the veil trailed from a thread. The dress, gleaming like pearl, hung off one shoulder leaving the other bare, one of my breasts almost exposed. The skirt was all angles, dimly outlined in the light. My feet were bare. My eyes were bright and my skin feverish with colour, my mouth a crushed blur. The reflection put its hands to its hot cheeks. Her hands were long, pale and surprisingly cool.

'Oh, Thomas,' I said.

He stood behind me, naked and big. I turned and buried my face against his chest.

'My wife,' he said.

'My—husband.' I tried it out, whispering.

'I shall dress now,' he said.

'Yes.'

He went out of the room.

The draggled reflection and I were alone together. I looked at this rakish person in the mirror. I liked her. She was sweet and funny, she was happy and sad. She

109

was surrounded by dusky light which was almost darkness. She was married in the mirror. She need not be lonely again.

I took off the flower wreath and the veil, laid them gently on the bed, undid the dress and let it fall. I lifted it. It was heavy. I laid it by the veil. Now there was just me in the mirror. Burning eyes and cheeks, untidy hair, not quite firm breasts, dark triangle, straight legs. Wide shoulders, long hands and feet. It was not a romantic body. It was a body for work, for walking and gardening. But Thomas loved this body. Thomas had married it. Aunt Jess came into my head. I covered my face. She would not approve.

'Forgive me, Aunt Jess, I need happiness so much.'

I got myself back into my serviceable clothes, ran my hands through my tangled hair. There I was in the mirror. Jen again. I was shy of meeting my eye.

And all at once I came to myself. I was here in Elizabeth's house. I had married Elizabeth's husband and made love with him. In Elizabeth's bedroom? Elizabeth's bed? Elizabeth's *dress?*

I ran out of the door and down the stairs. Thomas was taking food from the microwave in the spick-and-span kitchen.

'Thomas—'

'Go and sit down.' He did not turn to

me. 'Sit down in the living room. I will bring the food.'

'Thomas—'

'Sit down.'

I had not promised to obey. But I did. I sat upright on a dining chair, my hands spread on the table in front of me. Thomas's hands appeared. They placed two plates.

'Thomas—'

He had gone. The plates contained slices of pizza and salad. His hands came back. They placed knives and forks, napkins.'

'Thomas—'

'Eat.'

He sat opposite me.

'I have to ask a thing—'

'Eat.'

So I did. I was hungry. I ate every crumb, like a little dog, concentrated, grateful. I replaced my knife and fork on the empty plate. I folded my hands into my lap.

'Thomas—'

'And I thought I was to have a wife who could not speak.'

I looked at him. He smiled.

'Oh, Thomas. I'm so worried. I'm afraid that that was the room, the—the bed—where you and Elizabeth—'

'No!'

'No?'

'Jen, I have prepared all this for you.

111

Even the bed is new. That room was empty, the extra room—'

'Spare.'

'Spare room, yes. The sheets, the curtains, the furniture. Everything is for you. For you.'

'And the—and the—the dress?' My hand played with the handle of my knife. I looked at my hand and the knife and the plate with reddish stains and crumbs.

'I told you, Jen.'

'Yes.'

He was pale. His face was stiff.

'I looked in your clothes for the size. I looked to find the most beautiful dress. You think this might be Elizabeth's wedding dress? What a strange man you must think me to be.'

I looked sadly across the table.

'I've been lost,' I said. 'My life has been so—odd—lately. Even to speak is strange. Today is a dream to me. I can't follow things in the usual way. It's like forgetting how to read, or walk. I've forgotten how to live. I have to learn again.'

'I'm here to help you. To bring you back to life.'

'Yes.'

'My Sleeping Beauty.'

'No beauty, I.'

'Oh yes. To me. Oh yes.'

'You find me beautiful?'

'You want me to say it again?'

'Yes, oh yes. Three times each day. Well, I'm not greedy, say three times a week. Just till I get used to it.'

'This cannot be so strange to you.'

'You don't know how strange.'

'But why?'

Even Jean-Pierre had never gone further than to call me a *jolie laide*. And more, I suspected, *laide* than *jolie*. Thomas reached into his pocket and brought out his wallet. He opened it. Pulled out a photograph, looked at it, passed it across. His solemnity made me afraid to look at it. I saw a woman's face, high cheek bones, square chin, straight nose, steady eyes. The mouth was wide, set firm, the hair severe, pulled back. She wore a dark high-necked dress that suggested a straight back. There was about the image the suggestion of another era.

'Your grandmother?' I said.

'My mother.'

'Oh.'

'Do you see?'

I saw.

'It could be me,' I said.

'Yes.'

'Only my face lacks her strength.'

The bones of the face, the outdoor look of the skin, the width of the mouth—yes, yes. But this face could never be mine. So hard, so stern, so cruel almost. No.

Thomas took the photograph from me. He was its priest. He worshipped it.

'You see?' he said. 'Beautiful. Yes?'

'My eyes are brown.'

'Yes.'

'And hers?'

'Silver.'

'Her eyes?'

'Yes.'

'Silver eyes?'

'Yes. Grey. Like water. With light. Silver. You understand?'

I nodded. Was she alive or dead?

'Where is she now?' I asked.

'In the vicarage at—' An unintelligible word that sounded like 'Yoldrugh'.

'Where were you born?'

'In our home. Yes.'

'She lives alone there?'

His face closed up. He put the photograph away again. He started to collect the dirty plates. He didn't like to be questioned about his mother. Why? Well, it could wait. I sat alone in the darkening room and listened. Thomas washed up. The trees quivered and breathed. A car hooted far off. Thomas came back. His face was clear again.

'We should start back now, Jen.'

'Yes.'

I went upstairs. The dress, the veil, the diadem of flowers, hung on the carved cupboard, forlorn. I tidied my hair. On the landing I crept to another door, opened it a crack. Twin beds, mirror wardrobes. 'Their' room. I should have trusted him.

'Where do you sleep now?' I asked. We were halfway back to Kentish Town.

'In your house!' He looked taken aback.

'Oh, yes.' I blushed. 'I meant, where in your house.'

'Oh. I have slept on the couch in the living room. Ever since.'

'Oh.'

'I will only sleep in the special bed with you.'

'Oh.'

It was dark. Rain needled the windscreen. The wipers made their hypnotic passes back and forth.

'Oh.'

Conversation In Another Place

4

'Call this ten forty-five?'

'Sorry. Someone's off sick today so we're mad busy.'

'A-ha.'

'What is this then?'

She sat down.

'Let's call it—an inquiry.'

'You're not a policeman, you said.'

In fact he hadn't said.

'I'm a friend of the woman Peterson's involved with now.'

The girl blushed with shock:

'He's already got someone else?'

'A-ha.'

'Did he have her before—before Elizabeth—went off?'

'Not in so many words. I don't think.'

'What?'

'No. It appears not.'

'Oh... So what are you? Some kind of private detective checking up for her, or what?'

'Kind of.' He gave a kind of smile. 'Did you like Peterson?'

'I never met him.'

'You must have seen him around.'

'He used to collect her. I'd just see him then.'

'After her hair appointment.'

'Yes.' The girl paused. 'She used to tell him wrong times.'

'Did she now?'

'Yes. It was my idea. She had no freedom, you see. He wanted to know her every move. I said to her, "Listen your

116

hair'll be done by four. Tell him five or five-thirty. He won't know the difference." She was scared but she started doing it.'

'And what did she do with this hour and a half of freedom? Spend it with you?'

'At first she did. But then she— Well, look, I don't know what she did the last few months. She said she went for walks or round the shops.'

'You didn't believe her?'

'I did!'

'A-ha.'

His eyes made her feel funny, the way she felt at the dentist's when he said 'open wide'.

'Well, I believed her at the time. She was really innocent, you know, like a baby. It's only since. You know. You start to think.'

'You tell the police this?'

'No. Well, I believed her when they were asking me, didn't I? It was only after. When she—didn't come back.'

'A-ha.' He wagged his coffee spoon till it waved like rubber. She wondered if he was hypnotising her. 'Did you expect her to get in touch with you?' he said.

'Yes!' Her vehemence surprised her. 'Yes, I did.'

'And why do you think she hasn't?'

Her eyes filled up with tears.

'I don't know, do I?' she said. 'That's your job, isn't it?'

Chapter Nine

'You spoke to me!' Margot stared.

'Yes.'

'Oh, I have to sit down.' She plummeted into my sofa. Her hands hung like stones. 'Oh,' she said, 'I'm all rag doll. I don't know what to say.'

I smiled. She leaned forward.

'Is it real, Jen?'

'Yes.'

'Will it last, darling?'

'Why not?'

'It's so sudden.'

'How could it be anything but sudden? One speaks or one doesn't speak. There's nothing in between.'

'Well, I thought you might have started from scratch. Mamma, Dadda, Canna Habba Binka Bink? Slowly build up your vocabulary to its customary forty-odd words. I don't know how I thought it would happen. I began to think it never would. What did start you up again?'

'Thomas did.'

'The mind boggles. Thomas doing what?'

'Thomas—loving me.'

'Oh dear, I was afraid he might.'

'Why "oh dear"? Why "afraid"?'

'Don't be cross, Jen. But do you mean loving or making love? Don't mind my cheek. I hate the details to be blurred. I like nice black lines round everything. Like James's illustrations. You know me. You don't have to answer if you do mind.'

'I don't mind. I mean both.'

'My God.' Margot was silent for nearly half a minute. 'Was it the deflowering that did it, then?'

'Hardly deflowering, Margot.'

'You always seem so virgin, Jen. One can't help seeing it as that.'

'Spinster, you mean.'

'No, darling, no.' She gazed at me, searching for an attitude. 'Am I to be happy for you, then?'

'I think so, yes.'

'You do look—feverish.'

'Oh?'

'Yes. Hectic, a bit.'

'It's too soon for proper happiness. I'm still half-asleep.'

'Yes.' Margot was grave. 'Do you love him, Jen?'

'Sometimes I love him. Sometimes I don't know. He's a foreign country to me.'

'Denmark, love.'

We laughed.

'He thinks I'm beautiful.'

Margot's eyebrows disappeared under her fringe. 'That's nice,' she said.

'He means it. He can't lie.'

'Everyone can lie.'

'No. He really can't. And that's the best thing, Margot. He tells me the truth. I'm safe with him.'

'Hmmph.'

'Can't you be happy for me?'

'I hope I can. I'll try to be.'

'Okay. Shall we have Earl Grey?'

She followed me to the kitchen.

'Is this his house too then, now?'

'Well, he's been staying here for weeks, Margot!'

'Yes but it's always been your house. One could come and go as one pleased.'

'Except that until I was struck dumb you never did.'

'No, that's true. But I knew I could.'

'Well, you still can.'

'I'll have to ask Thomas's permission.'

'Be happy for me, Margot.' I could not stand her objections any more.

'Oh Jen, I wish you happiness. I do.'

'Thanks.'

We clinked cups.

'Here's to you.'

'Here's to me.'

'You're speaking!' James laughed. 'I can't believe it.'

120

'Amazing, isn't it?'

'Just as though you've been doing it all your life.'

'Like riding a bike.'

'Amazing she didn't come back speaking Danish.'

'Why?'

'She and Thomas are One.'

'What?' He pushed me to arm's length. 'Is it true?'

'Well, yes. Why all the fuss?'

'I don't know. I'd seen it coming, I suppose.'

'That's what Margot said.'

'Oh, he repeats everything I say, even before he's heard me say it. He does it naturally, like breathing.'

'We can't get married, of course.'

'No. Seven years, isn't it, for a missing person? Do you mind?'

That's when I recalled the conversation in their kitchen months ago. 'I want a husband!' I'd said. Now I had one, in a way. But I couldn't tell them that.

'It'll be just the same,' I said. 'Till death us do part.'

'Is that what you want?'

'Yes. Margot thinks it's awful, but I don't.'

'There are times when Margot should keep her mouth shut.'

'Oh, he can be bossy when he wants!

Why don't *you* boss me, Jen? Stop me? I just go till I'm stopped.'

'I'm not masterful like James.'

They laughed. James, the gentlest of men, stretched out his legs, crossing his feet.

We sat.

Thomas came upon this sad little scene. Margot got up, went to him, kissed his cheek.

'Thomas, you've cured Jen. God knows how, but however, congratulations.'

Thomas blushed and stammered, took refuge in his pipe. Margot, overcome with her generosity, went to make more tea. James and I smiled at each other. Sadly, quietly, sexily. How I loved James. Thomas sat on the arm of my chair and put an arm round me. I felt fine.

'So when will you be going back to work?' Margot marched in with the fresh pot.

'Margot, she's hardly recovered yet,' James said. 'Give her a chance.'

'Work's good for people.'

'You can't imagine it, but so is rest.'

'Too much rest kills, dear.'

'How much is too much?'

'That is the question, I think.' Thomas took out his pipe.

'Well, Jen?' James cocked his head.

I was just about to reply when Thomas

122

spoke again. 'I have today booked tickets for Denmark.' He cradled his pipe from which a spiral of smoke rose.

'What?' I said.

'A surprise,' he said to his pipe. 'A—a holiday.' He meant honeymoon, but not in front of Margot and James. 'Before you resume work.'

'People don't go to Denmark for holidays, darling.'

'To meet my mother. Who lives there, you know.'

'Oh, yes.' Margot had the wit to look confused. 'Sorry, I forgot.'

'It's perfect, Thomas.' I touched his hands. 'And afterwards, when we return, I'll go back to work.'

'It is what I thought.'

'Yes.' We looked at each other. Margot and James smiled. The four of us sat there smiling. It was silly and we all laughed.

Margot said, 'Jen, I hate to mention it but there's a bottle of very good champagne in your fridge.'

So that was the wedding reception for the secret wedding of the year. We drank the Dom Perignon and Margot rang up Ben who sounded puzzled and said he had been coming to see me anyway.

'Jen! You can speak!' Ben's face was a crumpled little bud, opening.

'Yes,' I said.

He brandished a bottle of wine and an armful of books, chanting. ' "And thou beside me in the wilderness!" ' He whirled me up and we jigged about. The champagne had made me floaty, feet above the ground. Things were happening to her-down-there. So must the dead watch life go on. Aunt Jess and I watched the happiness, amused, detached, neither happy nor sad. The doorbell rang.

John Bright stood on the step. He jingled the change in his pocket. His squint looked somewhere past me. Or through me. I came to earth.

'Happened again,' he said. 'They were supposed to be feeding me tonight and they turn out to be at your place instead. Margot left me a note.'

He held out a scrumpled paper. The evidence.

'Sticking out of the letter box. Asking for the place to be burgled.'

'Come in,' I said.

'You spoke!'

'Yes.'

'Since when?'

'Yesterday?' I shrugged. 'The day before?'

'About time too.'

I shut the front door. Noise came from the living room.

'I wanted to have a word with you,' he said.

'What about?'

'Well—Thomas Peterson.' He jingled his change again. I wished he wouldn't.

'Why?'

'I just don't think you should get too—involved.'

'What possible business could that conceivably be of yours?'

'You're right. None. But Reg Grant, you know, the guy in charge in Epping, is a mate of mine.'

Rubberface.

'Oh really?'

'A-ha. Really. Yes.'

I felt my skin would split and bring forth scorpions. But Aunt Jess's social training kept me mute.

'I'm sorry,' he said. 'Perhaps I shouldn't have said anything. I just thought— Look, take no notice. Policemen get suspicious minds. Everything starts to look like a crime. It's a nasty way to view the world. I don't know the guy. You do. I'll go now. Tell James and Margot.'

'Mr Peterson is here, now,' I said. He turned, paused.

'Oh yes?' He gave his still-face smile. Not a muscle moved. Then a short laugh. 'It's called tact,' he said. 'I'm famous for it.' Then his focus changed. He went still,

125

a gun dog with its ears up.

'Mr Bright, isn't it?' Thomas stood in the living room doorway. 'Will you come in to have a drink with us?'

The squint shifted back to me. Bright raised an eyebrow. I said nothing.

'Er, yes. Okay,' he said. 'Thanks.'

I went towards the kitchen without turning my head. 'I'll get another glass.'

When I came back he and Thomas were on the couch, deep in talk. Fear scuttled through me. I hurried over to them. I heard: 'megabytes, software, floppy disc, and backup'. Computers! Bright flicked me a glance as I handed him wine. He did not wink. Just.

Ben had found an alarming music station on the radio. He grabbed me to dance.

'Come on, Cinderella, you *shall* go to the ball.'

'Just till midnight,' I said.

'I always hate that. It's my impoverished upbringing. I can't stand that glass coach turning into a pumpkin again.'

'Poor Ben. And don't the footmen become white rats?'

'Yes! White rats scampering along in the dark pulling a pumpkin, and her inside all in rags again. Nasty, isn't it?'

'It ends happily, though. She marries the prince.'

'I'm no royalist, love.'

'Oh, *I* am.'

'What was it like being one of the disabled?'

'Curious.'

'Did you want to join the great able-bodied again?'

'Not entirely.'

'The reluctant returnee.'

'Returner.'

'Returness, surely.'

'Sexist.'

'I am.' He looked smug. 'Why did you return then?'

'All good things come to an end.'

'So do bad things, according to you.'

'Cinderella again?'

'If the slipper fits.'

'I think it might.'

'Oh it will, Jen. You'll get the prince in the end.'

We were at that stage in drinking when every silly word seems brilliant, profound and new.

Margot and James circled on the spot, inseparably entwined. I wanted Thomas to dance with me like that. I looked at him. He took out his pipe and smiled. John Bright stood up. He came over. He took hold of me.

'Dance?' he said.

I was too startled to object. And then my body was in his charge, held, caught, let go, caught again, tautened, loosened, turned, returned. I was surprised. Even Jean-Pierre had never danced like that. Bright grinned his unmoving ironic grin. I came back to myself.

'Don't stiffen, Miss Wren. You dance good.'

'I dance well.'

'Yeah.'

'Did you tire of interrogating Thomas?'

'I apologise.'

'Is it all taken down to be used in evidence?'

'You heard what we were talking about.'

'I should hate to have a job like yours.'

'Why is everybody always so rude to me?'

'I wonder.'

'Even a well-brought-up maiden like you.'

The little brown eyes challenged me. I did not respond.

'Do you accept my apology?' he said.

'What can your apology possibly be worth?'

'A-ha.' He looked straight at me for a moment. His squint did come and go. It had gone now. 'It's possible the case could be reactivated,' he said. 'I wanted to warn you, that's all.'

'Really.'

'There's not much I can—'

The doorbell rang. Margot yelled, 'Thai Take-away!'

Bright said quietly, hardly moving his mouth, 'But I'll have a word. I'll see what I can do.'

Eating with our fingers, I met Thomas's eye. His smile was not his usual wide quiet slow smile, but wolfish, hungry. A tingling started in my feet and twanged slowly up my legs. I wanted everyone to go, to be alone with him.

I cleared the debris after the food. Margot was dancing with John Bright. Then she even got Thomas to his feet. James danced with me, loose-limbed, boyish. John Bright looked on from the fireplace, working steadily through my bottle of whisky. Ben had no head for drink. He sat on the couch with a childlike smile. Thomas and I did not touch or speak. He did not dance with me. But each time I caught his eye I found myself breathless, almost scared.

At last they did go. John Bright shook my hand rather formally. His grip was strong, though he swayed on his feet. 'Thank you,' he said clearly, 'for a pleasant evening.' He walked with careful steps to the cab he was sharing with Ben. I felt suddenly sorry for my rudeness to him.

'Oh my ears and whiskers,' Margot said

when she felt the crisp night air. James took one of her dangling arms and draped it round his neck, almost lifting her off her feet. 'Darling,' she said, 'I thought you'd never ask.' He put his other arm round her waist. The four-legged monster, giggling and shushing, lurched down my street. I shut the door.

'Jen.' His voice was urgent. 'Come up.'

On the landing there was silence and no sign of him.

'Come and see.'

The door of my room was a little open. A dim light showed. 'Look.'

He stood, already naked, near the curtained window in the dim rosy light, the satin wedding dress draped in front of him touching his flesh.

'Oh Thomas.'

'I brought it with me.' He was whispering. 'Take off your clothes.'

'Yes.'

I dragged off my clothes. He poured the cool heavy stuff over me and fastened it. He took my hand and led me to the mirror. He ran his hands over the dress, over me. He held it, me, to him, he on his knees, I standing. He moaned and mumbled my name and 'darling' and words I didn't understand and supposed Danish. He lifted his face.

'Come,' I whispered. 'Come.'

I went to the bed, pulling him by the hand and drawing him down on top of me. He looked a Viking, magnificent, the reddish hairs on his body curling and sparkling in the light. Then my vision was blocked out. Again it was swiftly over, the lovemaking; again no time was needed. We both cried out in the same moment in the same deep darkness where we had gone. It seemed hours later that we returned to the bed, the room, the glow from the reddish-shaded lamp.

Conversation In
Another Place

5

'What sort of property would you be looking for, sir?'
'I *would* be looking for a nice little detached residence built in the reign of Queen Anne, with a lot of roses in the garden. If I was looking for a property. But I'm not.'
The young man in the blazer looked put out. But rallied with a watery smile: 'And what *are* you looking for, sir? If I may ask.'

'I'm looking for Elizabeth Peterson, mate.'

'I'm sorry?'

'Never heard of her?'

'Well, I—'

'You got to believe what they say about yesterday's newspaper. Young woman. Disappeared. A few months ago. Not a million miles from here?'

'Oh, you mean—? Oh, you're a—Oh. But I thought the case was closed.'

'No case is closed till it's solved.'

'Oh. No. Of course. But actually, sir, er, officer, I wasn't here at the time. I'm new.'

'New, eh? A-ha.'

'Well, relatively new. We have a rather fast turnover of personnel. Transfers from our other branches and so on. Promotions. You know. No, the person you want to speak to'—he called across the office—'Derek? Could you spare a moment possibly?'

A pale man in a good suit turned and looked at John Bright.

'Hello, Derek. You were working here when Elizabeth Peterson disappeared?'

'Who? Oh. Yes. I believe I was.'

'Can we have a word?'

'Oh but I wasn't actually here the weekend that— My wife and I were away on holiday.'

132

'You were away?'

'Afraid so, yes.'

'So you wouldn't have been questioned by the police at the time?'

'Well, no.'

Later the pale man and John Bright were seen deep in conversation among the dustbins behind the pub. Later still, John Bright dropped in at Epping Headquarters to talk to Reg Grant.

Chapter Ten

Thomas would tell me nothing about where we were to go in Denmark. Just: 'Its my home. It's where I grew up.'

'But where, Thomas?'

At last he said. 'Very well, it's in a region called Stayoons.'

'Staines?'

He grimaced. 'Nothing like Staines.'

'Is Stayoons a town, a city, a village? What?'

'None of these things.'

'A county?'

'An isthmus.'

'Oh.'

I had to be satisfied. He would tell me no more. Margot kept asking me where

133

we'd be going. I didn't care, was content to be taken and surprised. But for her sake I bought a map at Stanford's in Longacre. We pored over it.

'It's spelt with a "v",' I said.

'Very helpful. Everything is spelt with a "v". Copenhagen is spelt with two of them.'

'It's an isthmus.'

'Have you seen this coastline? What's the plural for isthmus—isthmuses? Which island?'

'He won't say.'

'I want to know where you'll be!'

'I'll let you know when I get there.'

'Not good enough.'

'It'll have to be, Margot.'

She pestered Thomas but he would not be drawn, just smiled with his teeth clenched on his pipe.

'Margot routed!' James said. 'A pretty sight. You have succeeded, Thomas, where all around have failed.'

A week had passed since the party, the night of wedding dress love. Every day I embraced him, touched his hair, his face, his hands. But he remained aloof. He gave no sign whether I should go further or stop. I was ashamed, slightly of my ardour, afraid to question him. Perhaps he felt guilty because of still being married to Elizabeth. Perhaps he simply liked to make the first move. I told myself not to worry, simply to wait.

Then one night he decked me again in the wedding dress, turned me to the mirror, made love to me in a rush of passion as before, and afterwards lay exhausted in my arms.

Next morning I said, 'How long are we staying in Denmark?'

'Oh, a few weeks.'

'I have to tell Grahame when I'll be back at work.'

'Who?'

'My chief librarian.'

'Say—the middle of December then.'

I went to see Grahame.

'That's fine, Jen. You're sure you'll be well by then?'

'I'm well now.'

'Oh no, I think not.'

'Why?'

'Well, I don't know. You look...feverish. Your eyes are too bright.'

'Oh.' For a moment I was quite cast down. 'I feel very good,' I said.

'And there's no need for you to hurry back.'

'But I want to come back!'

We stood on the gallery outside the staff room. I looked down at the library. Ben piled books from the trolley onto the 'recently returned' shelves. Suze, in her thick glasses, helped a student at the reference counter. The great unemployed of Kentish Town sat behind newspapers at the big reading table in the window. A big blonde girl issued books.

'Is she my replacement?' I said.

'Leila, yes.'

'I'd like to come back now.'

'We've got Leila till the end of December, Jen.'

'I'd be superfluous?'

'You must get well.'

'The first of January I'm coming back.'

'You look terrible,' Ben said.

'I feel fine.'

'Good party, wasn't it?'

'A surprise.'

'Funny bloke, that policeman.'

'John Bright.'

'Kept asking me about Thomas in the cab.'

'Asking what?'

'Too pissed to recall. Never off duty, are they, those bastards? I quite liked him though, somehow.'

'You have some esoteric tastes.'

'I like you.'

'Quite.'

We smiled.

'I'm coming back January the first,' I said.

'Can't wait.' He rolled his eyes in the direction of my replacement, Leila, of the long blonde hair. 'Bloody woman. All tits and no brain.'

'Ben!'

'She gropes me in the stock room. I'm terrorised.'

'That's no excuse.'

'It's sexual harassment. I'm going to sue.'

'I'd like to be back now. I miss it so, the dear old library.'

'Won't be long, Jen.'

He hugged me. I got the usual mouthful of warm yak. Released from this hairy darkness I said, 'Ben, p'raps I won't go to Denmark.'

'Listen, Jen, you really don't look well. You're pale. Your eyes are too bright. You even seem to be sort of shaking a bit.'

I looked at my hands. It was true. There was a tremor. How odd.

'You've had a rough time. You've been in a bad way. You need a holiday. It'll do you good.'

'Yes, you're right.'

'I mean, why not?'

'Yes.'

'What would you do here until you came back to work? Mope about, waiting.'

'I don't mope.'

'It's better to mope in Denmark.'

'I'm not moping!'

'At least it'll be different there.'

'Yes.'

I gave him a light kiss. I could, ridiculously, have wept into the brown reindeer crossing his chest. I patted a pair of antlers and said, 'See you when I get back.'

It was cold outside, bright. Dead birds and rabbits hung outside the fishmonger's, their fishy gamey smell drowning the mimosa at the flowershop next door. The bearded man in the red woolly hat hunched in a doorway. He held out his hand. I put a pound coin in it. I felt that I might never see any of this again. I told myself it was silly, but I had an overwhelming sensation of dread.

Chapter Eleven

Dear Margot and James,

Well, we're off!

'Today's the day,' Thomas said this morning when he brought me my tea. 'Tomorrow you will see my home.'

For the last few days I've had the silliest feeling of nervousness about going. Almost as though I might never come back!

You do realise, this is the only man who has taken me to meet his family since my first boyfriend aged six? It's no wonder I'm nervous, is it? I almost shed tears of gratitude when I think of the difference between Thomas and Jean-Pierre.

Thomas is even more excited than I am. Suppressed and glittery. His teeth are clamped on his pipe harder than ever; I can hardly see him for smoke. He still won't answer my questions about his home. I think it's because he loves it so much and is so afraid it may have changed. You know he hasn't been back for nearly ten years?

I'm writing this in our cabin, very quietly so's not to wake Thomas who is very deep asleep. I've never known a person sleep so deeply, as though he has dropped to the bottom of a very deep pit.

Anyway.

It has been a rather odd journey so far. Not at all as I expected. I hoped my nervousness would have gone by now but it hasn't. In fact it's increased. Thomas has hardly spoken to me since we set off. It upsets me rather, I'm afraid.

I tried to phone you from the harbour when he went to see about tickets or something. You weren't there and of course you hadn't switched on your machine so it's your own fault that you will have to wade through this mighty missive to get my news.

The boat is big and white and smart. Not at all like the scruffy little cross Channel ferries we're used to. Of course it's a Danish boat! I'm very impressed. They got all the cars on in minutes, so efficient, no fuss. And the inside! Thick carpets, luxurious velvet armchairs, three restaurants, two cinemas, a bar where they have cabaret. And everything is so beautifully designed, right down to the hand drying machine in the ladies' loo! Even the food is excellent. (I'm ashamed of my surprise at that.) Of course the North Sea is rather horrid, so deep-looking and cold, and if no one will speak to you you do tend to spend a lot of time looking at it! I've brought plenty of books with me, including your latest Felix which makes me laugh and cry, but at this rate I'll be through them before we land. As one who spent months without speaking to a soul it ill behoves me to complain. So I don't. But oh, I wish he would answer me. I'm starting to feel really alarmed. Silly midnight fancies. Sshh, Jenitha, go to sleep. It will all look better in the morning. Oh, dear Aunt Jess.

Next Day.

I thought he was even silenter when I first got up, till I looked in. the upper bunk and saw he wasn't there. He wasn't on the deck either, or in the restaurant, so I ate the gorgeous breakfast alone. Then I sat in one of the velvet armchairs and watched the people walk by. Numerous Thomases strolled past me. Yes, really. Tall and blond and beautiful: open faces, boyish mouths, and even smoking pipes. But none of them was my Thomas. I got really worried. Perhaps that terrible heaving sea had swallowed him up. (Or down.) I went onto the outer deck. The cold air was a slap in the face. I followed a sign to 'Observation Deck'—the only place I hadn't looked—at the top of steep narrow wet stairs, the wind like a whip. He wasn't there either, just an immense 'lawn' of wall to wall artificial grass, surrounded by glass, with striped deckchairs dotted about. Smoke was rising from one of the deckchairs and Thomas stood up! Yes, *my* Thomas. But when I ran and put my arms round him he didn't respond. Taut as a drumskin he was, with a slight tremor, a little like mine. What a pair we are.

I asked him, 'Are you nervous because you haven't seen your mother for so long?' He nodded. I said, 'Do you think she'll be cross with you?'

'For what?' he said. 'For coming back?'

'No!' (What an idea.) 'For staying away all these years.'

And he said, 'Oh no, she won't be angry with me for that.'

It was hot up there with the sun pouring through the glass, but a chill passed through me, I'm not sure why.

I said, 'So I haven't done something to offend you then?'

That was the first time he'd really looked at me since we set off! 'Jen! Of course not!'

'Oh, I'm so glad,' I said. 'Because I couldn't stand having to meet your mother if you were angry with me.'

'Oh, she'll love *you*,' he said and he put his arms round me and hugged me so close I should have felt better but somehow I didn't. Oh dear. I'm afraid I'm not all that well, yet.

Sorry, this letter is turning into a saga. I told Thomas it was a diary when he asked me what it was. I don't know why I said that, except that he was so keen on the whole trip being a secret. And after I said it I thought, Well, that's what it is really, a sort of journal. So I didn't lie after all!

Yes, he's speaking to me again! Such a relief. He showed me pictures of his mother from when she was a girl. She is so like me it's uncanny. It would worry me except that his childlike delight in her and me and the resemblance seems to make it all right. I feel such happiness when he is happy. It is so good to be instrumental in someone else's happiness, don't you think?

So when the big ship nudged into Esbjerg harbour I was feeling much better. Ready to welcome Denmark into my open arms as the harbour welcomed the ship.

And I'm amazed at how foreign Denmark is! Even the roofs on quite ordinary little houses are like lids, with four slopes instead of two like ours. At first the road was quite flat, curving along the coast. Glimpses of silver sea through a waving curtain of grass. Clusters of windmills on concrete stilts. Then we turned away from the coast and the land began modestly to roll and freisian cows stood in the protection of its little hills. The houses are long and low, painted white or ochre or a kind of faded Venetian red, a row of sometimes as many as twelve small square windows under the deep sloping roof. The houses, the countryside, are modest, austere, homely, beautiful. I am so *touched* by it all. When I told Thomas so, he reached out and held my hand. He was still holding my hand (you should be impressed—he's a two-hands-on-the-wheel driver at all times– when suddenly another big white boat appeared, on the far side of a car park.

'Another ferry?' I said.

'Yes.' (An answer! He hadn't spoken for miles.)

'How long on this one?' (I had fears of another night.)

'One hour only.' (I swear his accent and syntax have become more Danish since we arrived. It's nice. But I adore him, you know, whatever he is or says or does.)

On the boat we had tea, imagine, and he showed me again the pictures of his mother: 'This is when she was first married. This is when I first went to school. This is when I went back to visit ten years ago. This is in the orchard. This is outside the church...'

I am trying to like her but I must say, even though she looks like me, I find her rather forbidding. She is not smiling in a single one of the pictures. That's extraordinary, don't you think?

I asked him, 'Don't you have any pictures of your father?'

He collected up the photographs and said, 'My father died when I was very young.'

'So she lives alone now?'

'She lives with my brothers.'

'Your brothers?'

'Yes.'

'You have brothers?'

'Two. One older, one younger.'

'They live at home still? They've never married?'

He stood up and stretched.

I said, 'What do they do?'

'Sven is a carpenter. Bo is a— He dabbles in—art. I'm going for a walk.'

He went down the steps to the lower deck. When he came back I said, 'There are no pictures of your brothers either?'

He lit his pipe. 'Only she is of importance,' he said. Then he turned to the window and smoked in silence. He hasn't spoken since. So that's why I'm writing to you, you see! Nothing better to do. Imagine having brothers and not telling me. Well! Think of me as I am thinking of you. And think, if this is ever posted, it will be posted in Denmark. Where I am now the proud possessor of two common-law brothers-in-law!

Love always,
Jen.

Darkness fell before we drove off the ferry so that I saw nothing of Seeland except darker outlines on darkness and I must have gone to sleep because I woke, as one does, when the car slowed down, wondering where I was.

It was such a shock to think we had arrived. I felt unprepared. But the car swung suddenly left and stopped in a sort of courtyard, a high hedge on three sides shutting the house off from the lane. Nice narrow bricks and a white door, two windows above the door and a steep gable end. Thomas pushed the bell. We heard it echoing and the whisper of branches and dry November leaves rustling in the dark. I held tightly to Thomas's hand but let go when the door opened.

The light was behind her so it was hard at first to see her face. She was big-boned, straight-backed. She stood absolutely still holding the door. She didn't speak or smile, or even move. She just stared at Thomas. As though he had risen from the dead. Then she whispered something on an indrawn breath—'Thomas?' perhaps—and stepped back one step. Now I could see her better. The face was older of course, and bonier, and I hoped sterner and colder than mine. But the resemblance was uncanny and frightened me. She frightened me.

She swallowed and whispered, 'Thomas,' again but not in welcome, just in some sort of shock, it seemed. She had not looked at me at all, not once. She couldn't take her eyes off her son. A voice called out from inside the house. She made no response. Not even her head moved.

Thomas murmured something in Danish, subdued, almost pleading, and put his arm across my shoulders. Her eyes moved to me, then away, then slowly back again. Now she stared at me. As shocked as I at the resemblance? I smiled stupidly, a nervous reflex. She didn't.

'This is my mother,' he said.

The degree of my surprise may be imagined.

After a long hesitation she stood back to let us in.

The hall was big and square and warm, with two polished old oak chairs. One had 1781 carved into its back, about the age of the house, I thought. The floor was the palest driftwood colour, as blond as Thomas's hair. There were three doors, two ahead, closed, and a double one to the left, open. I clung to these physical details like a shipwrecked man to a life boat. The voice that had called out was talking from the room on the left, high-pitched, excited, voluble. Thomas helped me off with my jacket, opened one of the facing doors and hung the jacket up. He came back to my side. His mother turned away. She went ahead of us through the double doors into the room on the left.

This was a small vestibule, as it were, to the main room, with books from floor to ceiling and a big desk. It was in darkness but the long room through another double doorway was lit. At the far end two sofas, some comfortable chairs and some lamps were arranged round a huge ceramic stove. The floor was the same bleached wood as the hall, and there were Persian rugs.

I saw all this in my peripheral vision. In the middle of my eye a smaller version of Thomas sat on the sofa facing us. He took his pipe out of his mouth and stared. The high excited voice came from a wheelchair with its back to us. An expressive arm waved and a square small hand gave emphasis to the words. No head was visible above the back of the chair. Was it a child, then, who talked and laughed so elatedly? The voice was not quite a child's. The voice faltered, sputtered, stopped. Small-Thomas slowly stood up. He said, 'Thomas?' The squeaky voice from the wheelchair said 'Thomas?' also, with incredulity. The wheelchair turned to face us.

In the chair there was a head. Only a head. A head with arms. Black dots jabbed from the edge of my vision inwards to a point of light which contained just the Head. Then that was blacked out too.

A wet cloth wiped my face. I opened my eyes. I was lying on the sofa. Small-Thomas put down the cloth, held out a small glass of clear liquid and said some words which meant 'Drink this' as clearly as a label on a bottle. And I thought of

Alice but I drank. The liquid looked like water. It tasted like fire. I coughed. But I sat up. The mother stood by the stove, Thomas stood at the foot of the sofa. The wheelchair had gone. And the Head. I had, perhaps, invented it?

Thomas said, 'You fainted, Jen. It has been a long journey.'

I wanted to say it wasn't the journey that had made me faint, but: 'I'm so sorry,' I heard myself stammer. 'So silly. I can't think what came over me.' Idiotic, I felt.

'My mother you have met.' Thomas was very stiff. 'And this is my elder brother, Sven.'

Small-Thomas smiled. He handed me the fiery glass again and said, 'Aquavit.'

Thomas said, 'Drink, It will do you good.' Then he said, 'Steady,' as I drained the little glass in one gulp.

'I'm very pleased to meet you,' I said. Sven and the mother looked at me but said nothing.

'Don't they speak English, Thomas?'

Thomas didn't reply. Nobody replied.

'But how can I make myself understood? I don't have a word of Danish, not even please or thank you, not yes or no. I can't even say sorry for behaving so stupidly.'

'You won't need please or thank you and never sorry, and don't worry, I'll do all the interpreting. My English is tophole as

149

you will discover. I'm sure Thomas speaks English as he does Danish, like a farmer. No appreciation of the subtleties. I'm Bo. His younger brother. How do you do?'

The wheelchair bore down on me from the far end of the room. The Head said, 'More aquavit or she'll pass out again, poor girl.'

The others parted to let him through. The wheelchair stopped. I had not invented him. Who could? A head, wide at the top, narrowing to the chin. Two arms. Six inches of dark green sweater. Then less than six inches of small canvas bag which dwindled to a point on the seat of the chair. That was all. None of Aunt Jess's social injunctions could help me. Having first fainted, I now stared.

The face was alive with mischief, eyebrows up, teeth gleaming, even the ears seemed in the joke. He put out one of his neat small hands. His grip was fierce.

'Jen,' he squeaked. 'This is short for Jennifer?'

I shook my head.

'Give the girl more aquavit. I'm a very bad shock. Thomas, you didn't warn this poor girl. That's very bad. Not at all kind. To anyone.' He continued in Danish then stopped and grinned at me, showing eye teeth with points, like a fox. He had short coarse brown hair, unlike these two Thomases so white and blue and blond. He was a changeling. I had swallowed the aquavit too fast again. My head was a spiral, spinning.

'Now,' the Head said. 'You've very tired. And you are shocked. And lonely.' I opened my mouth. 'And quite drunk actually, so you must go to bed. No rooms are prepared because owing to Thomas's lack of—foresight, shall we say?—you were not expected. You'll be cold at first but you'll soon get warm. In fact you'll be asleep before you have time to think about it. I welcome you to Goltrup Vicarage and hope you will be comfortable with us. None of us—except me of course, because I am always ready for anything—is ready to welcome you tonight. Tomorrow we will start your visit properly and pretend tonight didn't happen. How's that?' The little hands lifted and opened in a conjurer's gesture: look, I have nothing up my sleeve—'Good. Bed! Thomas, take her up and put her in Aurora.' He clapped his hands. 'Come along. Jump to it, my little man.'

Sven looked at Thomas, warily perhaps. Thomas didn't smile. I got to my feet. The mother stood back to let me pass but Bo's chair was in my path. He reached out a hand. I gave him mine. He held it in both

151

his, pulled it towards him and kissed it. Then he laughed.

'How I astonish you!' he said. 'I merely wish to say sleep well and goodnight.'

'Thank you. I'm so sorry.' I looked at the three brothers in the glow of the stove. 'Goodnight then.'

I was standing next to the mother. Sven stared from me to her, as though the likeness only now struck him. She gave me a swift glance, and looked away.

Thomas led me through a large room with many windows and a big table, to a lobby with a small cramped staircase and a bathroom, which was all white porcelain and blue tiles.

At the top of the stairs I gasped. The space under the roof was vast. It must have been a granary once. I followed Thomas to the far end of this cold space where there were two doors. He opened the one with a porcelain plaque that said 'Aurora'. Two narrow mahogany beds with cloudy white duvets. A window between them. I sat on one of the beds. Thomas squatted to attend to a radiator. Then he turned. His face was pale, timorous. He knelt in front of me, buried his face against me. I draped limp arms over his shoulders and laid my head on his.

Conversation In
Another Place

6

'Margot?'

'Detective Inspector John Bright!'

'How did you know?'

'I'd know that horrible voice anywhere.'

'A-ha.'

'A-ha, yes! Are you coming to see us?'

'Listen, Margot—'

'We haven't seen you for ages. Haven't seen anyone, come to that. We've been promoting the latest *Felix*. You know, doing the rounds. Exhausting but over now. The damn thing can fend for itself from now on. Come round, we'll give you a copy.'

'Margot, I need to speak to your friend. The one who's going out with Peterson.'

'Jen?'

'Yeah.'

'Why? What's she done?'

'She hasn't done a thing.'

'Why d'you want to see her then?'

'It's confidential, love.'

'What's happened to her?'

'Nothing's happened to her, as far as I know.'

'Oh, God.'

'What?'

'She's gone.'

'Gone?'

'To Denmark. With him. With Thomas. She didn't even let us know. We only found out she'd gone when James popped round there and her little house had a definite shut up look. That's the first we knew. Oh, John.'

A small silence. Then: 'Give me her address in Denmark.'

Another small silence, then: 'We don't have her address.'

Chapter Twelve

It was warm when I woke, the room yellow with light. Where was I? At home? At Aunt Jess's? On the boat? Where? Why was I wearing bra and pants? The window curtains were gentian blue, a stiletto of light between them. The duvet was light as candy floss, the foot of the bed a narrow mahogany curve. Not an English bed. More like a French *bateau lit*. But this surely wasn't France?

Last night came back like an avalanche. I heard someone outside the door, swiftly sat and arranged the duvet up to my neck. A tray pushed the door open, followed by Thomas. He laid the tray on my knees.

On the tray was a white pot, a white cup and saucer, a white plate, a white egg in a white egg cup, two slices of bread (brown), a small white dish of butter (yellow), a Danish pastry, polished silver cutlery. The tray and the tray cloth were a pale bluish-grey.

'Dazzling,' I said.

Thomas sat on the bed.

'What time is it?' I said.

'Nine-thirty.'

'So late! Oh dear. Has everyone else had breakfast?'

'It's fine.'

'You're sure?'

'Yes.'

'Who made up this beautiful tray?'

'My mother.'

'Oh.' I tried the egg. It was perfect. 'How is she? This morning.'

He stood up.

'Has she got over the shock?' I said.

He turned to the window.

'That'll teach you to take people by surprise, Thomas. What possessed you?'

He pulled open the curtains.

'Thomas? You should have prepared us

all. The—Bo—was right. It wasn't fair.'
The anger didn't sound in my voice. I
couldn't get it there. I was dazed with
light. I poured some tea, a pale liquid the
colour of honey. I drank some. Darjeeling.
Perfect, too. 'Anyway.' I sighed. 'Is it all
right now? Has everyone recovered?'

He turned from the window.

'I introduced you as my wife,' he said.

I put down the cup.

'We're not really married, Thomas.'

'In my eyes, we are.'

'In mine too, but—' I looked at the ring
he had put on my finger. His father's ring.
What would his mother think of that? 'But
what about Elizabeth?' I said. 'What have
you told them about her?'

'They—never knew—about Elizabeth.'

'Never knew about her? You were
married five years and never told your
family?' I thought of Jean-Pierre. Were all
men the same? Or just the men I chose?
At least this time it wasn't I who was the
secret one. This did not comfort me.

'Thomas—'

'My mother could never have liked
Elizabeth.'

'Thomas, that's not the point—'

A huge reverberation shook the room. I
jumped, spilled tea.

'The church bell,' Thomas shouted.
'Each morning at this time.' It clanged

156

again. 'Each evening too.' And again.
After some minutes it stopped. The echoes
limped away.

'Will you tell them we are married,
Jen?'

I mopped spilled tea.

'Jen?' He gripped my hand till the ring
cut in.

'Ouch.' My thoughts were compacted,
my head full of bells. 'I won't deny it,' I
said at last.

He kissed me, gripping my shoulders
hard.

'But I hate lies and vaguenesses,' I said.
'I wish you'd tell them the truth.'

'My mother will see. She will understand. It will be all right. Everything will
be all right.'

That was no answer. But he was smiling
at me and the sun was shining into
this lovely room. I bit into the Danish
pastry expecting the heavy doughy dry as
cardboard thing that goes by the name in
England.

'This is wonderful, Thomas.'

'Just a pastry.' He shrugged.

'That is precisely where you are wrong.'

He looked puzzled. I smiled at him. I
drained the dregs of the delicious tea and
got out of bed. He didn't look at me.

'Thomas?'

He turned but again avoided looking at

157

me. Was this shyness brought on by being in his mother's house? It was silly, surely? I wasn't even quite naked, and anyway this was our honeymoon. I went to him to be hugged but he picked up the tray and held it between us.

'Thomas, don't leave me.'

'I'll come back.'

I heard him clatter down the stairs as I went to the window. It was immediately above the front door and overlooked the courtyard with the high hedges I now saw were beech. Thomas's car was still there. Beyond the hedge was a lane with bare trees. Beyond the trees small flat fields. And beyond the fields in the distance a glistening line of sea. His mother turned into the courtyard from the lane. She came through the courtyard, carrying a heavy shopping basket, and disappeared beneath me into the house.

My bag was on the floor. No thoughts of unpacking last night. I pulled out my dressing gown.

At the far end of the huge roof space where the stairs came up were some sofas on a rug, and an iron stove, now lit. Two doors matched the doors at this end.

A little nervous, I tried the right hand door. The room was full of faces, greenish and yellowish, animal and human, all round the walls and the huge old bath. At shoulder height the faces stopped. Above them, the walls were a glaucous green. Scalding water gushed out of the big-bellied tap. But I didn't stay in the bathroom long. The faces mocked me, peeping and grinning from their fringes of leaves.

Thomas had not come back. I told myself it was silly to feel abandoned. I put on a sweater and trousers. Then I took off the trousers and put on a skirt. Then the trousers again, then finally decided on the skirt.

I crept into the kitchen, at the foot of the stairs. It was a big square warm room smelling of coffee and bread. Bunches of herbs and dried flowers hung from the beams. Thomas had left my tray on the draining board. I rinsed my plate and cup at the big stainless steel sink and, timorous, opened cupboards. Their insides were a cool blue-grey, lined with white paper, the contents neatly stacked. I stowed the crockery, hoping I'd got it right.

From behind a closed door at the far end of the kitchen I heard voices. Thomas's insistent, and another, which I guessed to be his mother's, muffled and low. I crept from the door to the staircase lobby. I must not be caught eavesdropping, though I saw the irony of evesdropping on a conversation of which I could not understand a word.

In the dining room the polished table reflected scarlet berries on black branches in a white jug. Light dazzled the lace at the windows, so bright there was no view beyond. I crept into the long room. There was no one there. The door and the narrow bay windows on either side of it had small old panes with bevelled edges, glittering. Outside the windows red and yellow apples hung from leafless trees. High beech hedges cut this frozen orchard off from the rest of the world. I could not see beyond. The silence was as deep as the cold North Sea. You could as easily drown in it. I stood with my back to the windows and wondered if Thomas would come.

Everything in the room was white or grey or blue, except for the paisley cover on the shabby sofa, and the rugs. The huge white ceramic stove gave out a glowing warmth. A painted grandfather clock tick-tocked between the stove and a door in the corner of the room. I wondered where this door might lead. Then I heard a sound from the direction of the kitchen, a door open and close. No voices. I felt I had no right to be here, a thief about to be caught in the act. Footsteps. Not Thomas's I was sure. I took a step towards the dining room as the mother walked past. I stopped. She stopped too.

She stood looking at me. Her face was stern. I didn't know what to say. So I smiled. I thought for a moment she might speak. But she didn't. She simply took a jug from the sideboard and went back through to the kitchen. I heard a door again open and close. And then no sounds. I hovered in the room like a trapped moth. Then I opened the glass-paned door and let myself out.

The air was crisp and bright but so cold it hurt. I didn't mind the hurt, it was so good to be outside. A narrow flowerbed and a flagged path ran alongside the house. I turned right, passed the small bay window of the long room and reached another little window, just the same. I pressed my nose to the glass, my hands either side of my face to blinker the light. In the dimness I saw a big high bed with carved ends. The bed ends were painted, lovely faded greens and gold like the grandfather clock, with a cupboard that matched. The door in the corner by the clock must lead to this room. I somehow knew it must be the mother's room, full of dignity and history, private and dark. I backed away from the window in case she should come into the room and see me there.

I turned the corner of the house. This side was unexpectedly longer than the main house, and lower, with only one small window of stained glass. That must be the downstairs bathroom. The bricks, the colour of the dark bits of smoked salmon, were rough to the touch. I stroked them as I walked along. The apple trees continued as far as the end of the building. Then a hedge, not of beech but some evergreen with small leaves, divided the orchard from a vegetable garden, which was laid out in neat beds divided by brick paths, curly leaves of seakale and florets of broccoli, vivid grey green and purple in the frost. Thorny branches flung four or five frozen yellow rosebuds across a high brick wall. All this lovely husbandry. Who did it? The mother? Sven, perhaps.

A flagged courtyard lay between the vegetable garden and the back of the house, with flowerbeds where even now some straggling chrysanthemums and michaelmas daisies echoed the colours of the bricks. Along this side of the low leg of the L were eight small square windows; and in the elbow where it joined the main house, a door. I was so cold I had to go back in. I stood in the little lobby at the foot of the stairs. Warmth and the smell of coffee.

'Jen.'

'Oh!' My painfully thawing hands went to my heart. Thomas was standing at the dining-room door. His mother sat at the table with her back to us, drinking coffee. Thomas beckoned me in. I shook my head. I wanted to creep away upstairs.

'Yes.' His voice was loud and stern. 'You must have coffee. You are cold. You have been outside?'

The mother got up and went to the oak dresser. She took a white cup and saucer to the end of the table where there was a blue and white mat. She put a matching napkin and a silver knife and spoon on it. She poured coffee. Even the large white thermos jug was beautiful. She passed the frothy hot milk. She didn't speak, and she didn't smile. Thomas sat next to me. He didn't speak either. We drank. The coffee was excellent. But the silence was thick as flesh. She didn't look at anyone. Thomas didn't look at her.

'The coffee is delicious,' I said. The mother looked at me. 'Thomas?' I said.

He looked up.

'Will you tell your mother the coffee is very good?'

He glanced at her anxiously, said some Danish words in a subdued voice. Her expression did not change. She wiped her mouth with the blue napkin. She did not reply. Fear made me chatter.

'I walked round the house,' I said. 'What do you call the low bit where the kitchen is?'

'The sidehouse. It used to be a barn.'

'I thought so. What is it now? Apart from the kitchen, that is.'

'Kitchen, laundry, Bo's room.'

'The garden is lovely. Is it your mother who does the gardening?'

Again he spoke to her in the subdued voice. Again she answered with one abrupt syllable: *'Tak.'*

I gathered the answer was yes. I had no more courage. We finished our coffee in silence. Then she stood and began to clear things away.

'Thomas, ask her if I can help. Tell her I'd like to. I want to. Please.'

He spoke and she inclined her head a little, without looking at me. I followed her into the kitchen. She took the crockery from my hands and turned to the sink. She didn't hand me a tea towel or indicate where I might find one. I hovered in the doorway. Ignoring me, she opened the far door, from behind which this morning I had heard her voice and Thomas's, arguing. I saw a darkish room with a freezer, a washing machine, a hanging rack, another large sink. A farther door between the freezer and the washing machine was closed. That must be the door to Bo's room. She started to take clothes from the washing machine. I waited but she didn't turn.

'Thomas?'

He stood at the long room window and looked at the orchard, smoking his pipe.

'Thomas!'

He jumped, and turned to me like a stranger.

'Yes, it's me.' I managed to smile. 'I am still here.'

'Jen!' As though he'd forgotten my existence.

'Can we go for a walk?' I said.

Bright sun and a big sky, not like grey old England in the winter. It was good to get out of those high beech hedges and off down the lane. We turned to the right. Thomas said he wanted to show me the church: the sea was in the other direction and could wait. I put my arm through his, just like a real husband and wife.

'You had a talk with your mother then this morning?' I said.

He shrugged.

'I heard your voices in the laundry room. But of course I couldn't understand the words.'

No reply.

'What did she say? She doesn't seem delighted to see—well—me, anyway. Is she very—shy, perhaps?'

Then the lane opened out. A road came

up on the right and curved downhill ahead of us. Tucked into the bend was a long low white house, surrounded on three sides by bare brown trees. Thomas said it used to be the school house.

'It is not a school house, of course. I do not know who lives there now.'

'Did you go to school there?'

'Yes, till I was eight or nine.'

I could see them all, small serious blond Thomases sitting at their desks.

'Just one teacher I suppose?'

'Oh yes. He lived there too.'

School over, going down to his end of the house, stoking his stove

And opposite the schoolhouse on a green mound rose the church. It was bright yellow, with a red-tiled roof. The tower went up in steps to a bell house with a smaller red roof. Halfway up the tower, a round clock, duck egg blue like the sky, with golden numerals. All surrounded by a low white wall with a green picket gate. Showing above the wall, almost black against the sky, round-topped pines and tapering cypresses.

'Oh, so pretty!' I said.

He led me almost running up the little white path to the gate.

'Who rings the bell?' I asked.

'The sexton.'

'You have a sexton?' I laughed.

'Yes.'

Now I could see over the wall. Lovely avenues and little paths among the cypress trees. Low box hedges, a rich dark green, formed small enclosures perhaps six foot square. Within each little 'room' stood a gravestone or two. The floors of the little rooms were carpeted with fir tree branches newly spread.

'Is it always like that?' I said. 'The fir tree branches on the ground?'

'No. For Christmas, I think.' He was hurrying ahead of me through the gate.

Inside the churchyard I bent to read the names on the stones, in memory of Lars or Sven, Inge or Ane. They dated back to the seventeenth century and there were many Petersens but no Thomases, not one. It must be a rare name here.

'Thomas? Why are there no Thomases?'

But he didn't wait. He almost ran along the winding path. I wandered slowly behind, thinking of another churchyard by the sea and my little Aunt Jess.

Behind the church the path narrowed. The trees closed over it. Then all paths came to an end and rough ground sloped up to an ivy-covered wall. Thomas raced up this bank and stood quite still. He slowly shook his head.

'What is it?' I scrambled up.

'The gravel pit,' he whispered.

On the other side of the wall, the ground fell away into a round dell and, about twenty feet down, a deep dark pond all hung over with brambles and bushes and twisted trees.

'Gravel pit?'

'It was where we—played—as children. It was our—forbidden place.'

'I can see why it would be forbidden.'

'Why have they done this?' He was distressed.

'What?'

'It used to be grass, bushes, flowers. They have filled it up with water.'

'Thomas?'

But he was shaking his head, murmuring. He was unaware of me. So, after a while, I scrambled back down the slope and wandered again among the cosy little grave-rooms, round the other side of the church to the porch. I pushed the heavy door. A white silence. Cool white light. They had uncovered a mural, eleventh- or twelfth-century: Christ rising above a lot of little people and fork-tailed devils. I was entranced.

I came out into whiter colder light, blinking. Thomas was coming down the path alongside the church. His face was pale, his mouth trembling a little. I waited for him.

Then beyond him I saw a huge

man pushing a wheel barrow. He had materialised from behind the church, a character from the mural come to life. He parked his barrow by one of the graves. He wore a dark wool hat pulled well down, almost to meet his beard. He began to throw dead branches and leaves into the barrow. He stood up and saw us. Put a hand to his forehead to see us better.

I smiled politely. He didn't smile back. They were sparing with their smiles, these Danes.

'Come inside.' Thomas gripped my arm.

'But I've seen the church.'

'Come inside.'

He held me in the porch. His breathing was unsteady. We heard footsteps and the wheelbarrow crunch on gravel. Thomas shut the door carefully.

I whispered, 'Is he the sexton?'

Thomas nodded.

'Why don't you want to speak to him?'

He didn't reply. He listened till the sounds outside faded away. Then he eased the door open.

The sexton was pushing his barrow out of the gate. He appeared even bigger and darker than before, the barrow like a toy in his big hands. He stopped on the green mound. He was looking at Thomas. Thomas stayed quite still at my side. Both men seemed to be waiting, each perhaps for the other to speak. Then the sexton grasped the handles of his barrow again. He gave Thomas one last look then turned away and plodded up the lane. We watched him.

'Where's he going now?' I said.

'Home.'

'Where's that?'

'Just beyond our house up the lane.'

'You're neighbours?'

'We were at school together.' He looked at the schoolhouse. 'Over there.'

'And you don't like each other?'

No reply.

'What's his name?'

'Knud.'

'It would be.'

'What's funny?'

'I don't know. Everything.'

He suddenly gripped me by the upper arms and said, 'It's good to hear you laugh.'

Confused, alarmed, I smiled and couldn't look at him.

Then I saw that we stood right next to a large grave-room with two stones in it. One was engraved: 'Lars Petersen'; the other, a smaller one: 'Ketty'. A holly bush grew in the little enclosure and a small blue fir, but there were no branches spread on the frosty gravel floor.

170

'Lars Petersen,' I read. 'Is that your father?'

'Yes.'

'How old were you when he died?'

'Six.'

'How awful. Just like me.' I put my arm through his. 'Who was Ketty?'

'She was—married to Sven,' he said.

I looked at the small stone. She had died nine years ago.

Conversation In Another Place

7

'All I can remember is it begins with an S and has a V in it.'

'Christ.'

'And it's an isthmus.'

'And it's an isthmus. The place is littered with them.'

'I'm so sorry, John. But it was this big secret. Their secret honeymoon. Jen couldn't tell us because he wouldn't tell her. I tried and tried. Honestly I did.'

'Don't upset yourself.'

James put his arms round Margot. 'What's happened, John?'

171

'In Denmark or here?'

'Don't.'

'Let's say, developments.'

'You've found some evidence against him?'

'James! Don't ask, okay?'

'Oh God.'

'All right then. No. The one thing they haven't got yet is evidence. They'll get it though. If I've got anything to do with it. It'll just take time and manpower. Both of which are in short supply. Can I take this map away with me?'

'Sure.'

' 'Course, they might not have gone to Denmark at all. They could be anywhere She's a trusting soul, your friend.'

'You look so grim, John.'

'I feel grim.'

'Have a drink.'

Bright hesitated a moment. Then he said, 'No thanks,' and looked surprised.

Chapter Thirteen

His mother was setting the dining room table with its blue and silver and white. She looked at Thomas and said some Danish words. Thomas nodded, obedient.

I asked him what she'd said but he went into the long room without answering. I stood there, rather awkward, not knowing what to do. I said, 'Lunch?'

She held up five fingers. Without looking at me.

I said, 'Five minutes?'

She nodded without friendliness.

Trying not to feel rebuffed, I ran up to the roof space to tidy myself up. Perhaps the leering faces round the bathroom wall were to be the only Danish faces that would ever smile at me. No sound yet of people making for the dining room. I wandered to one of the row of windows under the roof. The windows overlooked the orchard and down there among the frozen trees a small girl galloped.

She was stocky, short. Two yellow pigtails stood out, stiff. They bounced up and down as she moved. She pulled up sharp, made a sudden swerve, and was off again, clip-clop, like a little horse. She wore a thick blue coat, red ankle boots, bright socks and mittens. I smiled, watching her. Who was she? I'd seen no sign of her in the house. Thomas hadn't mentioned a little girl. She must be a neighbour child.

Downstairs, Thomas sat with his back to the window, Sven next to him. Sven stood as I came in, ducked his head and blushed. Bo, from his wheelchair at the head of the table, said, 'The height of my ambition: to stand when a lady enters the room. Alas, it can never be.'

I smiled, though the sight of him was a fresh shock.

'Hello, Jen.' He raised his little conjurer's hand. 'It's good to see you again. You sit here, please. Next to me.'

Thomas seemed upset.

'Cheer up, Thomas,' squeaked Bo. 'Don't be jealous, my little man.'

Thomas made a convulsive movement, his fist clenched on the table.

'You see, my dear Jen?' Bo grinned. 'This Thomas is a dangerous fellow. You watch out.'

I smiled as best I could and said, 'Don't be cross, Thomas.' He focused on me. His face reorganised itself. I felt embarrassed in the silence.

'We went to see your church,' I said.

'You liked it?' Bo said.

'Very much, and the graveyard is lovely. You never see an English graveyard so cared for. They are like little green houses, the—enclosures.'

'And in England, how are they?'

'Like cold stone beds. Sometimes enclosed with chains.'

'Cold stone prison cells.'

'Yes! I liked the carpets of fir branches especially.'

'The branches are placed there for warmth in winter, you know.'

'For warmth!'

'Oh yes. We care for our dead there. We like to keep them warn.' He looked from the corners of his eyes. 'Don't we, Thomas?'

There was a silence.

'There were no branches on your father's grave,' I said.

'Knud will do it. Our sexton.' He looked at Thomas again. 'You saw Knud?' Thomas didn't reply.

'Yes,' I said.

'Did you like him?'

'We—he—didn't speak to us.'

'Ah. I wonder why. Can you think why, Thomas?'

Again Thomas said nothing.

'I saw lots of Petersen graves but no Thomases,' I rushed in.

'Thomas is an uncommon name here.' Bo looked again from the sides of his eyes. 'An uncommon name for an uncommon person.'

I heard the mother calling outside the room. Then she came in carrying a steaming meat loaf on an oblong brown dish. It smelt wonderful. Of warmth and garlic. She put it down, unsmiling, and went out again.

'A family recipe,' Bo said. 'Liver pâté,

175

traditional Danish, but the garlic—pure Mama Petersen.'

I heard a patter of footsteps on the stairs. The door flew open. The little girl from the orchard halted, panting, just inside the room.

I smiled at her. She put her head on one side. She had round blue eyes. She looked from Thomas to me and from me to Thomas. When she looked at him, Thomas became absolutely still. Expression left his face. Colour left his eyes. As though he had been shot through the heart and had just this one moment of paralysed life left to him before he fell. It was a curious hiatus. The room itself seemed to wait for him to fall, holding its breath.

Then the little girl trotted to Sven. Sven tugged one of her pigtails. She tossed her head and looked sideways at him. He put out an arm. She leaned against him. We breathed again.

Their faces were alike, hers and Sven's, their hair the same white-blond; but her bones had a rounded peasant solidity and her mouth a humorous strength. Sven said something. She raised her little white eyebrows.

Bo said to me, 'This is Luise. She is the head of the household. She rules the family with a rod of iron.'

'Hnn?' the child demanded.

While Bo translated, her eyebrows remained up though her eyes looked down. I heard my name. The round eyes came up again. She nodded twice, 'Hnn, hnn,' and put her hand into Sven's. Bo said Thomas's name. She did not look at Thomas. Still looking down, she said, 'mine onkel, Thomass?'

'You speak English!' I said.

The eyebrows went up again.

'She is a brilliant linguist,' Bo said. 'Aren't you, Luise?'

She rolled her round blue eyes to the ceiling and sighed. Abruptly she left Sven and cantered round the table to Bo. She reared up just past him, snorting through her nose. She wriggled onto her chair.

'She's not a girl, she's a horse.' Bo was solemn.

'I gathered,' I said.

The mother brought in a tray on which there were more kinds of herring than I had ever thought possible, and every colour of bread from quite black to quite white, with little pots of dripping.

Bo told me which kind of herring and dripping to spread on which bread. We each had a small glass of aquavit, ice cold, poured by Sven from the frosted bottle, and a green bottle of beer, ice cold too. It was not just the burning warmth of the alcohol, the heavenly flavours of

177

the food, that suddenly exalted me. It was the beauty of the house, the sturdy independent humorous little girl, her gentle father, Sven, and even the wicked little monster in the wheelchair.

'Oh, Thomas,' I said. 'It is wonderful here. I do love it so.'

Thomas had his back to the light. His eyes had not regained their colour, were silver perhaps, as he had described his mother's. He didn't answer me.

He said something in Danish, low and harsh, and Bo answered: 'Yes! The gravel pit, which used to be grass, is now a pond, and the village pond is now grass. Such are the ironies of life. About five years ago the gravel pit began to fill with water. No one knows why. It is now quite deep.'

Luise put out a hand and tweaked Bo's ear. She whispered something and he replied.

'Voder!' she said to me. 'Vell teep!'

'Water? Very deep?'

She nodded gravely, held up three fingers 'Dree maider,' she said.

'Three metres? Heavens.'

She looked at Bo and said, 'Heavens.'

'Heavens,' Bo replied.

He and I laughed. Sven smiled. Thomas looked at the child with his strange lack of expression.

'Do you teach her English?' I asked Bo.

The head turned fast, his eyebrows shot up, his expression, just like Luise's, said: 'Who, me?'

'She's good for such a small person,' I said.

He and Luise turned to each other, staring with a heavy frown, meaning: 'Is this woman crazy?' They were a good double act. I laughed again.

The mother said something to Luise. A gentle look came into the child's face when she looked at her grandmother, replaced at once with her air of private amusement. The mother spoke more firmly. Luise wriggled off her chair. She pulled Bo's ear, cantered round to Sven, put down her head, took his hand briefly in her teeth and let it go. He touched her head. She reared up, then leaned against her grandmother who put one arm round her. She nodded at me with a frown and said sternly, 'Gootpye.'

'Bye bye, Luise.'

I expected that next she would say goodbye to Thomas but, after the briefest glance in his direction, she wheeled round and cantered out of the room. I looked at Thomas. His eyes, still curiously colourless, were fixed on the doorway she had left.

The mother followed Luise from the room.

Sven stood. Blushing, he too said to me, 'Gootpye.'

'Where does Sven go now?'

'He takes Luise back to school in the town,' Bo said. 'And he goes back to work.'

'What is his work?'

'He teaches carpentry. At the school.'

'His wife was Ketty?' I said.

'Ah. You saw her tombstone.'

'Luise's mother?'

'Indeed.'

'What happened to her?'

There was a silence. I looked at Thomas. A deeper silence. Bo said, 'Luise was a small baby. She was found in the nip of time, just before the tide covered her. Ketty's body was washed up farther round the headland some weeks later, identifiable only by the teeth.

I could say nothing.

'She was a lovely girl, Ketty. Exactly like Luise. Except for two things. She was an inch or so taller. And she did not think she was a horse.'

'How did it happen?'

There was another silence. Thomas stared at the wall above my head.

Bo said, 'The verdict of the inquiry was accidental death.'

The mother came back. I helped her to clear the table. But in the kitchen, again she didn't look at me or speak. The cupboard and shelves were made of thick reddish wood. I touched one and said, 'Very nice.'

'Sven,' she replied.

One reluctant short syllable without turning her head. And I had still not seen her smile.

Thomas was in the long room piling logs into the stove. I waited. He sat on the reddish sofa and began to light his pipe.

'Thomas.' I sat next to him. 'This is a lovely place and I like your family very much. But—' I spoke softly—'I don't think we should stay any longer. Or at least, I don't think *I* should. Your mother—I really don't think she wants me here.'

'But I do!'

The lively voice jerked me round. The Head was working his wheelchair madly from the far end of the room where the books were.

'I want you here very much!' He smiled his devilish smile. 'I can practise my execrable English on you. And anyway you seem to be a jolly nice girl and I am going to take you under my wing.'

He screeched to a halt in front of the stove. The idea of such a scrap of humanity taking anything under its wing might have made me smile, had I not been so covered in confusion.

'I'll be your guardian angel,' he said. He turned to Thomas: 'Do you hear me, Thomas? I'll guard her well.' Thomas was tamping his pipe with a small silver instrument. 'Oh, how can you be bothered with this silent man? Look at him.' Bo waved a hand. 'He never speaks, just smokes his disgusting pipe. There are millions of Danish men like this. You will see.' He laughed his high-pitched laugh, baring those sharp white teeth. 'No, Jen-not-short-for-Jennifer, I'm much more your type. You like a chatterbox, I can see. You're a person full of fun!'

I thought of the ghastly events of the past few months, and smiled.

'That's it!' he said. 'You see?' He clapped his hands. 'What is it short for, however, this small name, Jen?'

'For Jenitha.'

'Fascinating. A name I have not met before. Its origin? Do you know?'

'I think it may be Quaker. Because my Grandma Jenitha was a Quaker, and all my Great-grandmas Jenitha. It's a family name.'

'All my Great-grandmas Jenitha,' he said. 'Oh, I shall adore to have you here. Come with me while I make a note.'

I followed him down to the study where he manoeuvred his chair between the desk and the shelves, opened a large notebook and wrote. He wrote with his left hand, a beautiful sharp script, like his teeth. He closed the book. Patted its marbled cover.

'This is where I collect all my knowledge of the world.'

'What are you collecting it for?'

'For? For? Are you a utilitarian? For my own amusement, what else? I need a lot of amusement, Jen-ith-a.' With a foxy look, he added, 'Placed as I am.'

'Only Aunt Jess ever called me Jenitha.'

'Aunt Jess?' he said.

Stupidly, for the first time since Jess's death, I started to cry. Unabashed, he went on looking at me. So I sat in the study with the shelves of books up to the ceiling and the light refracting off the small bevelled window panes, I sat on the corner of the big desk, looking at my hands, and I told him all about Aunt Jess and then I stopped. He pulled a white handkerchief bigger than himself from a corner of the chair, reminding me again of a conjurer. He looked thoughtful.

'This is a very bad thing.' He made it sound like somebody's fault.

'She was quite old,' I said.

'Yes?'

'Yes.'

I wiped my face with the handkerchief.

It smelled of pine. She had not seemed old. But had been, after all.

'So you have no one now?'

'I have Thomas.'

'No one but Thomas. Yes.'

I wondered suddenly where Thomas was.

'Thomas has been wonderful,' I said.

'Yes?'

'Without him I might not have survived.'

'May I have my handkerchief again, please?' He folded it with dexterity. 'Yes,' he said, 'my hands are marvellous. People always look at them. Of course, there's not much else of me to look at. You blush!' He laughed at my flustered face. 'I haven't seen anyone since Ket—I haven't seen a person for years who blushed, it's enchanting.' He had been going to say 'Since Ketty'. A silence fell.

'Where did you learn your English?' I said.

'It is remarkable, isn't it?'

'Yes.'

'From Shakespeare, from Dickens, from movies. From some delightful records the schoolmaster gave to me. That is why I sound like an Ealing comedy much of the time. Have you brought any books with you?'

'I have.'

'Oh, what?' He grinned like a fox in

a coop of hens. 'Some nice fat ones, I hope?'

I laughed.

He had never heard of Barbara Comyns, never read Kasuo Ishiguro, wanted to read Isabel Allende.

'You know about books,' he said.

'I'm a librarian.'

'Ah! I am a happy man.'

His whole face sparkled. I felt lifted up, flying, all head, no body, like him. Why, suddenly? There was no reason to it all. I laughed and Thomas appeared in the doorway. He stood looking down on us, a curious expression on his face.

'You have married a marvellous girl,' Bo said.

'You had better not take her away from me.'

'Oh I will, if I can.'

I stopped laughing. Bo was gazing at me, his expression sombre. 'You look like my mother when she was young,' he said.

In the sudden silence he looked at Thomas: 'Doesn't she, Thomas?'

The silence padded round like a thief, prying where it shouldn't look.

Thomas coughed, took out his pipe, banged it against the ash tray on the desk. Cold black ash spilled out.

'Yach,' Bo said. 'Take this disgusting little dish away, please. Sven is just the same. They are alike as a pair of peas, don't you think?'

'Like twins,' I said.

'Yes. I'm the changeling.' His smile was sly.

Thomas gripped my arm. 'Come, Jen.'

'Where are you taking her?' Bo called after us.

But Thomas paid him no heed. He said only, 'Put on your warmest clothes.'

And I ran upstairs for my hat and boots.

The wind whipped. The cold was fearsome.

'You didn't tell me Denmark was as cold as this.'

'I told you nothing about Denmark.'

'Where *are* you taking me?'

He turned away from me to light his pipe. I stamped from foot to foot. 'Thomas?'

We turned left up the hill. The opposite direction to the church and village.

'To the sea?' I said.

He didn't answer and high hedges hid the world on either side of the lane.

'Is it far to the sea?'

'Stayuns is a small round headland. Nothing is far from the sea.'

I couldn't understand his anger, or fathom its cause.

We reached the top of the hill where

the lane began to descend. A little way ahead on the right stood a white house, long and low like most of the country houses, the row of many small windows marching under its eaves. Smoke rose from the chimney.

'Is that where Knud lives?'

Thomas nodded but didn't answer me. He took my arm, quickened his pace.

The lane curved. Another house, on our left, was painted yellow like the church, with a red door in the middle and two red-painted windows either side. A gingerbread house. And Bo's wheelchair was turning in at the gate.

Thomas and I stopped in our tracks. I laughed. 'How did he get here so fast?'

Bo waved an arm and called my name. As I ran to join him he let out a piercing whistle. A face appeared at the window then disappeared.

The door opened and an old woman filled the doorway.

'Bo!'

'Nanna!'

Wrapped in coats and shawls she stumped out of her doorway and bent to embrace him.

'Nanna,' he said. 'The simple good woman of Goltrup. Ketty's grandmother. She loved us when we were children. Took care of Mother and of us when Father died. It was she who—. Well, she has been part of our family history. We like her quite a lot.'

The old woman beamed at me while Bo talked. Then she looked beyond me to where Thomas stood in the lane. She waved and called, 'Sven!'

Bo said, 'Thomas,' and the light went out of her face. When she turned to me again her smile had changed. She took both my hands and patted them. She said something to Bo. Then she trudged back into her house.

Thomas was going back up the lane away from the sea. I called his name but he didn't respond. Bo's chair had also turned back in the direction of the Vicarage.

'How long has your family been here?'

'Only three generations,' Bo said. 'My father's father came as pastor, and my father followed him.'

'You should have followed your father,' I said.

'Into the grave?'

'Bo! Into the pulpit.'

'Ha. Actually not a bad idea. Balanced on top of a pulpit, no one would know there was less of me than met the eye.'

We had reached the Vicarage. Bo stopped his chair. Thomas marched ahead. Bo turned in at the beech hedge. I trotted to catch Thomas up.

'What about the sea?' I said. 'Are we not going now?'

'Surely you would prefer to go with Bo.'

It was hard to tell if it was a joke.

The village was straight and square and brown. Houses right on the street, no gardens in front. I had expected something more ancient and romantic. I hoped my disappointment didn't show. Thomas pointed out the inn. The sign said *Goltrup Kro* but it didn't sound like that, the way he said it. It sounded like 'Goltrugh Krerl':

'Each village has a krerl. This is our krerl, the inn of Goltrup.'

It seemed the only building of interest in the one straight street. We had coffee in the Kro, a homely place with low ceilings, old beams, scrubbed tables. The coffee was excellent. But the cold was a shock again when we came outside. We walked fast. I put my arm through his and felt a little more courageous.

'Why are you angry?' I said. 'Is it Bo?'

Thomas loosed his arm from mine.

Dinner was a bowl of thick yellow soup, pea or lentil and, on a side plate, slices of belly pork and thick sausage with a sweet herb vinegar and a ramekin of mustard sauce. We ate thin slices of black bread and drank aquavit and beer.

Bo and Luise bounced a light banter between them. But the presence of the mother constrained me. Awkward silences entered the room with her and stayed among us.

But then after dinner we sat round the big stove. The lamps were lit. Bo in his wheelchair read Dickens in Danish. Luise, curled up on the sofa, her head on Sven's lap, listened with her sceptical look. Sometimes she and Sven laughed helplessly, while Bo sat with his eyebrows up—what could they find so amusing?—until the laughter stopped. The mother knitted. I felt warm and content, almost a member of this family. Until I caught sight of her stern face that shut me out.

Thomas sat to my left, his face in darkness. I put my hand on his. His hand made a small movement, not of reciprocation. Of escape. I removed my hand at once. His mother was not the only one who shut me out, it seemed.

At eight-thirty Luise was sent to bed. She came to me, took two fingers of my right hand, shook them. 'Goot nat,' she said with clownish solemnity. She gave Thomas a swift look from under her eyebrows, then cantered out of the room.

In Aurora that night, Thomas didn't kiss
me. He pulled out of my detaining arms
and got into his bed. He didn't say a word.
Soon he breathed deeply. I had to believe
him asleep.

Conversation In
Another Place

8

'Wake up, Reg.'

'Christ, John, what sort of an hour do
you call this?'

'The hour of the wolf.'

'Don't you ever sleep?'

'Given up the booze, mate. Creates a
lot of spare time.'

'The Peterson case again. I've got every
man I can spare on that.'

'And have all these genius cops found
her yet?'

'Estate agent's alibi checks. No question
he was where he said he was.'

'That's good, Reg.'

'Yeah, yeah. And the genius cops'll find
her, don't you worry, mate.'

'Never mind Elizabeth. We've got to find Peterson.'

'Give them time.'

'Time's what we ain't got.'

'I've got more time than I had in the old days, when you used to let me sleep, John.'

'I'm gonna phone the Copenhagen cops.'

'At your own expense?'

'Amazing how rich you get giving up the Scotch.'

'Come down the station and do it.'

'Haven't got time to get down the station.'

'Time...'

'Just wanted to get your go ahead, Reg. Okay?'

'What if I said No?'

Reg Grant was speaking to the dialling tone.

Chapter Fourteen

Next morning Thomas was not in his bed. I jumped up. I hoped to be in time for breakfast from now on. I should be embarrassed to be the recipient of another tray. A sound outside took me to the window.

The mother came out of the house. She crossed the courtyard, went out through the opening in the hedge and turned right into the lane. She walked with a stiff-backed stride, carrying a basket. Then Thomas came out and hurried after her. She must have heard his footsteps behind her, because she turned. They both stopped. They seemed to gaze at each other. He appeared to say something—I could see the cloud of his breath on the cold air. She didn't reply. They stood a moment longer. Then she turned from him and strode on down the lane. He stood still, watching her move away from him. I thought he would come back to the house. He wasn't even wearing a coat. But after a moment he trotted on after her. I watched them till they disappeared behind trees, he still going with small steps, keeping pace with her, a few yards behind.

I shuddered with anger at his humiliation. What sort of mother was she to treat him like this when he loved her so much? But then I knew that family things are hard to understand. Family hurts go deep. Aunt Jess and I had always been much too polite to quarrel but sometimes our little silences would last for days. Only days, however, not years. Well, he would catch her up. It would be easier to talk outside the house. They would surely come back reconciled.

And then, perhaps, he would be restored to me.

The place at the table I'd occupied yesterday was set with cup and plate and a pastry, the thermos of coffee next to it. I hated to think of her making these exquisite preparations with no warmth towards me in her heart.

Washing up the things in the kitchen, I saw the door to the washing room was open now and the door beyond ajar.

'Who's that?' Bo's voice.

'Me.'

'Come in, Jen-ith-a.'

I brushed past the hanging washing and pushed his door. My hand went to my mouth. All round the room faces, just like the ones in the bathroom, peeped, winked, leered. To one side there was a small cot with low sides, and also a sagging brown sofa. In the middle he balanced on his chair in front of an easel. He dabbed at a canvas with a long-handled brush.

'So it's you!' I said.

'The bathroom? Yes, I plead guilty.'

'You're a real painter.'

'Yes.'

'Do you sell them?'

'No.'

'Why not?'

'They'd come and stare at me. They'd write learned articles: "It is significant we feel that Bo Petersen who is nothing but a head himself should paint nothing but heads. We wonder if there could be a connection between the fact that Bo does not paint bodies and the fact that he has no body." No, Jenitha. I would not enjoy to do it any more if they came and looked. They would be buying not a painting but a relic, a piece of a freak.'

'Yes, I see.'

Half the pitched roof was large panes of glass. You might have been out of doors except that the room was warm. I wandered about looking at the paintings.

'Is that your whole name? Bo?' I said. 'Is Bo short for something?'

He yelped. 'How could any name be short for me?'

'What was it, Bo? An accident or what?'

'Do you believe in accidents, Jenitha?'

'Some.'

'My accident occurred in the darkness of the womb.'

'Oh.'

'Imagine! Out slid my head, very nice if a little mischievous, then my little arms feebly waving, and then—nothing else! They looked and looked but could find no more of me, search as they might. "This is all we can find, Mrs Petersen." "What, no legs, no feet?" "Nothing at all, I'm afraid. We've searched everywhere." "Is it a boy or a girl? Is it a person at all" '

'Bo, you are undeniably a man!'

'Well, about a sixth of one.'

'Much of the weight of the human body is in the head.'

'*Five kilos,* I believe.'

'And all the brains,'

'And the soul too, would you say?'

'I would now.'

'Nice girl. I'm No Body.'

'You're all spirit.'

'Bodies are no end of trouble. They bring people down. I wouldn't have one for the world.'

'You're half way to what man aspires to.'

'I'm the happiest man round here.'

His brush prodded the palette on a table by his side, trembled near the painting like a hoverfly, then pounced, leaving a dab of white that transformed a flat greenish blob into a winking face. He hovered, pounced, dabbed. There was no sound but his breathing and mine.

I watched him, wondering how all the necessary organs were packed into this tiny scrap of body. I saw that there was more of him from front to back than one might expect. And I noticed that at the dwindling point of the canvas bag there was a ring with a string through it by which he was attached to the chair.

'What amuses you?' he said.

'They tie you down. Is that in case you fly away?'

'Yes!' His high-pitched laugh. 'That's precisely it!'

I had a vision: the mischievous head and arms floating on the end of the string above our heads. There was a silence while this vision passed over us and returned to the chair. We smiled at each other.

'Oho, Jenitha,' he said. 'You have fallen in love with me.'

'Yes, I have. I've fallen in love with all of you here.'

'And have you fallen out of love with Thomas?'

'Not yet.'

'Ah, pity,' he lightly said, and bared his teeth.

'Bo.'

'Yes. Naughty. But it's nice to say naughty things. Don't you think?'

'No.'

'You think naughty words become naughty facts?'

'I don't know.'

'You're superstitious.'

'I'm fearful.'

'Speaking words is dangerous, thinking them is not?'

'Yes.'

'Unspoken words are ghosts waiting

behind doors. Get them out in the daylight where you can challenge them.'

'I'm too polite.'

He laughed. 'If the ghosts prefer the dark, it's not your place to disturb them there?'

'Something like that.'

'Very bad trouble you will store up for yourself.' He glared at me. I simply looked at him. 'Or perhaps not.' He sighed. 'Your innocence is great. Greater than my little Luise's even.'

I didn't like to ask what he meant.

'She's a wise woman,' I said.

'Oh yes. So maybe your innocence can win. It would be unusual, but—' His arms, one with the palette, one with the rush, lifted and dropped. 'I am your guardian angel.' He glared again. 'Don't forget.'

'I won't.'

We spoke lightly but there seemed an urgency under his words. Afraid of that, I let the subject go.

'I want to look at the sea,' I said.

'I will go with you when you go.'

'You will go with me and be my guide.'

' "In thy most need go by thy side." '

'Your Everyman editions. My Dickens, my Thackeray. Yes.'

'Bo.'

'Am I not a marvel? Don't go to the sea without me, please.'

'Now?'

'No. In the morning I must always work. It gives the illusion of meaning to my useless little life. But soon.'

'That's a hint that I should leave you to concentrate,' I said.

He grinned.

The rest of the house was silent, Thomas nowhere to be seen. I went upstairs but he was not in our room. Why did he never wait for me? Was he still following his mother pathetically round the lanes?'

So, dear Margot and James, here I am again, sitting by the stove in this huge granary where the chill is just off the air. I've tried to read but my mind won't concentrate, so you are my last resort! I'm forming a plan to get Thomas away. He is so changed here. After all, this is meant to be a sort of honeymoon, but so far he has hardly looked at me!

I crossed out the last sentence and gazed at the glow of the stove. How lovely this place was. How pleasant life here could easily be.

Later, a door banged downstairs and voices roused me from the deep reverie into which I had dropped. I stood, stretched, walked to one of the little windows under the eaves to loosen my stiff joints. There was Luise in the orchard, going at a bouncing trot. I watched her, smiling. Then I saw a movement near a tree ten yards behind her. A man, I thought. I looked again but the trees were frozen in stillness. No one was watching her but me. Was I starting to imagine things? And then Luise had disappeared too. As though spirited away.

Chapter Fifteen

Bo was in the long room, his back to the windows, absorbed in a book. Luise's rosy face appeared at the glass-paned door. She saw me, put her finger to her lips, opened the door with extreme caution. She tip-toed in, stopped behind his chair, put her small hands over his eyes.

He said, 'Is it Sven?'

Luise raised her pale little eyebrows at me.

'Is it Jen? No... Mama? Oh, no good. I can't guess.'

She came round his chair.

'Hah! Luise! It is you!' She pulled his ear. He said, 'She always fools me.'

She looked at him, translated for herself, said, 'Yes. Dis zo.' She came to me, took two of my fingers and shook them twice. 'Djenn. Mine aund.'

'Yes, I'm your aunt. You're my niece.'

'Knees?'

'Yes!'

She touched her knees, turned her face to Bo in mock surprise. She said. 'Bo hass no knees. Bo iss not your knees.' She marched to him, saying something in Danish.

'Lunch,' Bo translated.

'Lunge,' she repeated without turning on her way out of the room.

Luise was wriggling onto her chair opposite Thomas when we arrived. Settled, she sat quite still a moment. Then she lifted her index finger and moved it towards Thomas. She said quietly, eyelids lowered, 'Thomas. Mine onkel.'

Thomas turned colourless eyes on her, said something in Danish, very quiet. Sven turned his head, quick, asked Thomas to repeat what he had said. Thomas shook his head, lowered his eyes again. Luise, her face pink, had a puzzled look. There was silence. One of the silences that were always falling here, that I didn't understand, that I couldn't bear.

'Thomas,' I said, 'Where did you get to this morning? I always seem to be losing you.'

He turned the silver eyes on me. He was

about to speak, I thought, but the mother brought in the bread just then, and he remained silent.

Lunge was the lovely smorgasboard with aquavit and beer again. The meal over, Luise wriggled off her chair, trotted round the table performing her fond and comic gestures: tweaking Bo's ear, shaking Sven's hand in her mouth. She didn't look at Thomas again. She said something in Danish to her grandmother, who regarded me for a while, then nodded. Luise went into the stair lobby and came back carrying my coat, bigger than herself.

'Comm!' She thrust the coat at me. 'Oud.'

I was obedient. We put on our woolly hats, our boots, our gloves. She took my hand and led me to the kitchen door. We went round the side house and into the orchard, she at an almost imperceptible quiet canter, down a path among the trees to a huge old holly bush, where she let go my hand, reared up and came to a halt. She put a red woolly finger to her lips, then gestured to me to bend low. I bent double and followed her through an arched opening in the bush. Inside, the dying back of lower branches formed a small room almost high enough for me to stand upright. Wooden crates were arranged as a table and two seats. On the table was a small tin tea set decorated in willow pattern.

'Oh, Luise, it's very nice.'

'Huset,' she replied. 'Mine.'

'Huset?'

'Liddle house?'

'Luise's huset,' I said.

'Yo.'

We sat either side of the table. She lifted the teapot lid. The water was frozen in the pot. She raised her eyes and the palm of a hand in comic despair. I laughed.

'Never mind. We can pretend.'

She lifted her eyebrows, shrugging. She poured nothing carefully from the pot. We sipped nothing politely from the cups. She put down her cup and took mine from me. She held up a hand then bent to fish something out from inside the table.

She sat up, a little flushed, hiding something in her hand. She waited, then opened the hand to reveal a tiny black-and-white snapshot. I leaned closer. In the dim light I could just make out that this was a picture of Thomas, but a Thomas wondrously, heroically, ravishingly beautiful, aged about fifteen, standing at the rail of a ship.

'Oh, Luise,' I breathed.

She bent again to replace him in the crate, and this time she brought out an object about nine inches by six wrapped in a piece of blanket. She looked at me solemnly for a moment. She put her finger to her lips and raised her eyebrows in a question. I put my finger to my lips and nodded in reply. She slowly unwrapped the blanket and lifted up a round-bellied stocky white horse, carved in wood. The horse had strength, character, charm. Like herself.

Luise gazed at the horse, hopeless love in her eyes, then leaned closer to me. She whispered, 'Thomas.'

I sat upright: 'The horse's name?'

'Yess. Name. Thomas.'

'Oh.'

So Thomas was her hero, the long lost uncle travelling distant lands, conquering the world. She saw him as her Viking, perhaps. As I did. She treasured his crumpled picture. She named her most precious possession after him: her horse. I recalled that I too at her age had harboured secret loves that made me shy. I understood now why she hardly looked at Thomas, barely spoke to him. It was adoration that constrained her, not dislike.

We gazed at the horse in solemn silence for a while. Then she wrapped him again in his blanket and put him also inside the table. She came to me and shook my two fingers. It was time to go.

'Thank you, Luise,' I said.

She nodded briskly and led the way out, holding back prickling holly leaves for me. When I stood upright she put her hand again in mine. This time I did see a man move behind a tree and felt him stand there, still.

Luise had not seen him. She tugged my hand for attention, all solemnity gone. She rolled her eyes upwards. 'Shool!' She said, then let go my hand. She broke into a gallop and was off. I watched her disappear between beech hedges. I heard Sven's car start up.

The mother appeared at the long room door. She made a mime of drinking from a cup. *'Café!'* Her voice was deep, harsh.

'Thank you,' I said.

Thomas appeared from around the sidehouse. As though he too had come to fetch me for coffee.

As we went in Thomas, behind me, put a hand between my shoulder blades. It gave me a strange feeling. He had hidden behind a tree. I moved away from his touch. The mother silent, Thomas silent, I couldn't ask him why he had hidden. It would sound so silly. And after coffee, when his mother left the room to attend to Bo, he smiled at me. The first smile for so long, it parted the clouds that seemed to have gathered over me here.

'Would you like to stroll down to the

village with me, Jen?'

I almost cantered like Luise to get my outdoor things.

In the lane he kept an arm round me.

'Were you in the orchard just now?' I said.

'Yes. I came to fetch you for coffee.'

'No. I meant—'

He interrupted, gesturing at the old schoolhouse with his pipe. 'I found out. The new pastor lives there now. With five children.'

The scorn in his voice surprised me, daunted me.

Brown brick houses stood stiff round the village square where some boys helped two men on a ladder to raise the Christmas tree.

'It's early for Christmas preparations,' I said.

'We make a big thing of Advent here.'

We stopped to watch them. The boys jumped excitedly. They had shiny faces, bright eyes. I said, 'Do you want to have children, Thomas?'

'Why do you ask?'

'Well... We've never discussed it and—'

'There would be little point.'

'In discussing it?'

'Yes.'

'Why?'

'As things are.'

'With Elizabeth still missing?'

He didn't reply.

'Wouldn't you be prepared to have them, then?'

He looked at me slowly. 'Would you?'

'Oh yes, I—' I couldn't go on, suddenly.

'I had assumed—' He pushed at the tobacco in his pipe. '—that you had that side of things under control.'

'Yes. Of course. But—'

'No buts, I think? We couldn't think of it surely until Elizabeth either gets in touch and we can be divorced or until the seven years are up.'

'Thomas, I'm thirty-seven years old.'

He lifted his shoulders, sucked hard on his pipe. The nostalgic aroma drifted into the icy air. We walked on. When we came again between hedges and winter fields and there seemed nothing but white sky and crying birds in spirals, I said, 'But, Thomas—in general, I mean. If it were possible. Wouldn't you want? With me, I mean? Don't you want to have children, then?'

'I didn't say that.'

'No, but—'

'But.' He took the pipe from between his teeth, looked at it, put it back in his mouth, puffed a moment or two, removed it again. 'But it is a grave responsibility which I have never yet thought I could or should assume.'

'Oh.'

We turned to go back to the village. He walked faster. Angry, it seemed.

In the square, the boys and the men shouted and laughed as the tree creaked upwards into place. No one noticed us as we passed. Thomas strode ahead and for a moment it was as though I really did not exist. I let him go. I looked blindly into the window of a shop. When my sight cleared I saw it sold knitting wool and baby clothes. I smiled at myself. Lots of men felt like Thomas. And there was the example of Bo. Perhaps he feared heredity. I didn't. I feared nothing. Not even Thomas's anger, which surely arose from fear. I would have courage enough for both of us. I wanted a child.

I caught up with him at the green on the edge of the village where the road curved. He stared at it, gloomy behind a cloud of smoke. The sun was low behind him so I couldn't see his eyes.

I stood next to him. I was about to say, 'Don't let's quarrel', something to disperse his anger.

He said, 'Jen, go back to the house.'

'Are you sure, Thomas?'

'Leave me alone.'

I wanted to ask him all the things I

couldn't ask in the house. Why nobody was pleased to see him there, his mother least of all. Why he should hide in the orchard to watch a little girl canter among the trees. A man who didn't want children of his own. I hesitated but didn't dare to speak.

'I shan't be long,' he said.

I plodded back alone up the hill.

'Jen. Dinner time.' It was dark in Aurora.

He woke me all gentleness! He stroked my hair. He kept an arm round my shoulders as we went downstairs. I felt all would be well again between us. I had been right not to pursue the argument. I was glad I hadn't questioned him. I must have patience. All would surely yet be well.

After dinner round the stove, under the lamps, Bo read aloud from Dickens again. Tonight after her odd goodnights Luise stopped at Thomas's chair. She cantered round it once, came to a stop in front of it. She lifted her eyelids and looked at him. His face was shadowed by the position of the lamps. Neither moved. Neither spoke. She cantered out of the room. A listening stillness had descended. It made me uneasy, almost alarmed. No one looked at anyone. Fear seemed to flicker among us like a flame. I told myself my imagination was overheated. Too much good coffee after dinner, perhaps.

'Jen! You read now!' Bo started his chariot down the room.

'In Danish?'

'Naturally!' He raced back waving an Everyman edition with a ragged cover. 'There!' He put it into my hands. It was *Mansfield Park*. 'Jane Austen,' he said. 'So suitable.'

'You want me to read aloud?'

'I like the parsonage. So English. So unlike ours.'

'England isn't like that any more.'

'Oh yes! I have television. On television England is still like that. I have seen.'

'I can't read aloud.'

'Why not?'

I looked at Thomas for help. He would tell them I was too shy. He made no move. His face was still in shadow. I had a strong feeling only his body sat there. His mind was somewhere else.

'I'm not good at it. And anyway it wouldn't be polite. Sven and your mother wouldn't understand.'

'More than you think.' A wicked loud whisper. Sven smiled round the stem of his pipe. The mother knitted. She might not have heard. Bo opened the book. 'Here! The Parsonage!'

Haltingly, very quiet, I started to read. Mid-sentence I was forced to swallow, start again. Then I found myself gaining confidence. My heart slowed down. I began to follow the sense of the elegant words. It was the dinner party chapter, all about secrets, and poor Fanny who was excluded from the secrets, secrets which deeply affected her life. It was a scene that had always made me shudder with unease. The card game they played after dinner was *Speculation*. I had forgotten that. How oddly apposite: the game I seemed forced by Thomas into playing here. I was no better at my game of speculation than Fanny had been at hers.

Bo sat with his eyes closed in ecstasy, hands clasped. Sven chewed his pipe, eyes on the wooden ceiling. The mother knitted. Thomas, face in the dark, never moved. Nervous and not used to reading aloud, I quickly became hoarse.

'Enough.' Bo rolled to my side to rescue me: 'This was marvellous. Every night a little bit. Will you?'

'Bo—'

'Iss goot.' Sven removed his pipe and nodded earnestly.

Thomas got suddenly up from his chair behind Bo. His shadow was flung over us like black water. He stretched. Two black shadow arms with great spread hands

211

splayed over the couch where Sven sat, making a strange effect. I heard myself laugh nervously.

'Is it bedtime, Thomas?'

'If you like.'

'Good night,' I said.

Sven smiled. The mother actually looked at me, and nodded.

'Sleep well,' Bo said.

But no one looked at Thomas.

He undressed silently and got into his own bed.

'Thomas.'

Silence.

'Thomas.'

'Yes?'

'Are you angry with me?'

'What reason might I have to be angry with you?'

'Well, any reason. I don't know. Reading aloud so horribly perhaps?'

I had hoped to make him smile. He said nothing.

'Oh, never mind.' I left my bed in a movement and slid into his. I was naked. It was good to feel his body the whole length of me.

'Thomas?'

But he simply lay. As he was. On his back, eyes closed. I couldn't even put a hand on him to stroke him. I was absolutely refused. I sat up.

'Oh Thomas.'

He said nothing. I put my head down onto my knees. I said, 'Did you hide in the orchard today?'

Nothing.

'When Luise was there. I saw you go behind a tree.'

Silence.

'I'm sure I saw you. Why?'

He was not going to answer. The silence lengthened stupidly. I uttered a sort of voiceless scream. I got out of his bed and back into my own. As I lay down he whispered something.

'What?' I said.

'Why did she take you in there? Inside the bush? What did she show you in there?'

Luise had sworn me to secrecy. Vows to a child are serious.

'Nothing. She's a child. It's her special place.'

'Secrets! Why you?' he said.

He thumped the pillow with his fist, turned and buried his face in it. This was idiotic. Competition over the affection of a child? She had named the horse Thomas for the uncle she had never seen. The imaginary uncle she was now trying to square with the real. She was disposed to worship, in her ironic guarded way. I was the messenger, only. 'She is disposed to worship you.' I could have said that without breaking Luise's trust. But I was too cross with him even to speak. And too sad.

Again I slept alone.

Chapter Sixteen

Luise gave a final whinny and jumped into Sven's car. They drove out of the courtyard and disappeared up the lane. Thomas came out, got into his car and zoomed off after them. But at least this morning I need not breakfast alone. Bo was still in the dining room.

'Good morning, Jenitha. I trust you slept like a big top?'

I laughed. 'Like a very big top.'

He narrowed his eyes. He didn't like to get his idioms wrong. I poured him some coffee.

'Do you know where Thomas has gone?' I said.

'He's gone somewhere?'

'I saw his car drive off.'

'Without you? Poor Jenitha. What will you do?'

'Oh, I've letters to write.' I felt unreasonably upset. 'Friends in London,' I said.

'Letters to write. How sweetly old-fashioned. Other people use the telephone these days.'

'The telephone!' I said.

'Yes, it's an electrical apparatus or device which—'

'I mean, I hadn't thought. How stupid. But could I? I shouldn't like to impose—'

'Impose! Ha!' His high yelping laugh.

'And, Bo, I don't know how!'

We rolled down to the study end of the long room where he stopped at the desk.

'That is a telephone.'

'Ah, so that is a telephone!'

He wrote down the numbers for London and told me what to do.

'Bo!' The mother's harsh deep voice. She stood in the doorway to the dining room.

'I must go, Jenitha.' He glared up into my face. 'Bear up somehow without me?'

I smiled but, left alone again, wondered if I could.

I tidied the breakfast things into the kitchen. The door to the washroom was open but Bo's door was shut. While I washed up I heard the low murmur of voices. The mother and Bo. Bo grew louder, squeakier, insistent. He spoke Thomas's name. Then I heard him say my name. It's terrible to hear your name spoken like that from behind a closed door. The mother's voice deep and slow, also said my name. Bo argued with her. About me? About her attitude to me? Their voices became quieter. Some agreement had been reached? Then silence fell. At any moment the door might open, the mother come out. I ran up the stairs. I threw myself face down on Thomas's bed and uncharacteristically wept. I despised myself for this self-sorrow, so didn't indulge it long. Sitting up, mopping my eyes, I was struck by an idea. I opened the wardrobe. Thomas had brought two suitcases to my one. The smaller he hadn't unpacked. I opened it.

Three layers of white tissue paper whispered as I lifted them.

'Yes!'

I pulled the shining folds from the tissue paper. I sat back on my heels, hugging the crumpled stuff. I buried my face in the satin, soothing my hot cheeks in its cool embrace. Some day then he intended to make love to me again? He had never made love to me without the dress. Was I admitting then that he never would, that in some way the dress was more important to him than I? I hung the dress on the back of the door, smoothing its fleshy folds. I drew out the ectoplasmic veil, the pretty wreath, and arranged them with the dress. I was about to sob again like a silly young girl.

Urgently I needed to hear Margot's voice, brutal, sensible. Normal. I practised what I must say: 'Hello, Margot, I'm very miserable here. I could be happy if only Thomas—' No, that wouldn't do. 'Hello, Margot, it's lovely here but I think Thomas would like to stay forever.' Yes, that was better. Lies. Or perhaps not lies? I didn't know. 'So could you get Ben to phone from the library to say they need me back immediately?'—No, that was far-fetched—'Ben to phone from the library to say if I stay away longer I might lose my job.' Yes! 'Otherwise I doubt if I'll ever drag him away!' Yes! That was brilliant. Well, for a person who had never employed subterfuge, not bad. Anyway, it would do.

I ran downstairs into the long room, as the mother came in from the garden.

Her cheeks were shiny with cold. We regarded each other a moment. I blushed. Then she pointed outside and made a feathery movement with her fingers. She was speaking to me! What did she mean?

'Snow?' I said.

She gave a slight shrug.

'Oh how marvellous. I love snow.'

The sky was a heavy pale grey, full of it. She did not smile but she did not go away. We stood side by side and looked out. Her first sign of friendliness. Bo's argument had convinced her then? Made bold, not wanting our conversation to end here, I said, 'Thomas? Has he come back yet?'

At the mention of his name her face closed down. As though a shutter had descended. She turned and went into the kitchen. Chilled, I looked at the menacing sky. Then, 'Don't be an idiot,' I said to myself.

The long room, pale with snowy light, was darker at the study end. The phone was on the desk. I picked it up. While I pressed the numbers my mind ran over my prepared speech: 'Hello, Margot? I'm fine. It's nice here but Thomas loves it so much I think he'll stay forever. So can you get Ben—' It was ringing! I could hear it! Don't let it be the answering machine!

'Yes?' Margot's dear abrupt frightening phone-answering voice. It was a moment before I could speak.

In that moment a hand came down on the phone. And an arm came round me from behind. A mouth against my ear: 'Please don't, my dearest Jen.'

'Thomas!'

'Oh I'm sorry. I gave you a fright.'

'I didn't hear you come.'

'That's because I'm in my socks!'

'Were you here all the time?'

If so, he had seen his mother's friendly

gesture, her face set hard at the sound of his name.

'Didn't you see me lying on the couch?' He smiled.

'No.'

'Too eager to make your phone call.'

'I just wanted to—'

'Don't tell me. Let me guess. Margot, by any chance?'

'I just wanted to say hello.'

'It's only a few days since you saw her.'

'Yes.'

'Am I never to have you to myself?'

'But Thomas—'

'Where have you been this morning, for instance? I looked for you everywhere.'

'*You* looked for *me?*'

'I can never find you. And when I do, whom do I find you with?'

'Thomas, this is so unfair.'

'The inevitable Bo. Am I right?'

'But—'

'Am I right?'

'Thomas, this is silly. We merely had breakfast together, Bo and I!'

'And he tells you how to make secret phone calls.'

'Secret! Thomas, you weren't here to ask. You're never here. And no one knows where you are. This morning you drove off before I was up. Where did you go?

Why didn't you tell me? I might have wanted to go with you. Didn't you think of that?'

I had never been so forceful. Deceit makes people bluster.

'Oh, Jen.'

Being forceful worked! He hugged me close to him.

'It's true,' he said. 'I wake at dawn here. I walk. I drive. Miles. All the old places. This was my home. It is my home. I've spent too much time away from it. My childhood comes back. Good things and bad. It hurts me and makes me distant. I'm to blame. And now you want to go home to Margot and get away from me.'

'No. Thomas. Not that. I promise you.'

I looked at his face. His eyes in this light were their wonderful blue again, pleading. I put my hands either side of his face and pulled him to me. He kissed me, with the warmth and softness I had longed for since we left England.

'Oh, Thomas.'

We rocked together.

'I'll be better, Jen. Give me a chance. I'd do anything rather than lose you,' he said.

'You'll never lose me. I believe in our marriage.'

'Till death do us part.'

'Us do. Yes.'

'Us do?'

'Yes!' I smiled at him.

'Oh.' He stared over my head for a moment, oddly. Then, 'Oh yes,' he said. 'So.' He looked again into my eyes. 'So you won't make your phone call yet? Just give me a little time to have you to myself.'

'Thomas, it's just a phone call, it's—'

'Stroll down to the village with me? I need to buy tobacco. Now? Yes? Just the two of us?'

'Oh, Thomas, of course!'

We walked through and beyond the village to the headland, uninhabited and bleak. We could hardly hear each other speak in the wind. Thomas held on to me to stop me being blown away. We had lunch in the kro of the next village.

'Thomas?'

'Yes, dear Jen?'

'Where did you drive to this morning?'

'Are you checking up on me?'

For a moment I was alarmed. But then he smiled. 'I drove to the town. Time in Stevns just stands still. Nothing has changed in town. Apart from the school. The school is new.'

'Where Sven teaches and Luise learns?'

'All the little village schools have closed down now. So the new one is very big.'

'They must have been proud to show you round.'

'Who?'

'Luise and Sven.' I smiled.

His eyes did that strange trick they had. As their expression was sucked out, so was their colour. Silver eyes.

'They did not show me round,' he said. 'Let us go.'

I was afraid I had offended again without knowing why. But on the way back he talked and talked. I had never known him so voluble: the history of the region, landmarks, places he had played as a boy. He was excited, reckless, I might almost have said frightened. But of what? While he talked I phrased in my mind all the questions I wanted to ask, but I couldn't wedge in a word. And then the roof of the Vicarage appeared above the trees and with every step his spirits dropped. A silence hovered heavy like the yet unfallen snow. The silence was more impossible to penetrate than the talk, and outside the house he asked me to go in without him: he needed to walk some more.

After dinner, in the long room, Luise took my hand and led me to the window. She looked round to make sure no one was

listening. She had a great wariness of being mocked. She beckoned me down to her eye level.

'Yes, Luise?'

'Shall I say my reem to you?'

'Your reem?'

'It's English!'

'Your rhyme! Oh yes, please do.'

'Okay.'

She looked round again. Bo grinned at her. She waved him away with her small hand and he turned back to his book, mock-sheepish. She raised her brows at me and sighed.

'Okay.' She said in her light little guttural voice: 'Roses are ret, Wiolits are plue. Honney iss svit—and zo are you.'

'Oh Luise!' If she had not been such a reserved child I'd have hugged her. As it was, I didn't know whether to laugh or cry.

'Iss okay?' she said.

'It certainly is.'

'You know diss reem?'

'I do. Yes.'

'Oh.' She looked at me for a moment. Then she shook my two fingers and leaned closer. She swivelled her eyes to where Thomas sat by the stove. He was in shadow as he seemed always to be, in that room, in the evenings. She whispered, 'You tell him?'

'Thomas?' I whispered.

'Yess. Mine Onkel. You tell him diss reem?'

'You want me to?'

She nodded.

'It's for Thomas?'

She raised her eyebrows and gave a take it or leave it shrug, then she cantered to Bo, whose ear she tugged to tell him to read aloud.

Thomas was a lucky man. I'd have given a lot for that rhyme to be meant for me.

In Aurora that night he began to undress in silence, his back to me. I knew he would again get into his own little bed without even kissing me. His rejection, his silence, made me hot, foolish, timorous.

'Thomas?'

'Yes?'

He didn't even turn to look at me.

But he had kissed me today. He had said he wanted me for himself. I must remember that. And tonight I had something to give him. Two things to give him. I went close to him. I whispered into his naked back, 'Roses are ret, Wiolets are plue, Honney is svit. And zo are you.'

'What?'

'Luise told me to tell it you. It's from her.'

He shut his eyes. His head fell back a little. He gave a short deep sigh. Then he turned with eyes shut and hugged me so tight I could hardly breathe.

'Isn't it lovely?' I said.

He didn't reply, held on to me, swaying.

'Thomas,' I whispered. 'Look.' I made him turn to see the wedding dress which I had hung on the back of the door. He went quite still.

'Shall I put it on?' I said.

He seemed still frozen for a second, made no response at all. My fragile courage began to fail me.

Then he whispered, 'Yes,' and paused and again whispered, 'Yes.'

He didn't look at me while I undressed. He turned away to the window. I put on the lovely cool satin next to my naked skin with a trembling excitement that I felt he must share. This was to be the first night of our honeymoon.

'Thomas,' I murmured.

He turned to look at me. I could see no expression in his eyes. Hesitant, I stepped towards him. He moved out of my path. I wanted to see myself. Had I put the veil and wreath on wrong? Did I simply look a fool? There was no mirror in the room. No mirror in the room. He stood with his back to me again, near the door, almost as though he wanted to get out.

'Don't you want to, Thomas?' I was almost stammering. My attempt to bring us together had made an idiot of me.

But then he swung round and came to me. He gripped my shoulders and pushed me backwards onto the bed. He dragged up the skirt of the dress so that it covered my face, blinding and choking me. He dragged my legs apart, kneeling then lying between them, pushing them wider apart till I thought they would break.

'Thomas! Please! No!'

'Be quiet, you'll wake the girl.'

The girl?'

'She is next door.'

He pinned down my flailing arms with rough hands as I tried to pull the suffocating stuff off my face, thrusting and thrusting at me.

'Thomas! Please!'—trying not to make noise because Luise was next door—'Think of Luise. Please, no! Think of Luise if not of me. Please!'

And then it stopped. The frantic activity stopped. He lay heavy on top of me, his face turned away. He was trembling. He said something, muffled by the pillow so I couldn't hear. It sounded like, 'I can't.'

Can't what? Can't rape your not quite lawful wedded wife? Can't make love to a reject approaching forty and no beauty to start with? Can't do it without a mirror? What's wrong with you?

I said none of that. He lay there

226

trembling. And after a time the surge of pure anger left me.

'It's because of your family,' I said. 'It's because we're here. If we were to go somewhere else, somewhere by ourselves, it would be all right. Don't you think so, Thomas?'

His head turned slowly on the pillow. His eyes stayed steady on mine.

'Is it because of your mother?' I ventured.

'You understand nothing,' he said.

Conversation In Another Place

9

'Have you got an officer there who speaks English?'

'Sir, all our officers speak English.'

'Oh. Right. A-ha. Have you got one who speaks it good?'

'Most of us speak it reasonably well. Might I enquire what is your problem, please?'

'I need to find—trace someone. Danish bloke. Possibly in Denmark now. Gone to see his folks. Connected to a crime

227

in England. I want to know if he's got a record.'

'I see. Just a moment, please.'

Bright jingled the change in his pocket. Then: 'Hello? Detective Inspector Bright, is that right?' A new voice, friendly, lively, with hardly a trace of accent.

'That's right, yeah! Who are you?'

'Lars Knudsen. Detective Inspector also. How's things? I hear you want an officer who speaks English.' Knudsen laughed. 'Do you think I might do?'

'Okay, okay. Ever tried to find an English cop who speaks Danish?'

'You have a point.'

'I do, mate.'

'So what can I do for you?'

'You can find this bloke Peterson for me.'

'Petersen?'

'That's right.'

'What would you say if I called you in England and asked you to find a bloke named Smith?'

'Like that, is it?'

'Very much like that. His description, please?'

'Big. Thick blond hair.' Bright's heart sank as he spoke. 'He smokes a pipe.'

'You know, that is a description of quite a few Danish men.' Knudsen laughed again.

'Yeah, I know. But this isn't funny, mate. Let me tell you a story.'

Bright talked at length and fast and when he stopped Knudsen wasn't laughing any more.

Chapter Seventeen

The first thing I saw when I woke was the stupid wedding dress hanging on the door. I wished I had hidden it. I wished I had never discovered it in Thomas's bag, or, having found it, left it there. I had acted out of character. Thinking myself so clever, I had ruined everything. Thomas's duvet was folded neatly on the chair by the stove. So that was where he'd spent the night.

It was only on the way back from the mocking faces in the bathroom that I saw the snow. Grey lumps jostling against the paler sky. His mother had been right about that, then. I watched the soft stuff settle on the knobbly trees, the stiff grass. Luise's holly house.

I hoped the horrible scene last night hadn't woken her. I hoped nobody knew. I feared everyone must know. Everyone must see the contamination I felt.

But there was nobody about. Bo wasn't in the dining room. I saw the mother in the vegetable garden burning frosted leaves. I wanted to join her. But I didn't dare presume on her friendliness of yesterday. She was happy there, burning the leaves. She wouldn't want me. Then I saw Thomas.

He came round the hedge and stood watching her. At first she didn't notice, went on happily attending to her fire. Then she saw him. He took a few paces towards her but didn't come close. He said something. She didn't reply. He spoke again. His hands made a small pleading movement. She turned away, as though to gather more leaves with her rake. He rushed to her, speaking, put out his hands and touched her, trying to make her turn to him. She thrust him away as though he was attacking her. She shouted. She took one pace towards him, and made a gesture of dismissal so final I felt it like a stab in my own heart. He hesitated. Then he lowered his arms and turned away. I couldn't bear to watch any more.

I thought of knocking on Bo's door. But he would be working, he wouldn't want to be disturbed. I crept back upstairs. For a long time I sat by the stove. Then I fetched my long silly letter to Margot and James. Though I tried to sound cheerful I knew what I wrote was sad. I finished it anyway, huddled by the stove, and I decided I must post it whether Thomas wanted me to or not. He could no longer be allowed to cut me off from my friends. Someone who loved me must be told where I was. This act of defiance lifted my silly self pity. I signed my name with a flourish, found an envelope in my writing case and sealed the letter up, bang bang, with the side of my fist on the flap. But then I remembered I had no stamps. Never mind, I'd ask Bo later. It would be no use asking Thomas. I put the letter in my writing case on the bedside table and left it there, for now.

Then I tried to read, but failed to engage my fractured mind. All at once I couldn't stand to be indoors any more. I wanted to feel the cold flakes on my face, I wanted to taste the snow on my tongue. I wanted big mouthfuls of air to hurt my lungs. I had to be out.

Smoke from Knud's chimney scattered on the sky. After Nanna's house the land sloped suddenly down. Breaks in the confining hedges showed small square fields, black and livid green, striped and spotted with snow. The grey flakes fell thicker, collecting on the eyelids, small cold fingertips patting the skin. Now that it snowed, the weather seemed less cold. I began to feel the glow from walking fast.

And then, behind the thick grey curtain of snowy lace, lay the sea. White water, white sky, no horizon line.

To my right a gravelled path sloped away to some steps where two stone arms made a wide cradle for five or six fishing boats. To my left the cliff was twenty foot high, sheer, crumbly white rock topped with grass; like little white cliffs of Dover, but yellower, creamy against the snow. The path was narrow, bumpy, close to the edge of the cliff. I struggled down it, buffeted, stumbling, blinded by the snow, deafened by the wind. And, suddenly, quiet fell. I was down on the shore on a concrete platform among the pebbles and boulders. The platform was protected on both sides by wings of cliff, a cave without a roof. I sighed, relaxed a little, watching the snow fall on the sea. It was too cold to stand still long. I came round the projection of rock to continue along the shore. And he gripped my arm above the elbow.

'Jen?'

'Thomas?'

'Were you following me?'

I shook my head. 'You gave me a shock.'

'So what are you doing here?'

'A walk. I came for a walk.'

He let go my arm.

'The tides are dangerous. Didn't your

precious Bo tell you that?'

'*You're* here.'

'And that makes you feel safe? That makes you think it's safe to come down here?'

'Thomas—'

'Go back. Go back to the house.'

He started to walk away. I stumbled after him.

'Thomas, please let's talk. Please.'

'What is to talk about?'

'Please!'

'Anyone will tell you not to be down on the shore with me. My mother will tell you. Hasn't my mother told you?'

'Why should she? She doesn't speak to me.'

'You can't understand.'

'You said that last night.'

'It's better if you don't.'

'It's never better not to understand.'

'Oh, you think so?'

'Yes!' He was still walking away. 'Thomas, please help me to understand.

He turned on me so suddenly I nearly fell. 'You want me to help you *understand,* do you? All right, why not? I'll help you to understand. Now where shall we begin?' He held me by the scarf at my neck. 'Ah yes. Shall I help you to understand about the girl? How would that be?'

He'd called Luise 'the girl' last night:

233

'Don't wake the girl.'

'Luise?' I said.

'Ketty! Yes.'

'Ketty?'

'Of course Ketty. Who else but Ketty? Who else does everyone love so much? Who else died on the shore? Who else am I accused of doing away with?'

'No one could believe that!'

'My mother believes it. She always believed it.'

'She couldn't.'

'Why not?'

'It couldn't be true.'

'It's true.'

'Oh Thomas, no.'

'Poor Jen.' He pulled me to him by the scarf and gently touched my face. I jerked the scarf away from him. I slipped. Fell. He dragged me to my feet, over the slimy pebbles to the sand. He held my arm, speaking as fast as he walked.

'You wanted to understand you *shall* understand. You want to know why my mother thinks I'm a murderer? I'll tell you why. Then you can think me a murderer too. After all, you are exactly like her in every other way.'

I stumbled and slid like a dog on a too tight leash. His hand on my arm was like a machine gripping me. His other hand grabbed me, turning me to face him. He breathed out, two or three hoarse breaths as if to calm himself. His speech became slower, quieter.

'Do you really want me to tell you?'

'Yes.'

'Very well.' He loosened his grip a little and gave an odd smile. 'Ketty wanted me, you see. More than she wanted Sven.'

'She married Sven.'

'She never wanted Sven. It was to be close to me she married him. And after she married him she followed me. All the time. Everywhere. There was no way I could escape her. Nowhere I could go. Her eyes were on me always, like slime. My mother knew this. And Bo, of course. Only Sven didn't know, it seemed. It made me *sick*. After the girl was born it became worse. Ketty became unhinged. She was always—after me. "Thomas, come for a walk." "Thomas, come and tend your father's grave." "Thomas, come and pick apples." "Thomas, Thomas..." '

'And you? How did you behave towards her?'

'I walked away. I was always walking away. On the day she—I had walked to the sea to get rid of her. It was a cold windy day. Like now but without snow. I did not know or care if she followed me or not. I walked and walked along the shore. I walked fast. I ran. Miles.

235

Till it was late. Hours, I was out. I came back across the fields. I was tired. There was nobody at home. They were all out looking for her. Even the village people had come to help. It was dark. The church bell ringing, ringing. Torches down on the shore. The child was missing too. Sven found it behind a boulder just along there, out of the wind.'

It. Luise. It.

'My mother—' He stopped. 'She could not accuse me out loud because of Sven, because of family honour, because she could not prove. So she simply stopped speaking to me. I could not defend myself. She would not listen to me. She would not even look at me.' He shook me in his grip. 'It went on for months. Months of this. Begging her to listen to me. Begging. It did no good. She was harder than this rock. That is why I had to leave. There was nothing else for me to do. I got a job in England again. I've been there ever since. I thought after all this time—ten years—and bringing her my wife, a good wife, a good woman, just like herself—I thought she would see. She had to see. She had to forgive. I thought she would forgive. Instead, what happens? The girl's still here. They love the girl like they always loved the girl. Nothing's changed. Nothing will change. Except that you have learned to fear the monster too. Thomas Petersen the monster. Just like her in that, as you're like her in every other way. You'll always be the same. You'll never forgive. You'll never forgive.'

He was shaking me back and forth till I thought my neck might break. The cliff juddered in my sight, shards of snow stabbed my eyes and the metallic taste of snow was in my mouth. The sounds that came out of me were feeble, babyish. I had no breath. And then I heard shouting. And then Thomas threw me away from him and I was lying, awkward, on a rock and Thomas was hurtling away from me along the shore. Bo's wheelchair was lurching down the cliff path to the concrete platform between the wings of rock and Bo was calling my name, his high voice thinned by the wind.

I picked myself up and half crawled, half slithered to his roofless cave out of the wind. He caught my hand. We watched Thomas and Knud, farther along the beach. The snow revealed and concealed them by turns like swirling fog. The wind blew their voices away but there was no need for sound. Thomas was a big strong man but Knud towered over him. His whole body rocked with rage. He shouted. His clenched fists made hard gestures to emphasise his words. Thomas's arms were

folded across his chest. He seemed to be
barely speaking at all. Then we watched
Thomas clamber up the rock and become a
speck among swirling specks, disappearing
from our sight. The huge man followed
him up, stood high on the clifftop watching
him go.

'I told you never to come to the sea
without me,' Bo said.

'How did you know I had?'

'I couldn't find you anywhere else.'

'I see.'

'So now I expect you think I saved
your life.'

We looked at each other a moment.

'I don't think it's me he wants to hurt,'
I said. I didn't know why I said that. I
didn't know what I meant.

'Oh, don't you, Jenitha?'

The sharp head turned to me. He was
wrapped in a heavy fur coat with a hood.

'What fur is it?' I said.

'Wolf.' He snarled, baring his teeth.

He looked terribly funny in his wolfish
coat. The funniest thing in the world.
Laughter bubbled out of me like blood
from a wound. He held my hand tighter.
The laughter stopped. We were silent,
hand in hand.

'Your mother said it would snow,' I
said.

'My mother *said?* She spoke to you?'
I imitated her gesture.

'Mother is always right.' He looked at me sideways, raising his brows at me under the wolfish hood. I looked away. Knud was on his way back, striding above us along the top of the cliff.

'Come on,' Bo tugged my hand. 'We have to leave my break-wind. What's funny now?'

'Wind-break.'

'All right, wind-break. Okay. Not that funny, is it?'

'No.'

'Sven and Knud made it for me, my wind-break.' He turned the chair and pointed it up the cliff path. 'I like the sea but the chair's no good on the pebbles.'

'It's not too good on the path either.'

'Don't worry, the chair won't run away with me.'

'The dish ran away with the spoon.'

'What does it mean, that beautiful rhyme?'

'No one knows.'

'The little dog laughed. That's me.'

'Yes, that's you.'

'But I'm not laughing now, Jenitha.'

'Nor am I.'

He stopped the chair at the top of the path and turned it to face me. 'He told you about Ketty?' he said.

'Yes.'

'He told you what Mother thinks?'

'Yes.'

'That he followed Ketty to the shore that day?'

'He says she followed him.'

'Ah, yes.'

Knud marched ahead up the lane, disappeared at the brow of the hill. Bo slapped his arms across his tiny body, out like furry wings and back again. 'Run, Jenitha! Come on, look sharp!'

Knud came out of his house without his black wool hat and his sheepskin coat. I was afraid.

Bo waved to him. Knud folded his arms and waited.

'Knud, this is Jen. Thomas's wife. We got cold down there.'

'Come in. Drink aquavit.'

'Good fellow.'

I held back.

'Come along, Jenitha!' He grinned at me sideways. 'Jump to it!' He knew I was too polite to refuse.

The room was low, white, with the usual, I now saw, bleached wood floor and big tiled stove. The furniture was also of pale wood with linen cushions. My brain began to come to life again in the warmth, pins and needles in the head. Knud came back, ducking his head in the doorway. He seemed too big for the house, the bottle of aquavit and the glasses miniature in his hands. His red face shone.

'Waters off life,' he said.

'Thank you.'

Bo grinned. 'Have you put the carpet of firs on my father's grave yet, Knud?'

Knud looked for help. Bo translated.

'Oh yes. I did.'

'Good. Jen will be glad about that. She likes to protect everyone. Now he will be warm for the winter.'

'And Ketty also.' Knud's face filled with rage.

Bo spoke softly to him. Knud replied in rapid Danish. He said 'Thomas' once or twice, and 'Ketty' several times. His rage swelled. He turned his angry face on me.

'We love Ketty. She is as Luise. Like so.' He held up, side by side, the index finger of each hand.

'Yes.'

He growled some Danish at Bo.

'What does he say?' I was weary.

'He says, "That—bastard—should go away from here and stay away. He should never have come back." '

A tiny pretty woman appeared, flanked by two big boys. Knud stopped growling. Bo bared his teeth: 'Ah, Karen, Lars, Steen! Please say hello to Jen.'

They came in to shake hands with me.

241

We stood, awkward, smiling.

'Lovely furniture,' I heard myself say.

'Sven!' Karen beamed. 'For our marriage gift.'

Bo took pity. He pointed a finger at me. 'Jen is as tired as a mouse.'

'A mouse?' I said.

'You want to curl up in a little small hole where the big cat can't get in his paw.'

'Yes. I do.'

'I'm taking her away now, Knud.'

'Oh. Yes.' He stood, towering over his big boys, his little wife. He looked at me without friendliness.

'She's so tiny,' I said in the lane.

'Yes. "They only need one chair." That's what they say round here. True, she could sit in the palm of his hand. And yet the boys are just like Knud, no? Without of course as yet the big black beards.'

I said, 'Why does Knud hate Thomas?'

He stopped his chair inside the beech hedge yard.

'Would you like to come into the orchard for a moment? Or have you had enough of cold and despair?' He waited.

'I will.'

'You will not like to but you will.'

'Wouldn't it be better indoors?'

'Walls have ears.'

'So have trees.'

'Well?'

'You want to tell me terrible things.'

'You can say no.'

'No,' I said wearily, and led the way to the orchard. Trees weighted with snow and the yellow and scarlet orbs. A fairy tale orchard, everything unseasonal, therefore magical. Apples in snow, like the pictures in my childhood story books. I wanted life to be like those pictures. Like it used to be. I saw life now as a huge hand, a hand like Knud's but bigger, approaching from above, ready to press down and crush me to the earth. It could seem a protective hand, if you didn't know. It hovered over the orchard, waiting.

Bo's chair stopped by a swing which hung from a branch by two thick ropes. We looked at each other.

'Sven,' we both said.

I brushed the snow off the swing, and sat. Bo pushed his hands inside his sleeves. Now he was just a wolf's head in his hairy hood.

'You should have left the ears on that animal,' I said. 'They'd suit you.'

'Oh, good. Angry. That's better.'

'Nothing's better.'

'Anger will help you to—'

'Just tell me, Bo.'

'Okay. He pursed his lips, glaring, and

243

took a breath. 'Okay. Years ago when we were all children—'

'Once upon a time.'

'It's not a fairy story, I'm sorry.'

'No.'

'They all played in the gravel pit.'

'Behind the church?'

'You've seen it. It's a lake now. A pond.'

'Thomas was very upset about that.'

'Yes. When we were children it was grass, brambles, flowers in their seasons. The trees made it secret. The children were forbidden to play there. It was dangerous, so steep and overgrown. Because forbidden, it was a most exciting place.'

'Yes, of course.'

'Ketty was a little girl. The age of Luise now. Very sweet. We all were in love with her. Even I who was only five, six. But Knud most of all. And she loved Knud. They were sweethearts. Only ten, eleven years old. But they were serious, these feelings. One day—' Bo stopped, then went on. 'There had been a wedding in the village. White dresses, flowers, wreaths for the hair, processions up by the church. You know.'

I stopped swinging.

'Next day of course the children played at a wedding. In the gravel pit. Knud and Ketty the bride and groom. She got a white dress of her mother, long, down past her feet, and they gathered flowers. Ketty had flowers in her hair, so pretty. Someone was the parson. Thomas, who knows? It was quite a solemn affair.'

'You were not there?'

'Naturally not. It was told to me by my friend Knud. Thomas's friend Knud.'

I did not look at him.

'In the middle of the wedding game, someone appeared at the churchyard wall. As it happened this person had not seen the children, but they scattered silently as they were wont to do from that forbidden place. They went all their separate ways so no one knows what happened. She was not found till much later.'

I said nothing. The wedding dress.

'She had fallen, it was thought, hit her head and rolled down the slope. The dress was too long. Her feet could have caught in it.'

The orchard grew dark. The wedding dress.

'She was not dead. But nearly. They saved her but she was not the same. She remembered nothing before the incident. A lost little life. Between her and Knud it ended. As though she had forgotten him.'

'And Knud thinks Thomas hit her on the head and threw her down the pit.' I was scornful.

'Thomas was a—jealous boy. He was jealous of his friend Knud. All the children knew that.'

'So?'

'Thomas was missing for many hours. Before we found Ketty and after. We had to search for him. He was down in the village, swimming in the village pond. With some village children that he normally despised.'

'A perfectly innocent thing for a boy to do.'

'Yes. Except that he never played with the village children. None of us did. Thomas never swam in the village pond, he swam in the sea.'

'And is that all?'

'Yes.'

'It's just isolated country suspicion. It's like believing in witches. It's like saying fat Nanna is a witch because she lives alone.'

'But no one does say that.'

'It's just Knud's belief.'

'Yes.'

'Well, it's not mine. It's stupid childish nonsense. You live here cut off from the world. You have nothing better to do than to make up these Grimm's fairy tales in which Thomas has the role of villain.'

'We're only sixty kilometres from Copenhagen.'

'Well, you wouldn't think so. It's like the Middle Ages here.'

'You believe it,' he said.

'I don't.'

'My mother believed it.'

'Your mother seems to believe nothing but the worst of Thomas. No wonder he is so unhappy here. My God, I certainly will take him away. He was crazy to think you people could ever love him again.'

'You said it was not you he wanted to harm—'

'Of course he won't harm me! He has never harmed anyone. This whole fairy tale is based on the suspicions of a schoolboy who was jealous of him and a mother who couldn't love her own son.'

'It's good to cry.'

'You unspeakable smug little monster. Reduce me to this and then tell me it's good to cry? You can find your own way back indoors.'

'It's not me he wants to harm.' What had I meant? That he wanted to harm someone else? He had confused me with his mother. Was it she who was in danger, then?

The wedding dress. The wedding dress. The wedding in the mirror. A child's play ceremony. Thomas both parson and groom. He had never made love to me without the wedding dress. Till death us do part. Whose death? When?

I didn't feel the cold. In fact my body burned. I passed the village green, the main street with its few shops, the square where three men and the boys were now decorating the tree. I reached the end of the village street. To the right, flat fields. To the left, flat fields and sea. Seagulls gathered in crowds and screamed. The snow started again. It was too cold to stand still. There was nowhere to go but back. Back through the village to the house. The Christmas tree was lit up now, the boys cheering.

A postman got off his bike by a letter box. He opened the box and put letters into his sack. I ran faster back up the lane.

Conversation In
Another Place

10

'It has been a hard job. We have got information from all over Denmark. We have not found him, of course. But we think we have narrowed it down.'

'A-ha?'

'Yes. There are of course many head-lands in Denmark. Many begin with S and contain a V. But there are only certain ones where the family name Petersen is common. The computer has given us these.'

'You know what Petersen does for a living? He's a computer expert.'

Knudsen laughed.

Bright said, 'I take back every word I ever said against computers.'

'I have set inquiries afoot in these places. It is somewhere to begin. At least we may rule these places out.'

'I've got some more information this end. Been asking a few more questions.'

'Yes?'

'Yeah. His old man was a clergyman.'

'His old man?'

'Gotcha.'

'Oh, his father, yes!'

'Died when he was a kid. We're talking thirty-odd years ago. They lived in a vicarage, parsonage, whatever you call it. His mother's still alive. Still lives in the parsonage apparently. That's all we know. Told to my informants by Peterson's wife.'

'She is not found yet either, I take it?'

'Not yet.'

'You need a good computer expert maybe.'

'Shall I tell you something else an

informant told me? The guy used to make
her wear some other woman's wedding
dress. It was the only way he could
do it.'

'Do it?'

'Come on, mate.'

'Oh, do it. I see.'

'A-ha.'

A pause.

'Don't worry. If he's in Denmark we'll
find him for you.'

Chapter Eighteen

I opened my writing case. The letter was
gone. Perhaps I'd moved it and forgotten?
I searched my pockets, I looked under the
pillows, even under the bed. Though I
knew really there was no hope of finding
it, I opened Thomas's bag. Feeling sick,
I even went through his pockets. Stealing
and spying. Death had parted us. Not my
death or Thomas's. Ketty's. I didn't dare
think further.

The wedding dress had gone too, from
the back of the door. Thomas must also
have taken that. I wondered what he had
done with it. I didn't care. I wanted never
to see it again. I could never wear it again.

'I need to send a letter. To some friends in London.'

Bo rolled to a chest of drawers, fished out paper, rolled to a table, handed me a pen.

Dear Margot and James,
I am at Thomas's family's place, on a rather ancient headland, surprisingly isolated for a place only sixty kilometres from Copenhagen. It is spelt Stevns though pronounced Stayuns. And the nearby village is Goltrup. His family and the house—the old rectory opposite the church—are wonderful. Only Thomas is not happy here so I think we shall not be staying long. Miss you.

'What is the address here, Bo? And the phone number?'

He told me. I wrote the phone number large and underlined it. 'So you could ring me if you cared to!' I wrote. 'I'd love to hear your voices. Hope you're both well.' Et cetera. Bo held up an envelope and a stamp and dipped them into my hand.

'You could telephone these friends,' he said.

'No.'

He grinned. 'I could telephone for you.'

I went to his chair and put my arms

251

around him from behind.

'Was I right to tell you those things?' he said.

'Who knows?'

His hands covered mine.

'You be a brave girl,' he said.

'What do you mean, be a brave girl? What do you expect me to do?'

'Whatever you decide to do, you will have to be brave.'

'Meaning my choices are not great.'

'Yes.'

'I can abandon Thomas or stick by Thomas.'

'Yes.'

I heard John Bright's voice speaking the words in my pretty little house in Kentish Town: 'They are still investigating him.' But suppose Elizbeth turned up safe and well, all the suspicions surrounding him, about her death and Ketty's, mere fabrications, as Thomas said? What if I were to confide in Bo? Where could be the harm? Bo was not his enemy as Knud was. Bo might know what to do.

'Bo,' I said.

Thomas opened the door. He stared, pale. Then he said, 'Excuse me.' And left, closing the door carefully.

My head was an engine, seized. Cogs were stuck. Nothing would move. My hands covered my eyes.

'Bip bip bip bip!' Bo waved his arms. 'Don't you get paralysed, Jenitha! It's nice to go to sleep. You like to go to sleep, not to fight.'

'Yes, I do!'

'You're not to, now.'

'I'll do what I like.'

'You'll do what I say.'

'Why should I?'

'Because you know I'm right!'

His eyes were bright, his cheeks glowed, his fists were clenched. We were yelling quietly so as not to be heard. He was pure spirit, he might take off, disappear in a puff of smoke. He was incredible. I started to laugh. So did he. High-pitched like a little dog. Then we stopped. We just sat, in the glaring white light.

'You were about to tell me something,' he said.

'No.'

'Yes.'

'I have to go.'

'About Thomas.'

'I'm Thomas's wife. My loyalty is to him. Not to you. Until I know more, I can't speak.'

'Ah,' he said.

'All I know is, I have to get him away from here, before he—'

'Yes?'

'I have to get him away.'

'I'm sorry about my behaviour down on the shore. Please forgive me. I was carried away. You understand?'

I strode out of the courtyard without answering. If he could once confuse me with his mother, let him do so again: beg my forgiveness, follow me down the lane to explain himself.

'You know the gravel pit behind the church?' I said.

We stood between the church and the schoolhouse. His black woollen hat pulled well down obscured his beauty. He was any big man wrapped up against the cold. I waited while he lit his pipe.

'Bo was telling me about the—accident there. When you were children.'

He took his pipe from his mouth, looked at it.

'Yes?'

'It must have given you a great shock, Ketty being found like that.'

'Yes. We were all very—quietened. It taught us a lesson. I don't recall that we played in the gravel pit again.'

He was calm again now. He talked so normally. Said what any adult would say, looking back to a tragic incident in childhood softened by time. But his hands shook a little, I thought.

'Bo said Ketty was a sweet child. Just like Luise.'

'She was.'

'That she and Knud were sweethearts.'

'What else has Bo been telling you? That I was supposed to have banged her head with a stone and flung her down the pit?'

I looked at him. He sighed, shaking his head.

'Why? Because I was jealous of Knud?' He laughed. 'My God. My whole life and I have not lived down that childish fairy tale.'

'I told Bo I thought it was just that.'

'Did you?'

'Yes.'

We walked. A car hooted past us. We flattened into the hedge.

'Was I right?' I said.

He sighed. 'I ran away like the other children. I don't know where the others went. I made for the village. Naturally: they wouldn't think of looking there for me. It was hot. June. Some boys were splashing in the village pond, so I did too. Eventually of course they found me there.'

'You were playing weddings when it happened.'

'Yes.'

'What part did you play at that wedding?'

'The parson, I think. Well, my father had been the parson, you know.'

I covered my mouth with my hands.

'What is the matter, Jen?'

He put an arm round my shoulder. I shivered with disloyalty.

'You're cold,' he said.

'I'm not.'

We were at the edge of the village, approaching the post box. I pulled the letter out of my pocket.

'What is that?'

'Just a little note to Margot and James.'

'Instead of making your telephone call.'

'Well, they won't get it for days and—'

'I told you I wanted this to be our private honeymoon. I wanted no one to know where we were.'

'I didn't think you meant forever. After all, we might have left here by the time this reaches them.'

'Don't post it.'

He came, persuasively, close.

'Oh, Thomas, don't be silly. It doesn't make sense.'

'Don't you want this to be our secret?'

'No, Thomas, I don't, I don't.'

A different sort of woman might have resorted to tears. A younger prettier woman. He took the letter from my hand.

'Just for me then. For my sake. Don't

post it, Jen. Let's be secret just a little longer.'

'How much longer?'

He smiled.

'Thomas, listen. I don't think it's good for you here. Wouldn't you like to leave really soon and go somewhere else? I'd like to see Elsinore for instance, I'd love that. Couldn't we just go off on our own? After all, people don't usually spend their honeymoon with their family. Honeymoons are normally to get away from your family!'

'In my case, to get away from your friends.'

'My friends?'

'Yes.' He put his arms round me. 'To have you to myself.'

I was pressed into his chest. I couldn't breathe. I tried not to panic. 'To have you to myself.' The words would once have delighted me. What, then, did I believe?

'But Thomas,' I pushed myself away from the stifling stuff of his jacket. 'You haven't got me to yourself!' I smiled up at him. 'Your family are my friends now.'

'But they can see you are mine. You are my bride.'

He stressed 'my' so strongly I saw the brides who had not been his. Ketty, twice. And myself, too. I was only a make-believe bride. A looking-glass bride. Brought for his mother's approval.

'Yes, I am yours,' I said. 'But your family have seen that now. So it's all right. It's all complete. We can go off by ourselves somewhere and come back here another time. You've re-established contact now. There will be other times.'

He rested his chin on my head so I couldn't see his face. He said, 'It's Mother.'

'Can't you see, Thomas, it's no good?'

'What do you mean?' He stood away from me. He was white. Even his mouth. I was afraid. But I went on: 'Well, she—she never will—come round—unbend—give you—what you want. Bo says she loves you very much but—'

'Bo says, Bo says. Yap yap yap. Bo the Brain. Bo the Head. Bo the Mouth. He should have been born just a mouth.'

I gasped. He thought I was about to speak.

'Of course!' he said. 'Of course she does. She loves me best! I know that.'

'Well, isn't it enough to know that? Why ask her to forgive as well? It's hopeless, Thomas.'

'It's *not!* It's not enough. She will forgive me. For something I didn't do. Something not my fault. Forgive me! For what? For being falsely blamed!'

'You've been falsely blamed then all your life?'

'Yes.'

I can't say what was the look in his eyes. He suddenly became gentle.

'You believe me, don't you, Jen?'

'On one condition.' I smiled.

'What is that?'

'That you let me post my letter.'

'No!'

'Very well. If I don't post my letter we must leave here tomorrow. Take your pick.' A woman needs more confidence in her female power than I possessed, to get away with being charmingly masterful. I wasn't the type. Thomas smiled too, matching uncertain flirtation with uncertain flirtation.

'Very well,' he said.

'Oh Thomas!'

'We shall see.'

My heart dropped. ' "We shall see" is not a bargain.'

'We shall see.' He put the letter in his pocket.

'That's mine!' I cried out.

'There should be no secrets between husband and wife.' He smiled sideways at me.

'There's nothing secret in it. Read it if you like.'

'We shall see.' He left it in his pocket

and with the protective arm round my shoulder moved me away with him.

All evening he stayed at my side, left me alone not an instant. Though his face was as always in darkness I felt his gaze on Luise. She didn't look at him. Surely she hadn't heard us, last night? I prayed not.

Luise glided through the orchard in my wedding dress. A man in black crept from tree to tree. I raced headlong after her to warn her, calling, 'Ketty!' Calling, 'Elizabeth!' But because I couldn't get her name right, she ran from me. Her veil caught on a branch. I freed it as I ran. The veil stayed in my hand. The girl in the wedding dress had gone. I roamed the orchard all night searching for her. And I woke, my head thick with dreams.

My sullied bridal gown.

Thomas's place was still set. The others had finished breakfast though a jumble of napkins and coffee cups remained. I carried my coffee to the window. I saw the mother in the vegetable garden, in boots, thick coat and woollen hat. She gave me a feeling of safety. I wanted to be near her. On impulse I too dressed warm and went out.

She bent to pick up her basket, then

stood, ruddy-faced from cold and exertion, and saw me. She looked almost happy, in her unsmiling way. She held up, to show me, a bunch of seakale she had picked. I smiled. Something in my face seemed to touch her. She beckoned me to walk with her. I took the basket. We went round the sidehouse. When we reached the corner and could see into the orchard she put a hand on my arm and a finger to her lips. We stood still.

Luise cantered in and out of the trees. She cradled something in her arms. I couldn't tell what. Every now and then she reared up, shook her head about and whinnied. The mother and I watched her happily. And then I saw him.

He moved out from behind the tree. Luise had not seen him. He trod carefully ten paces behind her, gaining on her. The mother and I froze for a moment. Then she and I moved at the same time.

The mother walked past Thomas to Luise and stood behind the child, her hands on Luise's shoulders. She said something to Luise. The child turned. It was her horse she had been cradling. She saw Thomas. A blush clawed from her neck up to her eyes.

'Oh,' she whispered.

She tried to hide the precious horse in her arms. The mother spoke again.

Luise whispered, 'Huset.' Her grandmother nodded. Luise attempted a canter, faltered, righted herself, walked with dignity to her holly house.

The mother waited till she came out of the bush, then, again with a hand on the child's shoulder, guided her to the high beech hedge. We heard Sven's voice and hers and then the car drive off.

The mother came back towards Thomas and me. As she came closer he made as if to speak to her. She brushed past him into the house, saying only one word in her low harsh voice. She didn't look at him.

Thomas's face stiffened, in pain or shame. He stood.

'Thomas?'

He came back from far away.

'We're leaving,' he said.

'What?'

'You heard what I said.'

'When?'

'Now.'

He crossed the long room, went through the dining room, took the stairs three at a time.

My chest felt empty. Perhaps because I should at any moment be leaving my heart behind me, here.

She'd gone from the kitchen. I put the vegetable basket on the shelf. I heard her voice and Bo's beyond his closed door. A pad and pencil hung on the kitchen wall for shopping lists. I wrote a short note, thanking, missing. Love.

Chapter Nineteen

'Where are we going?'

Silence.

'Back home or somewhere else in Denmark?'

Both hands on the wheel, both eyes on the road.

'Are you taking us to Elsinore? Is it a long way? I've always longed to see Elsinore. Is that where we're going? Aren't you going to tell me? Is it another secret destination? Am I not allowed to know?'

The snow glittered. I chattered. Thomas's silence filled the car. Filled my head. I closed my eyes in terror. Nobody knew where I was. Nobody knew where we were going. It didn't matter. I had got him away from the house.

'Or are we going home? Back to England, I mean. Straight to Esbjerg for the boat. I'll be glad to see my little house again.'

Then he said a Danish word. The word sounded, as many Danish words did to me,

263

like something said backwards. 'Erglererl', perhaps.

'What, Thomas?'

He said the word again.

'What does it mean?'

He wrote in the steam on the windscreen: Hojerup.

'Is it a place?'

No reply.

'Is it where we're going?'

A shrug.

'Is it a town? A village? A monument? A castle? What sort of place? Let me guess.'

We had been driving in narrow roads between fields, passing the occasional farm with lovely barns, cobbled courtyards, stables. The car turned drove through a break in a hedge, bumped over grass, stones. And stopped, facing the sea. To our left a long low building, a restaurant, but closed. Ahead a small church. Not as pretty as the yellow Goltrup church, but older, it perched over the sea. To the right bare black woodland and a house like the Goltrup schoolhouse.

Thomas strode ahead to a wall at right angles to the church. The wall too perched right on the edge of the cliff. As at Goltrup, the cliffs were not high but sheer, creamy crumbly rock topped with a line of green under snow. The sea crawled with suppressed anger below, over the round grey boulders of the shore. The bay curved. I craned my neck to the left. The church, poised on the edge, looked odd, curtailed.

He spoke, at last.

'Half of it fell into the sea.'

'Half of the church?'

'Yes.'

'Were there people in it?'

'I believe it was a wedding.' He smiled.

They fell before my eyes, bridge, groom, parson, guests, turning over and over in the air. Pretty hats and bridesmaids' posies lifted on the breeze, then dropped and floated away on the pewter sea. Arms waved from the water then sank. I held on to the wall. Thomas had gone.

He stood up at the church porch and beckoned me. A large square faced man sat at a table in the porch selling tickets. The man smiled at me.

The door from the porch into the church was of thick cinnamon coloured wood. Each panel contained a different bas relief: a hand, a foot, a heart. This anatomical dissection, literal carving up, disturbed me. As we moved from the porch into the church the big man spoke.

'What did he say?'

'To close the door behind us,' Thomas said.

The door was heavy, the closing slow. I tried not to think of a tomb.

On each pure white wall, just as at Goltrup, an old fresco was half revealed. Pathetic humans poured headlong into the open mouths of animals. Or were they devils? Some had horns, tails. People also tilled the earth, plucked flowers, harvested corn, in ignorance of their coming fate. God overlooked it all, distant, detached, thinking of something else.

I walked between the tumbling people fixed halfway between their inception and their doom, towards the altar. But where the altar should have been, the church was open to the sky and sea. Only a metal rail stopped us tumbling like the painted people down onto the rocks.

I was never good at heights. I stood, back to the rail, gripping it. It felt cold even through my gloves. My hands might grow there, stuck fast.

Thomas sat in a pew. The light off the sea flickered on his face, pale, pure, unblinking, half smiling, quite calm now, like the moon.

I saw him clear. Separate from me. Separate from the idea I had had of him. We were alone, entombed here in this scrap of church. Why had he brought us here?

His eyes came to rest on mine. My

back was to the sky. How much of my expression could he see? The waves sucked at the rocks below. A bird shrieked.

'Why have you brought us here, Thomas?'

He started to talk, in a calm voice, quiet, detached.

'Before it was born, I beat my mother's stomach with an iron bar. When she was sleeping.'

I had a moment of incomprehension, then I said, 'You're talking about Bo?'

'I wanted to kill it.'

'Why?'

'I wanted her to myself, of course. She bled but unfortunately didn't abort. It waited its term.'

He talked matter-of-factly, taking me on the tour of his mind: This is the drawing room, this is the hall, this is the staircase that leads to—

'That was the first time she sent me away,' he went on. 'She should not have done that.'

'Where did she send you?'

'An aunt in Copenhagen. Dead now. A horrible apartment. It overlooked a park which she pretended was the country. I refused to eat. They had to take me back. The monster had been born. My father had died. I had learned my lesson.'

'What lesson?'

'To bide my time.'

His hands, clasped, rested on the pew in front of him. He stared out at the big white sky. His face was empty. His eyes were empty.

'And then, you see, came Ketty.'

He leaned back, folded his arms.

'Ketty was six when she came to live with Nanna up the lane. Her parents worked in Copenhagen, visited at weekends. I took charge of her, showed her everything: the sea, the gravel pit, where to find birds' eggs. The house in the holly bush. Oh yes, that too. It was our house. Ketty's and mine. Every day I ran back from school to Nanna's house where she waited for me. Till the day I saw her with Knud. Knud was also my friend, you know. They were standing in the field. She was looking up at him. He held out his hand and she put her hand in his. I called out. They didn't answer. They walked away together across the field. After that day she didn't wait for me. Her eyes were only for Knud. I did not show what I felt. I told you, I had learned to bide my time. Two whole years passed before—the wedding in the gravel pit. The wedding of Ketty to Knud.'

The calm voice stopped. The eyelids closed a second.

'She sent me away again. To school this time. Even though Ketty had not died. Again I did not eat or sleep there and again she had to bring me back. Ketty came out of hospital. And do you know? She was cured. She had eyes again only for me! Not for Knud. She had forgotten him! She was mine again. She went everywhere with me. She was my shadow. Of course, Sven tagged along as he always had but we hardly noticed him. He had always been there, always the same: dull, obliging, easily pleased. I had still to bide my time. She was younger than me, you see. But the waiting was hard, so when I was sixteen I sent *myself* away. I went to sea. I wrote to her long letters saying what I couldn't say in words. I came back from England qualified, able to earn much money. She was eighteen now. Old enough at last. I went to see her. I told her we should be married soon. You know what she said? She said, "Oh Thomas, I'm so sorry, I'm going to marry Sven." '

He got up from the pew and came towards me. The light hit his eyes, reflecting silver sky.

'I had had the wedding dress made for her. It was all prepared. A foregone conclusion. We had been waiting only for my return. At first I thought she was joking, teasing me. But no. She and the carpenter were married amid rejoicing. And Knud was the best man! That's amusing, isn't it? By then I had a job in Copenhagen, a year's contract. It was a good excuse to stay. I could not leave, you see. I was waiting. My mother watched me. But she could say nothing. However, it was hard to live in that house with them, oh so happy. Everyone so happy. Ketty made them happy, you see. All of them. Just as she does now.'

Now? She?

'I believe it was the hospital that changed her. She went there to have the child. When she came out she turned away from Sven! Just as she had from Knud the first time. It was like a miracle. I had bided my time and now it was my chance. I began to follow her, speak to her. I never touched her, you understand? Never. She had to choose me. Not be forced. That day on the shore I said, "You must come away with me, Ketty. You are not happy here." '

He stopped speaking a moment. The silver eyes reflected sky and sea. I even saw a seagull fly across. Two seagulls: two eyes.

'In the hospital she had remembered, you see. She told me she held me responsible for everything she had lost. She would never come away with me. She would never marry me. She hated me. She called me a terrible thing.'

'What thing?'

'She told me I was a psychopath.' He smiled. 'So I began to shake her and I went on shaking her and we fell and I was kneeling over her and I still shook her so that her head hit the rock, hit and hit and hit again, and there was blood all over the rock, sticky, and in her hair too, much more than there had been that day in the gravel pit. And this time I made a better job of it. I made sure she was dead. And this time of course the tide was coming in, already wetting my legs. I went into the sea to wash her off me. Not the village pond this time, you see. And when I came out she was gone. The sea had kindly taken her off my hands. Then I ran and ran for hours. To dry myself.'

He had stopped speaking. He looked out at the white sky, I inwards into the dim church. Even the gulls were silent.

'You spared the baby,' I said.

He laughed. 'Dear good Jen, always looking for good. Even in the monster. You like monsters, don't you, Jen? Why should that be, I wonder? No, Ketty had laid the child down when I began to speak to her. Out of the wind and the reach of the tide. In what you might call the heat of the moment I forgot the child. That's all.'

'I'm a monster too,' I said.

He wasn't listening. 'And do you know,

while I was banging her head against the rock, I wanted her to be wearing the wedding dress, just as she had been the first time? Yes. But afterwards, when she was dead, while I was running, I thought: no. It's better this way. After all, I may need the wedding dress again some day. I may need it for somebody else.'

His eyes drew back from the sea to me. I saw myself, twice reflected, white sky behind my head.

'For Elizabeth?' I could barely speak.

He smiled. 'Not just Elizabeth.'

'Ah no. Not my wedding dress? You said you had it made especially for me.'

He leaned to my ear and whispered: 'Ketty's. Always Ketty's. Ketty's wedding dress.'

He leaned back again and we looked at each other.

'What a pity we don't have the wedding dress with us now. We could have our marriage blessed. Wouldn't you like that, to have our marriage sanctified by our holy mother church?' He closed his hands over mine on the rail. He shut his eyes. His cheek brushed mine.

'Is this why you brought me here? To confess your sins?'

'Not only that.'

'So why have we come here?'

'Because I am tired of it all.'

'Then why bring me?'

'You are my wife. In sickness and in health. Don't you think married people should do things together?'

This time he looked at me as though he saw me. His eyes were blue again.

'Yes,' I said.

His mouth, soft and hot, opened my trembling mouth. All right, let's go then, I thought. Let's gently float hand on hand, mouth on mouth, over the cliffs and the boulders and over and over and into the sea.

His arms came tight around my arms, pulling my hands from the rail. Probing my mouth, filling my mouth, he forced me back over the rail. The rail cut into my lower back. That was how it was going to be, then. We would go together. He deserved it, and so did I. If he had killed two people, so had I. I had killed my parents. But I could save Luise. He would no longer be a danger to Luise. I would make my sacrifice for her. I held on to him tight. I didn't try to pull away.

The door opened with a scream. Thomas stood away from me. The big man said something. Thomas did not reply. The man stayed, holding the door open. Thomas made a sound between a sigh and a laugh.

'The church is closing now,' he said.

'For lunch! What a shame.'

He clasped my arm above the elbow and strode down the aisle. I looked at the man as we passed through the door into the porch. His eyes were kind.

'Do you speak English?' I said.

His kind eyes smiled. He lifted his shoulders. Thomas's hand slid down my arm, gripped my wrist. Politely I smiled at the man and went hand in hand with my unlawful wedded husband to the car.

Thomas drove just anywhere, in circles, it seemed. We took small roads. Twice we came back to the same level crossing in the back streets of a town. Stopped. Backed off. Turned again.

It was market day in the town. In the square, people bought Christmas things: trees, candles, advent wreaths. But we didn't stop. He drove through the back streets out of the town again. He didn't look for a way. He let the car do it, nose first, down the darkening lanes.

There were no other cars in the lanes. The sun was low and lowering, blinding.

Something crashed against the windscreen. We had hit something. No. Something had hit us, was hitting us, rushing at the windscreen, all the windows, pouring, running, glittering. The noise was frightful. It surrounded us. The car seemed to be spinning in a vortex of noise and flashing light.

The car stopped, just short of the railway line. The train passed. The water splashed by the train rolled down the windows. The noise of the train faded. A train. That was all.

We breathed out, like panting dogs, in short gasps. I looked at Thomas. Shaken, he sat up straight.

He murmured, 'What have I been thinking of?'

He turned the key in the ignition.

'Where are we going?' I said before the car moved off.

'Back to the Vicarage.'

'Thomas, no.'

Thomas had beaten Bo with a stick in the darkness of the womb. Bo might have given up then. But Bo was brave. He had decided to survive. I saw his boney thrusting face, all fire, all spirit, breathing life into me: 'Be a brave girl. Don't go to sleep.' My hands were pressed against the dashboard in front of me, long, thin, like his mother's hands, the knuckles white. I heard my voice.

'Thomas, we could drive to Esbjerg now. We could get on a boat and go straight to England. It would be all right there now. The investigation's closed after all. We don't have to go back to Goltrup.

I'm yours. I've made a vow. Whatever you've done, I'll stay with you. But let's not go back to the Vicarage. What's there? A few clothes, some suitcases, nothing we need. Let's go now. We can leave this nightmare behind us. We can wake up and start again.'

'Start again. Start what?'

'We—'

'We?'

'Yes, we. You were going to take me with you. Back there in the church. Weren't you?'

'Ah, you knew that?'

'Of course I knew it.'

He sighed. 'You know me now. Like her. You know me.'

'Your mother.'

'When I saw you I didn't understand at first. But soon I did. A face like hers. Her faithful nature. But a forgiving heart. When she saw you she would understand. You were my way of coming back to her, coming home. She'd see it was possible to be like you, to forgive. Instead, you have become like her. And, like her, you put them all before me. The monster. The stupid Sven.' A spasm shook his mouth. 'The girl. The so sweet dear little girl.'

'Luise?' I said with spasm of fear.

'Ketty. Yes. Oh, she comes first with everyone.'

'And if I were ever to be having a child. You would want to kill that too?'

'You?' He turned to me so fast the car rocked. 'Are you? Are you?'

'No.'

'Are you?'

'No!'

He sat back.

'I have to have things to myself. Just for myself.' He spoke factually. Quietly. 'I will not share.'

Side by side we stared ahead. There were no cars, no lights. Just us in the car. At the crossing. In the dark.

'Why did you tell me everything?' I said.

'I had to give you the choice. Like Ketty. Like Elizabeth. They chose to leave me.'

'I chose to stay with you.'

'Even unto death.' He smiled.

'Yes.'

'Poor Jen.' He moved his shoulders, put his hands on the steering wheel. 'There is something for me to finish, however. I always finish what I have begun, I told you that. I wasn't thinking straight back there. I was tired, you see. I'd forgotten the thing I have to do.'

'What thing?'

'You had confused me, you see. Like Mother. You have the capacity to do that.'

'What is the thing you have to do?'

'Oh, you know that too, I think, don't you?'

He stared at the black road ahead. His mouth smiled. It had the naked look, without the pipe, that I remembered from Kew Gardens, the day he had made me pity him. I pitied him still. But now I pitied others more.

'You're right, of course,' I said. 'We can't start again. If we hadn't come here I would have loved you always. It's my nature, as you know. Of course it's impossible, now I know everything. Impossible for you, I mean. I realise that. But let's go now. Together. We said till death us do part. But we needn't part. Just drive and let go. Anything. Go with me.' I put my hands out to touch him. He flinched away from me. 'Just drive to the sea. We can jump, like the people who fell from the church. Just as you meant us to. It's so cold, we'd be dead in an instant from shock. We'd know nothing. Then it would all be over. For both of us.'

'No, dearest Jen. There's the thing I have to do, first.'

'Don't harm Luise, Thomas—' The words were torn from me. The last words in the world I should have spoken aloud.

He went quite still. Then he started the car. He drove across the level crossing into the black lanes. He drove fast. The car rocked at corners, on bends. Then slowed and stopped.

'Thomas—'

'Sshh.'

He leaned across to me. His hand reached for the seat belt and unlocked it. The hand came up across my body, brushing my waist, my left breast, my shoulder, my neck. His white face came close. I saw the pure whites of his eyes in the dark, felt his warm breath on my eyelids. His broad white hand covered my face. I tasted his flesh, soft almost comforting. The hand moved over my face, closing eyelids, outlining nostrils, learning the bones. In a way it was the most intimate gesture he had yet made me. The warm, comforting hand moved down, closing nostrils, mouth, and now gently caressing my neck, now closing round my neck. Now his face came close again, closer, his mouth, dry, warm, on my mouth.

'Jen.' Then a sigh. Then: 'Mama, Mama, Mama.'

My hands clawed at his hand. Then his hand came away from my neck, throwing off my hands. It brushed across my breast. Black branches screeched on metal. The cold air stung. The rough road surface tore my elbow, my face. A blow in my

279

back rolled me into undergrowth. His face hovered over me.

'Thomas, take me with you. Please.'

He said, 'I'll come back for you. Don't worry. It won't be long.'

I tried to scramble out from branches and hard earth. The car moved away from me, picked up speed. The tail lights diminished, were swallowed up, the headlights no longer swooped over the hedges. The last strip of light had gone from the bottom of the sky.

Chapter Twenty

I got to my knees panting. I had no idea where I was. The market town whose name I did not know might be near, might be far. The cold might be lethal if I kept still. I started to run.

I saw the headlights before I heard the car. He had changed his mind, had come back for me, to run me down perhaps? I hurled myself into the ditch. Brambles tore my face, my knees scraped on ice. The headlights blinded me. But when the car passed I saw it was not Thomas's but a Danish car, the driver on the left. I scrambled out of the frozen brushwood leaping and screaming: 'Please please please help. I have to get to Goltrup.'

But the car was gone. Ridiculous, anyway, he could never have heard. I stood dashed, for a moment ready to give up. But time was passing. Thomas could be back at the Vicarage by now. I forced my legs to run again. The pain helped. It came between me and thought. And after a while I crossed the threshold even of pain. I had never experienced anything like this: the co-ordination of my body, the speed, the cold starry night as clear as my mind which worked by itself as my body did. If I kept running I must reach a house. From where I might telephone. The Vicarage. The police. I had no Danish. But I would make myself understood. I must also phone England. I must not be too polite to ask. Aunt Jess's voice: 'You must never take advantage, Jenitha, especially of those who are doing you a favour.' I sobbed a laugh. Another car. Again I leapt into the ditch. I had no choice. I must not be caught by Thomas now. The car, again not his, roared past the way I had come. I must call the Danish police. They would deal with everything. Two lights, headlights, again I was flagging. Could I keep running, take the risk? Thomas was unlikely to return now, surely? Too much time had passed. No, he was back at Goltrup by now. He had to be. I kept running. The lights bobbed about, small, impossible to calculate their distance, not travelling fast. They grew clearer, larger. They were not travelling at all. They disappeared, appeared again. They were square. They were not headlights. They were windows. They were contained in a long low shadow which must be a house. My body became all strain, all pain, aware of itself, my leg muscles liquid as treacle.

Yes, it was a house, long, low, at the side of the road. But the windows were gliding further away. I could not get closer to them. I was running on the spot. I was going to collapse before I reached the squares of bobbing light. How yellow they looked, how warm. Thus the Vicarage at Goltrup must look if you could see it through the fastnesses of beech. 'Oh God, let me get to the light, let me get to the light.'

I banged on the low door. I must make myself neat. I must not frighten the people. Nobody came. 'Oh please, oh please.' My legs trembled. I had to sink to my knees. I was on my knees, banging on the door. The door was green. Or looked it in the dark. 'Red looks green in the dark.' The window, not lit, to the left of the door, opened a crack. 'Oh God it's a child. A scared child.'

A small voice spoke in Danish. My jaw was stiff, my lungs too tired. I said, or tried to say 'Telephone', and 'Please.' 'Telephone, Telephone.' Everyone surely must understand telephone. The window closed. An endless silence. Only the little noises of the night, and my breath rasping. She was not going to open the door.

I almost fell into the house.

She was a short, round-breasted girl, in her twenties, her blonde hair thick as cream. She wore a flowered cotton dress with a big sweater over it. She did not help me up, I pulled myself up by the door frame. 'Telephone,' I said.

She nodded. She kept her distance, moving round me to look out into the night before closing the door. She led the way into a long room with a glowing iron stove. She pointed to the phone.

One word per breath, each breath a pain, I said, 'I don't speak Danish. I need to phone the Vicarage at Goltrup. I don't know the number.'

She handed me a phone book. There were thousands of Petersens.

'What name?' she said.

'Petersen.'

'Vicarage? At—?'

'Goltrup.'

'Oh!' She repeated Goltrup as I could

283

never pronounce it. 'I know them,' she said.

'You know them?'

'Well, Stevns is a small place, you know. Sven Petersen is my colleague. At the school. I will get the number for you.'

I didn't cry until Sven spoke.

'Jen!'

'Yes—Sven—'

'I get Bo.'

'Hello? Jenitha!'

That soaring, eager, excited, intelligent, positive flight of voice.

'Bo.'

'Stop crying please. What has happened?'

As best I could, I told.

'He is not in the house, no,' Bo said. 'His car has not come back.'

'Is Luise all right?'

'Yes, she is here.'

'You must tell the police.'

'Tell them what?'

'That he, that—'

'Sounds convincing, doesn't it? That ten years ago he may or may not have drowned someone, and that he has pushed you out of a car.'

'Bo, there's real danger.'

'Very well, no laughing. Sven will come for you.'

'No!'

'What?'

'Sven must stay there. I believe you are all in danger, but especially Luise. Sven must not leave you. I'll get there by myself, phone for a taxi. Please be careful. I'll get there as soon as I can.'

The girl's eyes were round.

'Thank you,' I said.

She took my arm and led me to the stove.

'Coffee?' She gave me a thick white cup and an anxious smile. She had small, even, very white teeth.

'I must phone England.'

'Oh yes.' She dialled and held the phone to me.

'It's engaged.'

'All lines. This time of the evening.'

'Are we far from Goltrup?'

She shook her head. 'Thirdy kilomeders.'

'I must phone for a taxi.'

'I will bring you.'

'Oh no, I mustn't trouble you.'

She smiled. 'So English you are.'

I saw the absurdity, in the circumstances, of turning down a lift.

'Yes, I suppose I am.'

Her face became serious. 'I don't know Thomas. You spoke of him.'

'Yes.'

'Don't cry more. Don't tell me. Drink the coffee. I must go, one minude. Please.' She left the room.

She came back in woolly hat and boots. I drank the coffee. Nothing had ever tasted so good. When she returned I was under control.

'I have driven to the door. Come.' She put me in the car. 'One minude.' She went in the house again and after one minute came out with a child wrapped in a blanket. She stowed the bundle on the back seat. 'My girl,' she said, making a U-turn.

'Oh, I didn't know, I'm sorry. I wouldn't have—'

She laughed. 'Ane is Luise's friend. They will be happy.'

'Are they the same age?' I forced myself to speak.

'No. Ane is small. Not yet six years old. Luise is her hero.'

'Oh.'

'But good friends.'

'And your husband?'

She laughed. 'No husband.'

'Oh I'm sorry, I—'

'He was too young. He ran away. He was afraid. Ane was not then born. She has face like him. Is good.'

'It must be difficult for you.'

'No!'

'No?'

'Ane and I are most happy.'

'I see.'

Silence for a while. A car passed in the other direction. I ducked. But it was not Thomas's.

'Why do you live so far from the school?' I had to talk.

'My house. I like it. Also very—ah—' She rubbed two fingers against a thumb.

'Cheap?' I said.

'Yes, most sheap. Because so alone and so far.'

'Aren't you lonely there?'

'Sometimes yes.'

'Afraid?'

'Yes, sometimes.' She was smiling. 'I was afraid this evening. From you.'

'I'm sorry,' I said.

'I'm sorry, I'm sorry,' she quoted me, smiling.

I could not talk to her of Thomas, the only thing in my head. Hurry, hurry. Please.

'We are not far now,' the girl said, as though I had spoken. 'Sven too is alone mother. For Luise.'

'Yes!' I smiled.

'You like Sven?'

'Very much.'

'And Luise also?'

'Oh yes!' I turned to her. 'She's *my* hero too.'

'Luise takes good care of Sven.' She nodded at my shining eyes.

'I like the whole family. I don't want to leave them.'

'Therefore don't.'

If only it were that simple She didn't know.

Chapter Twenty-One

Thomas's car was not in the courtyard. Sven lifted out Ane. At the end of the long room the mother knitted. Bo sat in his chair with a large volume propped up on the arms. Luise was curled in her place on the sofa. There was a wonderful smell in the room. I stopped and sniffed. Bo grinned.

'We are roasting apples in the stove. 'Goo'day, Inge. You have brought Ane. Good.' They spoke quietly in Danish. I heard Luise's name. The mother got up. She came to me. Her hard hand brushed lightly over my hair. My eyes filled up. What a sight I must look. She too said, 'Goo'day, Inge,' and went to the dining room. Sven laid Ane on the window seat. I was glad of their all speaking Danish together. I could gather myself. I was glad to be in that room again: the shadows, the lamps, the low wooden ceiling, the glowing stove. And my Luise.

But something about Luise was not right. She didn't move. I went to her. She lay on her side. Her face was wet. I sat on my haunches in front of her. She didn't look at me. In her hands she held her horse.

The horse was in two pieces. A jagged break.

She held up the pieces, one in each hand, and dropped the hands again.

'How, Luise?'

But I knew.

'I must phone England,' I said.

Margot's kitchen. The coloured tiles, the jumble of china on the dresser, the clutter round the phone. Margot groaning at the interruption to her work. But she would answer. She would call John Bright for me. It rang. It rang. But no one came. And they had forgotten to turn on the answering machine. They were always forgetting.

I put the receiver back and looked at Bo. His eyes were enormous. We stared at each other. At least the lines to England were no longer engaged.

The mother came and put coffee on the desk with a pastry. She placed her hand briefly on mine. And went back to the stove and her knitting. Such smells of coffee and apples and the pastry and wood smoke.

Life could be full of simple happiness. Thomas destroyed the simple happiness of life. A child's most precious possession. As a sign. Because he had to have everything for himself. And I could not hate him. My head fell forward, so heavy that, like Bo, I might overbalance. Even knowing Thomas, I could not wholeheartedly wish him caught. This family too had protected him. We were prepared then to let him go on? And on?

I lifted my head. I looked at Luise.

I said to Bo, 'Please get Directory Enquiries for me. The number for the Headquarters of the Epping Forest Police.'

We waited. At last Bo said some words in Danish and wrote a number neatly on a pad. 'Tak,' he said. He handed me the pad and the phone. I dialled. The silence went on, in London and in this room. Forever, it seemed. Then a woman said 'Hello? Epping Police Station, how can I help you?'

'I'm speaking from Denmark. It's a matter you have under investigation. Concerning the—the disappearance—of the wife of Thomas Peterson.'

Heads lifted. No one looked at anyone. Then at last a young man's voice questioned me. I couldn't recall the name of the rubber-faced inspector who had come to my house in Kentish Town. I asked for the person in charge.

'I'm the duty officer, madam. What seems to be the trouble?'

Seems to be the trouble. I almost laughed. Bo stared at me.

'About six months ago a young woman, Elizabeth Peterson, disappeared from an address in Epping Forest... I believe the matter is still under investigation.'

'The Superintendent is not in the station just at the moment, madam. Do you have information concerning the missing person?'

'No, I—not exactly. Well, I have reason to think...'

The mother was taking sizzling apples out of the stove at the other end of the room to distract Luise, and Ane who was now awake. A cosy scene. 'I think his family or some member of it may be in danger. He is in his car, you see, possibly close by. I wondered if it might be possible for you, for instance, to inform the Danish Police. I don't think they'd listen to me.'

'I'll pass on your message to the officer in charge, madam.'

'Can you tell him quickly? Speed is of the essence, I think.'

I think.

'As soon as I can, madam, yes.'

Helpless, I gave the address of the Vicarage, the phone number. I put the phone down and looked at Bo's eyes.

'Another wife?' he said, very quiet.

Very quiet too, I told him.

How a story can change. It had once been the story of a heartbroken man whose wife had decided to run away from him., Because he was a 'dull old stick'.

'But you?' he said. 'Jenitha?'

I told him the tale of my 'wedding'. I left out the mirror but I told our vow: 'Till death us do part.'

'Whose death?' Bo said.

'Yes.'

He sat still, hands clapsed tight. He might spontaneously combust, little tongues of flame flicker over him. Also, in my tiredness, his eyes were two black tunnels into which I was sucked, safer, darker, than the world outside.

'Knud is in the garden,' he said.

'I thought you didn't take me seriously?'

'That was before Luise found her horse.'

'When did she find it?'

'This evening after supper.'

'She was in the garden alone? In the dark?'

'She did not go into her holly house at midday. The horse could have been broken this morning before you and Thomas left. It does not necessarily mean he has returned here.'

'But Knud is in the garden.'

292

'Better safe than sorry? That's right?'

'Where is Thomas then?'

'I don't think we shall hear from him tonight.'

'Why not?'

'He will like us to fear and wait. His pleasure will be galore.'

'Will be what?'

'Galore?' He questioned me with outrage. 'My English is not correct?' He beat the arms of his chair. 'Thomas is to blame!'

'Even now you joke.'

'Especially now. Come and eat roasted apples. They're good.'

Luise and Ane, a little round child also with pigtails, sat side by side on the sofa. I was introduced to Ane in Danish.

'Goo'day, Ane,' I said.

'Jenitha speaks Danish now!' Bo said.

'Yo.'

'Two whole words. It's absolutely galore!'

The mother didn't smile. No one did. Luise stared ahead, the two pieces of horse in her lap, one hand on them, protecting. In the other she held a roasted apple which she attempted to eat.

Inge said, 'Sven can mend the horse.'

Luise's eyes moved in Inge's direction. Stopped. Moved back again without hope. She was right. Sven could mend the horse. But worse things than the horse were broken. These it might not be possible to mend.

A great clang shook the walls. We leapt. The church bell, heard every night at this time, sounded different.

'Knud's boys do it tonight,' Bo said.

'Oh.' I didn't like to think of them in the tower alone

'They are big boys. They are two.'

'They are absolutely galore.'

'Correct!'

Sven knocked out his pipe. He crouched in front of Luise, spoke gently. She nodded. He made to lift her. She gave one shake of the head, wriggled off the sofa. She performed a pale version of her goodnight ritual, limply shaking two fingers of my hand. Last, she took hold of Ane's foot, gave it a little shake. Ane too wriggled off the sofa, followed Luise to the door. Inge and Sven went with them out of the room. No cantering.

Bo spoke quietly and at length to his mother. She listened with her hands still on the knitting. She had long strong hands. Like mine. Once, as he spoke, she lifted her head and looked at me. Then she lowered her head again. At the end of Bo's story she sat still for some time. Then she picked up the needles and resumed her knitting. The wood settled in the stove. Floor boards creaked upstairs as the little girls were brought from the bathroom and settled in their beds. The mother spoke a short sentence without looking up from her work. Bo looked at me.

'Mother says you have done well.'

I was moved, and weak. I could only nod.

Sven came down, spoke to Bo, looked at me.

'Sven says will you mind if Inge sleeps in your room?'

'Of course not. No, Sven.'

Sven went back upstairs.

'Sven will stay in the roof space. He won't sleep. He has lit the stove. I will be down here. I don't have legs but I have a big bell. Not as big as the church bell but loud.'

The phone trilled in mockery. Bo rolled fast down the room, spoke, listened, spoke, put the receiver down.

'The police.' He rolled back to us.

'The Danish Police?'

'They've had a call from the London Police, so they're going to keep their eyes on us tonight.'

He told the mother. Her hands faltered on the needles then gripped again. It was the only sign of what she felt. Never think it easy to set the nets to catch someone you love, or have loved, or have trusted more than daylight. Even if that person may have killed. May kill again. It is a hard, hard thing to have to do; to betray.

Bo looked from her to me.

'You are worn out and must rest now. No, we won't sleep but we should rest. Try. Go.'

Upstairs, Sven was pushing logs into the stove. Inge sat on the arm of a chair. I said goodnight to them. I did not enjoy walking alone across the huge roof space that never lost its chill. I turned at the door of Aurora. Sven and Inge were standing close together. I felt a pang. He looked like Thomas, standing there so close to her.

Aurora hadn't changed. The cloudy white duvets, the little boat beds. Cosy, clean, innocent. I leaned back against the door, closed my eyes, felt the cool satin of the wedding dress. It hung there again? How had it come back? When? And I became aware of the smell. A filthy rotten smell, like the smell of a pond in winter when you break the ice: the smell of filth and corruption and dying and death. As I turned, the smooth stuff slithered from the hanger, lay shining, moving, on the floor. In parts the satin gleamed, still creamy white. The rest was sticky with black mud, smeared with green slime that hung in webs, ripped down the front in a jagged raw hole from the bodice to six inches below the waits. The edges of the hole were stiff with dried mud.

I stopped the scream with my slimy hand but a sound must have escaped me. The dress moved again as the door pushed against it. Inge stood, Sven behind her, staring.

'I'm sorry,' I said.

Inge squeezed round the door and knelt beside me. 'Such bad thing.' She touched my arm. She looked up at Sven. Between them they lifted me, got me out of the room and into the bathroom. I'd never get the smell off my hands, the slime off the back of my neck, the terror out of my stomach. The terror he meant me to feel: 'I have come back. I can get into the house. I could be in the house now, even. I learned my lesson: to bide my time.'

When Sven brought the clean white duvet to wrap me in in the chair by the stove, I felt no better. Even though the house had been searched. Even though they had found no further sign of him.

'It was your bride dress?' Inge whispered, tucking the white cloud round me.

And Ketty's. And Elizabeth's. In any language it would be hard to explain.

'Yes,' I said. I should not be able to sleep.

Chapter Twenty-Two

When I woke it was a bright day. The roof space was empty. The stove glowed. There was a hint even of warmth. I ached all over. I wondered how far I had run yesterday. Yesterday. There was no sound but the logs shifting in the stove.

Downstairs too was silent. Coffee in the thermos, pastries on the lovely china still warm, but no one about. From the dining room window I saw smoke drift over the vegetable beds, the mother at her bonfire. Any winter morning. I went out.

She stood on the path with her hand on the back of Bo's chair. With desperate slowness she lifted leaves into place on the long-handled rake, thrust them down into the fire, lifted more leaves. Stared at the column of smoke.

Bo said, very quiet, 'Sven threw the wedding dress out here last night. When she lit the fire this morning to burn the thing, I'm afraid it had disappeared. During the night. She thinks if she keeps the fire burning—'

He had been there in the night. He had

taken the wedding dress.

I went backwards down the path. And thudded into somebody. A large somebody who clasped my arm when I cried out.

Knud's rocky face expressed hostility. As though he blamed me for Thomas's coming back here. For everything. As well he might. I felt oppressed by this, and by his size and his ruddy health. There was no language to talk with. And nothing to say.

I ducked into the holly house. The dress wasn't there. Nothing was there except the little tin tea set on the packing case, still filled with ice. On the way back I gave Knud an awkward salute and went in at the long room door.

Bo wheeled in from the dining room. 'The police phoned this morning. They have found no sign of him. He may have left Stevns, who knows?'

'I don't think so. Where is everyone?'

'Inge and Sven took the children to school as usual. They will be safe there. And it keeps things normal.' He gave a short laugh. 'Normal.'

I said nothing.

'Something has happened to you, Jenitha?'

'No. I met Knud.'

'Ah yes. The hatred.'

'And the—the—fire.'

'My mother so wanted the thing burned. She loathered it.'

'Yes.' I smiled. 'It was somewhat loathersome.'

'Jen!' He banged his hands on the chair arm. 'Don't. Don't go depressed. Don't let your mind go to sleep. You were good yesterday. Brave. You ran. You phoned. You made things move. Don't forget that. He must be stopped. He must not go on. He was always sent away, always went away. You have an expression: "Out of sight, out of mind?" We are all responsible. He is out of sight now but he must no longer be out of mind. Wake up!'

'I will.'

'That's better.'

'What are the police doing?'

'Looking all over. The ferries and airports. In Copenhagen too.'

'And nearby?'

'Yes. Patrolling the area, I think you say.'

'It doesn't comfort me. What can I do?'

'Wait.'

'Wait?'

'That's all.'

'For what?'

'Ah, yes.'

'Sven took Luise to school just the same?'

'She'll be safe there. Happier perhaps too.'

'It's Luise who—' I said.

He wiped his face with both his hands. He was so helpless. So imprisoned.

'You know what she called her poor horse?' I said.

'No.'

'Thomas.'

'No?'

'But you knew she worshipped him?'

'It was her secret.'

'I wouldn't have betrayed it. Before.'

'Nor I. For a king's ransom.'

'Why, Bo? She has two wonderful men in her life. Sven and you.'

'There was always a space in the family album. Thomas up to a certain age, and then no Thomas. A mystery. She would ask, but naturally nobody wished to tell. We wanted to protect her from such wickedness, such sadness. So's not to mention his misdeeds, we would say he ran away to sea, he was only sixteen, and so on. "Did he go on big ships?" "Yes, on big ships " "Where did he go?" "All over the world!" You see? I am responsible. Sven too. We told her stories. Thomas the Hero. We raised him from mere mystery to the status of myth. And then, you know, her mother too disappeared at a certain age from the family history. It was as though her little mind put them both together in a dream place of her own making.

Her mother and Thomas the brave. We thought that, like Ketty, he would never come back.'

'But he did.'

'I'm afraid it is always wrong to try to protect children from the truth.'

I thought of my parents' death and no one telling me, and my long silence. 'Oh, yes,' I said.

'You have done what you can. For the moment she is safe. Come to my studio. I can daub at a painting while you read to me. We can't do anything else.'

'He named a character after you! Read!' He found the page and handed me *Our Mutual Friend:* Dickens's Jenny Wren, the dwarf with hair down to her feet, lavishing love on her frightful father, faithful to the end, going up to the rooftops to play at death. Grotesque nightmare. Bo's sense of humour knew no bounds. This time I couldn't be amused. I closed the book. The mother announced lunch.

She handed me a bowl of thick soup and some sausage and aquavit on a tray, saying, 'Knud.'

Her face was streaked with black from the bonfire. Her eyes were red.

Knud was in the orchard still, piling frosted leaves into his barrow. It was something to do, I supposed. And the wide-toothed rake was a good weapon. He said nothing when I brought him the food. He sat on the bench to eat.

Bo was on the phone when I returned. 'That was Sven,' he said. 'He is keeping Luise there at the school for lunch. Better away from the house, he thinks. She will be safer with her teachers and the other children.'

We ate lunch in silence.

After lunch I called Margot again. The phone rang and rang. I went out to fetch Knud's dishes. They were on the napkin on the seat, but there was no sign of Knud. I stood in the orchard shivering. The white sky bulged with snow. I wished it would fall. I wanted its soft white violence to blot out everything. The light was already going, the sun low. It was the light for sacrifice. 'Thomas,' I wanted to cry out, 'come and take me and leave these people in peace.

Thomas came hurtling through the beech hedge and along the house. No sound came out of me though I tried to call. Before he got to the door I ran. Within five yards of him I called 'Thomas!' He looked round, wild. He was Sven.

He pushed me in ahead of him. The door crashed back. Crying, he spoke. I watched the faces of the others. Everyone was still. Then Bo said, for my sake, 'Luise is missing. A child brought a note to her teacher. The child said the note came from Sven. The note asked the teacher to send Luise to her father. The teacher sent the child with Luise. She did not fear, because the police were round the school. Luise has not been seen since. The child says she delivered Luise to her father. Only of course this so-called father was not Sven. It was a man who looked like Sven. We know who he was. He even spoke to the policemen. They too thought he was Sven. They didn't know how like Sven Thomas looks. None of us thought to say.'

'He has a car,' I said. 'They could be anywhere.'

'The police too have cars.'

'Knud?' I said.

'He is looking in the woods behind the old teacher's house, Mother and Knud's boys are searching the shore.'

Sven came down the stairs, speaking fast.

Bo said, 'Sven had looked over the house. They are not here.'

'The gravel pit,' I said.

Sven ran. I ran after him.

'They', he had said. 'They, they.' My running feet repeated the word: They. They. They.

Sven went through the church gate in

front of me, sprinted past the cypresses, up the winding path between the neat tidy kindly little graves. He reached the bank, leaped up it, vaulted the boundary wall. I scrambled after him into the wildnerness. Brambles tore at our legs, snow bouncing and flying. Sven, yards ahead, was in my sights, appearing and disappearing through trees and scrub. Then suddenly he was gone. As though he had fallen off the world. Slipping, sliding, tearing, I threw myself after him down the slope and by hanging on to a branch stopped myself hurtling over the lip of the pit.

I saw then the black water down there through the trees, congealed in places into greyish whorls of greasy-looking ice. Sven had gone to the left, making hardly a sound, grabbing branches so as not to slither down the steep bank. My legs hurt. Every breath was a pain. I liked the pain, was glad of it. Neither of us called out to Luise; secret, silent, we were hunting wolf. I went the other way round the rim. Apart from our snow-muffled movement, I heard no sound. I'd lose sight of Sven, feel fear, see him again. I prayed all the time, 'God, God, God, God,' though I had no belief; the word was a mantra, an incantation, a way not to think of the worst.

Ten yards away I saw Sven stop. I stopped. I saw it. The small figure in the long white dress, lying face down at the edge of the pond. It didn't move. On the back of its head was something black, like a spider. It was blood.

The sides of the pit were slippery, treacherous. The undergrowth clawed, tricking your ankles, snatching at your feet. Sven reached her. He knelt. He placed his hands on her back. He pounded, calm, rigid, desperate. She did not respond. He pumped her arms up, down, up, down. He shouted, 'Luise! Luise! Luise! Luise!' The little body convulsed. Water trickled out of the mouth. He shouted 'Luise!' again, in a different tone. Water spurted out, and spurted again, then reduced to a dribble once more. He turned her on her back, held her nose, breathed into her mouth, once, twice, three times. He pressed her chest with flat hands. She breathed, a painful shaking feeble sucking on life. He pressed again. She breathed again. And breathed. But she didn't open her eyes.

Scrambling over the wall, running through the dark churchyard and down the lane to the house, I forgot to feel fear. Bo was in the beech yard outside the open door.

'Doctor,' I said. I ran past him into the house, brought the phone.

'Where?' he said, dialling.

'Gravel pit.'

'The doctor speaks English.' He gave me the receiver.

'Blankets,' the doctor said. 'And I will come. Make her warm and keep her still.'

'Thank you.'

'I will be ten minutes at the most.'

I pulled rugs off the sofa, ran back up the lane. Footsteps behind me. Whoever it might be I could not stop. The footsteps gained. Still running I turned. Knud, huge against the streaky sky, pounded behind me. He snatched the rugs and out-ran me.

Covered with the blankets and Sven's anorak she was breathing shallowly. Her eyes were still closed.

'The doctor will be here in a few minutes.' Speaking hurt. Everything hurt.

We surrounded Luise as though our closeness could make her all right.

The doctor told Knud to carry her up the bank. But Sven insisted he do it himself. So Knud clambered behind them to break any fall. There was no fall. No obstacle existed for Sven.

The warmth of the stove brought no colour to her face. Even her freckles had grown pale. The doctor gently removed the wedding dress. She didn't stir.

He said, to me, 'The police will need to see this. Will you take care of it?'

I took my wedding dress, wet, stained now with Luise's blood as well as the mud and slime, and carried it out of the room. I hung it in the laundry room where it dripped brown drops onto the stone flags. I washed my hands.

The doctor came into the dining room where Bo and I hovered, silent. He would like to take her to hospital in Copenhagen. He had called the ambulance.

Sven was shaking when the ambulance arrived.

'May I go with you?' I said.

But the mother was already in her coat. She and Sven climbed into the small white van with Luise, and we were left, watching the ambulance tail lights as they faded down the lane.

When we came back indoors, a policeman was putting down the phone. He spoke to Bo.

'There is no news of Thomas,' Bo translated. 'He has not been sighted. Neither his car. Apart from the child at the school who believed him to be Sven, no one has set eyes on him.'

'Will he come back here?' I said.

Bo lifted his hands. 'Who knows?'

'I don't think he will,' I said. 'Not now.'

'Why?'

'He thinks he has killed Luise. That's what he wanted to do.'

'Unless he has been watching everything, and knows it is not done yet.'

My throat made an inarticulate sound.

The policeman spoke in English for me. 'One colleague will come. Stay here for the night. I go in the car. I search.'

'May I go with you?' I said. 'Perhaps I could help.'

'Okay.' He nodded. 'But wait for colleague now.'

Wait, wait, wait.

I went upstairs. The roof space was chill again, the stove burned down. I thrust some logs onto the embers. Sparks rose, and fell as fine white ash. And there, stuffed under the logs, a thick wodge of paper not quite consumed: my letter to Margot and James. It would burn now. As Thomas had desired.

I stood at the window. Bare branches, silver apples, frosty grass, glittered under the moon. Only a few days ago, my first view of the orchard, the little girl in pigtails cantering among the trees. Did he believe he had killed her?

The three men were gathered round the stove, Knud's head almost touching the ceiling. I crashed into the room.

'I know where he has gone!' I tugged at the policeman's sleeve. 'We must go now. I know where he is. Come, please.'

'My orders.' His face creased in doubt. 'I must wait here.'

'Please,' I said. 'Please!'

'Okay.'

He spurted a few words at Bo and Knud. I was already out of the room. He spoke on the car phone too, in the lane.

'Hojerup,' I said.

Incomprehension. 'Where, please?'

I wrote in the steam on the windscreen.

'Oh! Erglerergl!

'Yes?'

'Broken church?'

'Yes!'

He spoke on the radio which spat speech back. I closed my eyes.

The church was locked and dark but lights from the house flickered through the trees. The big ticket man came to his door, bleary eyed. The policeman explained. Unbearably methodical, the man went inside to put on his coat and hat. And I wondered why I wanted Thomas found so urgently. I wanted him taken alive. Why?

Another police car squealed into the car park. A light came on in the restaurant. The ticket man stolidly clomped up the slope to the church, carefully placed a

310

key in the lock, stomped to the carved door, creaked it open, ducked his head. The doors of Denmark were so small, the people so large. One of the mysteries.

The paintings of the falling people wriggled and leered in the dim light. The policeman and I reached the balcony rail together. Clouds over the moon, just a dull glimmer on the water far below, and the noise of the sucking sea. Then a dance of torches like insects down there on the rocks. My policeman climbed onto the rail. A big floodlight that normally lit the outside of the church, he manoeuvred to illuminate the beach. Someone outside swung another lamp round. As the lights hit the black figures below, throwing long shadows, one of the men down there turned and shouted up. But before he shouted, I saw.

Like Luise, he lay half in the water, half out. His head and shoulders lifted and fell with the movement of the sea. My policeman climbed down off the rail and looked at me. Hands frozen to the rail, I stood and looked at Thomas.

Then I freed my hands and followed the policeman down the steep cliff path and over the boulders of the shore.

They were turning him over. His body was broken. You could see that, when they moved him. It flopped in ways that even a dead body should not. But his face, except for a smudge on one cheek bone, was not harmed. I tried to rub the smudge away but it would not go away, it would not rub off.

The policeman asked me, 'Is this Thomas Petersen?' and I said, yes, it was.

It. Was. It. Used to be. Once.

They found traces on the rocks and the church rail that showed he had climbed over the wall at the side of the church, scrambled his way across ten or twelve feet of sheer rock face to reach the rail. He had spent time in the church. Enough anyway to remove his coat, his hat, his gloves. They were found neatly folded on a pew. Then he had climbed onto the rail and flown down to where the tide came to meet him. Half an hour later and we should never have found him at all. I was sure he had not meant to be found. He wanted to stalk the nights of Goltrup forever, no one knowing whether he was alive or dead. I knew why I had needed to find him so urgently. Now I could be sure.

Couldn't I?

The policeman took me back to Goltrup. He told Knud and Bo what we had found. Bo looked into a distance, not at anyone. Knud clenched his huge fists, wishing Thomas had not pre-empted him. He would have liked to have had a part in the destruction of Thomas. And I found myself glad that at least Thomas had cheated him of that.

The news from the hospital was that Luise still lay in her pale sleep. No change. The tests had revealed no internal injury. The head wound was bad. The results of the brain scan were still being analysed. The doctors were perplexed at her refusal to wake, suspecting something worse than concussion.

The doorbell rang. My policeman went to answer it. He returned, followed by a slighter man, dark, wiry, light on his feet. I watched them come down the length of the room, transfixed. The smaller man halted on sight of Bo, a mere hiatus in his step, almost imperceptible. Then he came steadily on.

'Don't be alarmed, *Miss* Wren, you're not seeing things.' He thrust a hand in the direction of Bo. 'Detective Inspector John Bright,' he said. Bo's chin came up, his look sharpened, his hand went out. Their hands were alike. They weighed each other up in a swift comprehensive stare.

'I'm Bo, Thomas's younger brother. This is Knud, a friend. You need a drink, I imagine. Forgive Jenitha for her

313

silence. She has just identified Thomas's body on the shore farther up the coast.'

'A-ha? Is that so? Cheers.' He downed the aquavit in a gulp and said, 'Christ.'

Bo smiled.

'You'd better sit down, Miss Wren.' Bright put a hand under my elbow. 'You want to know what I'm doing here, only you're too polite to ask. Well, I'll tell you. This might be a shock, okay?'

I sat down.

'Yesterday morning Elizabeth Peterson's body was dug up in Epping Forest. Yeah. The guy in charge is a mate of mine, you know that. I've been giving them a bit of unofficial help. He was for telling you over the phone, but I thought, well, I've got time on my hands and if they were going to pay my fare—! And then I thought they'd need a bit of help here too. Liaison, you know. So here I am. So, if there's anything I can do—' He raised another little glass of aquavit, emptied it. 'Cheers.'

'Thank you.' My voice was faint. 'Does Margot know?'

'I couldn't reach them. Their phone—'

'They must be away.'

'Out of order.'

'Oh.'

'Good old British Telecom.'

'I miss them.'

'British Telecom?'

'Margot and, Margot and—'

'Give her some of this fire water. It'll do the trick.'

'I'll be all right.'

'You will, yes.'

'I'm sorry.'

'She's sorry,' Bright said to Bo.

'We guessed she might be dead. His wife.' Bo rapidly gave the sad details of Thomas's life. He held his chin high from shame, that so much knowledge had been withheld. 'So, the death of this poor Elizabeth could have been prevented perhaps,' he said, 'had we told what we knew.'

'You can't prevent people dying. They all do it in the end.'

'Sophistry.'

'A-ha.'

'At least Jenitha has not been—' Bo stopped. 'I was going to say harmed but—'

'But you meant killed.'

'Clearly.'

'Luise,' I said.

'My brother Sven's daughter, nine years old.'

'You said.'

Knud growled into his beard.

'The big fellow,' Bright said, 'wishes Thomas was still alive and well enough to be battered to death. I know the feeling.'

'They were good friends as boys.'

'I see.'

Shock and aquavit had their effect. I woke on the sofa to the murmur of voices. And to instant recall. Daylight lapped across lamplight, negating it. Without moving I looked at the room and at the three men, all bleached by the strange light. Knud, dwarfing the chair he sat in, was as dependable as a land mine. He frightened me. But the other two: a little scrap of fire and mischief, and a wiry cockney with unspeakable manners—I'd trust both of them with my life. I recalled the moment in Margot's conservatory when I had looked at Thomas and thought I could trust him with my life. And I had been justified: he had spared me my life. I turned my face into the cushions and groaned and slept again.

I woke to broad day and the smell of coffee. I was alone in the long room.

Chapter Twenty-Three

Bright deftly laid out crockery on a tray in the kitchen. 'Nice things they have here, don't they?' He poured coffee. 'Good morning, Miss Wren.'

'Where's Bo?' I drank the coffee leaning

on one of Sven's cupboards. Bright gestured with his head towards Bo's room. 'I put him to bed.'

'He let you?'

'That surprising?'

'Normally only his mother is allowed.'

'He was high on lack of sleep.'

'He's always like that.'

'A-ha?'

Silence. It was good to be eating breakfast. I dreaded to ask certain questions so I asked others.

'What did you talk about all night, you and Bo?'

'Proust.'

'Proust?'

'A bit of an insulting level of surprise if I may say so, Miss Wren.'

'No, I—'

'You don't have to blush. It's my sabbatical project, *Remembrance of Things Past*. Bit ironic, the title, as it happens, in my case. Good books though. Number three's a bit of a problem, but once you get past that... His nibs in there is all brain. Well, he'd have to be. Being all head. Little cracker, isn't he?'

'Yes,' I said.

The silence of the unasked questions descended again.

'Just the same,' he said.

'What?'

'The little girl. Isn't that what you wanted to know? Still unconscious.'

'No better?'

'No worse.'

'Same thing.'

'Different way of looking at it.'

'Yes.'

More silence. He poured more coffee.

'What you going to do? Now.'

'Do?' I said. 'Now?'

'Yes. Stay on here? Go back home? What?'

'I haven't thought.'

'A-ha.'

'I can't do anything or think anything till Luise—till I know how Luise is.'

'We'll go and see her.'

'In Copenhagen?'

'Why not?'

'What about Bo?'

'The giant will keep an eye on him?'

'Yes, I suppose.'

The silence deepened, moving with possibilities. Like Bo, Bright was trying to tell me, Don't go to sleep. Think about the next step. Walk to meet life, don't wait for life to creep up on you.

A little bell sounded from Bo's room.

'His nibs wants me.'

I sat on the sofa where Luise used to curl up in the evenings. Thomas must not be

allowed to control lives even after ending his own. Her life must not be broken in two as her mother's life had been. As her horse had been. I saw the horse in her hands irretrievably broken, and remembered her look at Inge which had said that more than the horse was broken. The horse was called Thomas. The horse was her dream. Thomas. The horse. Where would it be now? What would she have done with it?

Darkness. Thick as a blanket after the fierce cold sun outside. I felt around inside the table crate. Only the tea set and a conch shell. My eyes adapted. The childhood house was deserted, was desert.

Sun ballooned to fill the room. Two little beds. Under one bed a pair of small red boots. Under the pillow the horse, in two pieces.

'Do you see?' I said.

'All the king's horses and all the king's men.' Bo held the horse, a piece in each hand.

'The original Humpty Dumpty, that's you,' Bright said.

'You are right!' Bo rolled to his table and rummaged on its crowded top. 'There.' He rolled back to his desk. He laid the pieces down, wiped them carefully. He mixed stuff in a small dish. Applied the stuff to each half. Pressed the halves together. Stood the horse and carefully wrapped tape around the join to hold it tight. 'There.' He put a finger to his lips, then to the join. 'One hour will be enough.'

In the kitchen he stopped his chair suddenly. 'And after your visit to the hospital, Jenitha? What then?'

'It depends.'

'Ah, yes.'

Packing is usually a problem: what do you take? What do you leave? I left a scarf. An old chiffon scarf dating back to Aunt Jess's youth. The only thing I had taken from her house. The only thing I could leave here. I left it under the pillow for Luise to find as I had found her horse. The rest of my things were still in Thomas's car. But his towelling robe still hung in the cupboard.

The robe was blazing when Bright came out to the bonfire to fetch me. He squinted sideways at me but said nothing.

Bo unwrapped the horse from its bandage. He scraped away a little hardened bead of glue. Then he took a fine brush, dipped, mixed, dabbed, stroked, till there was no sign of a break, no hint of a join.

'If you did not know, you would not know,' I said.

'It will do for one glance.' Bo laid it in my hands.

'Will you ask Knud to come and stay with you?' I glared at Bo's hawk face which flamed up at me. We were in the hall.

'Come back here, Jenitha.'

'I will.'

Bright came back from the car. They shook hands.

'I wish I thought we might meet again,' Bo said to him.

'So do I. My English grammar could do with a bit of help.'

The car was in the lane. Bright went ahead. At the gap in the beech hedge I turned to wave.

The church bell was ringing in wintry sunset light. A bright moon hung to the left of the tower. Low down to the earth, red streaked the sky. I turned in my seat and watched till the lane folded the church and the moon out of my sight. Then I closed my eyes. But in the dark behind my eyelids people fell, turning over in the air, breaking. Or worse, lay in hospital beds, preferring sleep to life.

Bright had said nothing. I turned my head. His face hung in sadness, his mouth

321

slack. He didn't drive like Thomas in rigid concentration. You felt the car react to the slightest pressure of his will, that he and the car were one. Yet his mind seemed elsewhere. Far away.

'You're awake then, Miss Wren.'

'I wasn't sleeping.'

'No.'

The car sped on.

'You brought no luggage,' he said.

'No.'

'Travelling light.'

'I have no luggage.'

'Oh shit. Of course.'

'I left my luggage with Thomas.'

'Probably a good idea.'

'You think so?'

'Shed your luggage every now and then.'

'Mmm.'

'That mean England after Copenhagen?'

'Why does everybody want to know what I'm going to do next?'

'Well... You know. Concern, Miss Wren.'

'I'll see.'

'A-ha. Okay.'

White walls, white light, high narrow white bed. The mother sat by the bed as she had by the big stove, knitting clutched in her hand. Sven sat hunched, head hanging, I thought in sleep until I reached the bed. But his eyes were wide, their whites yellowish. He looked iller than Luise whose weak breath came and went, freckled face pale as the pillow. The mother looked at me.

'No change?' I whispered.

She shook her head.

'Sven, I have something.'

I unwrapped the horse from its blanket. Sven's hands came out slowly. He examined the horse.

'Bo?' he said.

'Bo.'

He sat for a while with the horse in his hands. Then he coughed. He said, 'Luise.' He leaned over her. 'Luise.' He went on speaking. As he talked he placed the horse on her chest. He lifted one of her hands then the other, and placed them on the horse. He guided her hands all over the horse, but when he let go they dropped back, limp. He tried for a long time, always replacing her hands on the horse, holding them there, talking. But when he didn't hold them there they slid away. The horse lay on her chest. Her hands lay on the coverlet, inert.

He stood and went to the window. There was only darkness out there.

I could hardly think that I was the only person Luise had entrusted with her secret. But it was possible. I hesitated, feeling an intruder, presumptuous. I said to the mother, 'May I?'

I went to Luise's bed, stroked her hair back from her forehead. I knelt and put my mouth close to her ear. I whispered. 'Luise? It's Jen. I've brought your horse. He's well again. He's all one. It's Thomas. Your horse, Thomas. Thomas Horse. He's all well. He's good. He's mended. Bo mended him. Horse name Thomas. Thomas, your horse. He's okay, he's good, good. He's come back. He's here.' My words were no good, they were English words. 'Sven,' I said. 'Tell her in Danish Thomas is mended, please. Tell her he's mended and is good again. Bo has made him good.'

Sven was not looking at me but at Luise.

Her hands moved, feeble at her sides. The fingers lifted like butterflies trembling above a leaf. Sven gently placed them on the horse. They wavered like blind things in the air. He placed the small fingers round the horse. Luise whimpered. The mother's knitting dropped. Luise's eyelids fluttered. Sven took his hands away and we watched Luise's hands move over the horse like blind hands, learning it. There came a point when the hands seemed to recognise, began to caress, first tentative, then firm. Then both hands brought the horse close to her face and she opened her eyes. She lifted the horse and looked at it. She rubbed it against her cheek. She said, 'Thomas,' like a sigh. Then she turned on her side, brought her knees up, and cradling the horse between knees and chin, went back to sleep.

Half an hour later she woke, saw the horse, said 'Thomas' again, sat up, saw the horse's blanket where I had dropped it on the bed, reached for it, wrapped the horse in it carefully, and placed it under her arm. She sat back and looked at us. She said something in Danish to her grandmother, who poured orange juice, which Luise drank as a desert rain, then held out her glass for more.

Chapter Twenty-Four

Narrow cobbled streets. Antique shops, book shops, three steps below street level. Pubs with scrubbed wood floors and tables. People sitting round the tables. Restaurants with bright lights. Lights for the light. I was light. Light of foot, light of brain, moving in John Bright's wake, will-less, thought-less.

'It comes recommended,' he said.

Van Gogh's *L'Arlésienne* in a green frame. Lace curtains on brass poles across the bottoms of the windows. Cotton table cloths, red, yellow, green, black, thick yellow Provençale crockery. People, warmth, light. Where was I?

'Christ.' Bright squinted at me. 'You need a drink.'

'And delicious smells,' I said.

'Can I get you something to drink?' The nice brown-haired woman wore spectacles, and a red cotton napkin tucked in the side of her immaculate apron.

'You certainly can, love.'

Her English was immaculate too. She gave him a reserved smile. I sipped the golden wine while Bright ordered. I might come back to life. As Luise had. As Thomas would not.

'It's called The Provençale,' Bright said.

'Well, you could knock me down with a feather.'

'Oh, I see. You're waking up.'

'Recommended by whom?'

'Danish detective. Mate of mine. Name of Knudsen. Likes good food.'

'Do you?'

'One of my hobbies.'

'And mine.'

The nice woman brought our first course on the earthy yellow plates. Delicious garlic scents wreathed us round like smoke.

'The menu is small,' he said. 'But deep, know what I mean?'

Awaiting the next course, wine slipping down like silk, he said, 'Love him, then, did you? Peterson.'

I didn't answer for a while. Then I said, 'I thought I did. I wanted to, you see. But how can you love a person you don't know? I didn't know him at all. So it could never have been real.'

'That make it better? Or worse?'

'I feel stupid. And wicked. That I allowed myself to be tricked. That I failed. But it would be worse if it had been a real love. Surely. Even worse.'

'A-ha.'

'Why do you want to know?' I said. 'How I feel?'

I watched his face. It was the stillest face I'd ever seen, yet it revealed much, in gleams and glimpses. I remembered then. 'You'd know more about this than I,' I said.

His eyes sharpened. I had the sensation of being stabbed, as when I'd met him first.

'Oh, I'm sorry,' I floundered. 'I shouldn't have— It must be the wine.'

'It's okay.' He rubbed his forehead with an awkward gesture. 'Got to talk about it sometime. You put it off. It's only words, but—'

The brown-haired woman brought the second fragrant course. I thought the subject dropped, but later he said, 'My case is complicated by the fact that she—that—Millie—is quite likely to be swanning round the world somewhere still alive.'

'I'm sorry. I thought she—'

'Her note said she would.'

'But—'

'No body was found.'

'But—'

'Millie was a trickster. High class. No way I'll ever know.'

'So you can't even mourn.' Did I remember Thomas saying that? About Elizabeth?

'That's right. Got it in one, Miss Wren. She did it to save my career. Ironic, isn't it? As I may never go back to being a copper again.'

'What are you doing now?'

'Eh?'

'Why did you come out here?'

'Oh. Well. That's personal.'

'How?'

'Well...Reg Grant, the bloke at Epping, is an old mate. And then the James and Margot connection. And I met the guy, see? Peterson, I mean. I was intrigued. And then, I mean, well... There was you.'

'Me?'

'Well, I knew you.'

'I see.'

We looked at each other.

'Yeah, well. I felt kind of responsible.'

'How?'

'Well.' He drank some wine. 'It was me got the file reactivated, you know.'

'You?'

'A-ha.'

'You.'

'It was your aunt dying that did it. It didn't feel right. I couldn't ignore the feeling. Kept thinking about it. Asked my mate Grant could I poke about a bit. Unofficially, you know. Had time on my hands. Made a change from pushing my old mum round South Norwood. Pruning the roses. Kept me occupied. Got me off the booze a bit too. Taking over a bit, it was, the sauce. Does that quite fast, given half a chance. And I gave it more than half a one. Don't remember being sober much, from Millie's—little note—for nearly a year. Christ. Don't remember anything else much either. You saved me from a fate just a shade less permanent than death, Miss Wren.'

He raised his glass. The candle flame, and I, were reflected in wine. My mouth being dry, I couldn't speak. He drank and put the glass down.

'Well, I unearthed enough odd things to

justify reactivating the file. I tried to warn you, didn't I? Trouble was, every time I met Petersen I changed my mind. The guy was so dependable. He was so—simple. But then you disappeared and no one knew where. Look, shall I save this till another time?'

I shook my head.

'I didn't find out about the other man till after you'd gone.'

'Other man?'

'The one Elizabeth was seeing.'

'Oh no? Thomas said she—chose to leave him. I didn't know what he meant.'

'Yep. He worked in the estate agent's next to the hairdresser's where her friend worked. The friend didn't know. No one knew. I go into the estate agent's one day on the off chance. I find out one of the blokes was away the weekend Elizabeth disappeared. He comes back after the weekend, but he's not all that well. The day I go in he still looks a bit on the grey side, you know, even though it's months later. Face doesn't go with the natty suit. So I put a little bit of pressure on. Next thing we're out the back of the pub and he's throwing up. Spilling more than the chicken-in-a-basket too. Sorry.'

'So Thomas didn't kill Eliz—'

'Don't get your hopes up, love. The

330

estate agent bloke's got a proper alibi. He's married. Natch. This thing between him and Elizabeth was a big deal. In love, all that. He's going to leave his wife. Elizabeth's going to leave Thomas. That weekend he takes his wife away to break the news. People at the hotel remember them well. Well, the estate agent chickened. Never told his wife. But I guess Elizabeth told Thomas.'

'Oh, God.'

'The estate agent couldn't come forward, you see. Didn't want to be suspected. And didn't want the wife to find out. Not a hero, this bloke, to put it mildly. I promised his name wouldn't come into it if he agreed to a DNA test. Didn't have to push him too hard. Then we started digging in the forest. She wasn't all that far away from the house. And not all that deep. In some brambles. Good ground cover, brambles.'

The proprietress came to collect the plates. Bright asked for another bottle of wine. She suggested a dessert wine. They held a serious discussion. I waited. I tried to prepare myself. He poured the last of the Château Simone. Drank. Rubbed his face with a square small hand that reminded me again of Bo.

'Well. There was no doubt. The DNA was all Peterson. You only need a hair,

331

you know, to check. Well...' he looked at me. 'I had one.'

I looked at my hands on the table cloth. I wondered when Thomas had decided on me. Before Elizabeth told him about the other man or after? If she hadn't told him, would he ever have—? And I decided to stop wondering. For now.

'You said something about my aunt—' I couldn't continue.

'Yeah. Look, it's only speculation but... The neighbour—Mrs Bowyer?—saw a man at the back door the day before your auntie died. Not the doc, that's for sure. We never found out who he was, but we can guess. And she seemed to be over the flu by then, so the relapse was funny. And then her death isolated *you,* you see, like the death of Elizabeth's folks isolated her. It made you vulnerable. More dependent on him. I don't know. It was just a feeling I had, that's all. And then... Well, Reg told me something else: Elizabeth's parents died after she met Thomas, but before she married him. See?'

I put my hands over my face.

'I'm a tactless bugger, I shouldn't have mentioned any of this, But the truth is the truth. I mean, how can I put it? Well... Once you know the truth, you can't discover anything worse. See what I mean?'

'How would he have—done it?'

'Your aunt? Plenty of stuff you can get. Put a bit of strain on the heart. Not so hard to come by.'

'How can I find out?'

'Have her dug up.'

He looked at me. I looked back.

'Thought you wouldn't fancy that,' he said.

'I wish Aunt Jess to remain in peace.'

I got up and found my way to the tiny lavatory. I bathed my face. I tidied my hair. I looked at the person in the mirror. She was a stranger. Perhaps she always would be from now on. Perhaps it's right that the person in the mirror should always be a stranger. Perhaps I might even get to like this stranger, in time.

Bright gave me the look I was coming to recognise as a smile: 'I ordered *Iles Flottantes*,' he said. 'That all right?'

They were as sublime as the wine, subtle implosions in the mouth.

He said to the brown-haired woman, 'Tell the chef he's a genius, love.'

She gave him a smile, grave but a touch less reserved. 'I think my husband knows that, but I'll tell him just the same.'

'You see'—I had to explain—'I trusted Thomas. Completely. I didn't fall in love with him. I fell in trust.'

'Trust is the mother of deceit.'

I stared at him. 'What?'

'Where you most trust, you can be most deceived.'

'That's a chilling thought.'

He shrugged. 'Just fact.'

'And you see'—I had to make him understand—'I wanted a husband so much. I really needed a husband.'

'Necessity'—he slipped me a look—'is the mother of disaster.'

I groaned.

We gazed past each other, sipping the wine, the taste of the *Iles Flottantes* faintly lingering with it on the tongue. The place was still full of people, the sound of Provençale folk songs not loud but raw. I'd remember this little restaurant always as a haven of good things. Of life and peace. Of hope, even, perhaps.

'Come back.' Bright's voice.

I focused on him.

'What now?' he said.

'Now I try to trust myself. Depend on myself. I have decisions to make.'

'What decisions?'

'Well.' I paused. 'There's my job. There's my house.'

'Why should they change?'

'Well...' I raised my chin. 'I seem to like—Denmark rather a lot.'

'A-ha!' The small brown eyes glinted like blades in the candle light. 'They're a nice family,' he said. 'If a family is what you want. If you wanted a ready made daughter you'd go a long way to find anything handier than that little cracker with the pigtails.'

I slapped the table, to my surprise though not, I suspected, to his.

'Don't get cross, *Miss* Wren!'

'Don't call me that.'

'Okay.'

'My name's Jen.'

'Okay.'

'And if I wanted a daughter, it's not totally impossible that I could have one of—' I stopped.

'What?' He screwed up one eye, looked at me straight with the other. I swallowed and looked straight back.

'I think I might be pregnant,' I said.

He laughed. A short sharp sound I hadn't heard before. He nodded.

'A-ha.'

Now I had spoken the word I dared to believe it, for the first time. The thing I had wanted most in the world and had hardly ventured to hope for.

'And you're going to have this kid, are you? Going to go through with it? Things run in families, you know. You're not worried that it might turn out like—'

'Like Thomas? No. I'm not. I'll make sure of that.'

'I was going to say, like Bo.'

'What's wrong with Bo?'

We laughed.

'Yeah, you could do worse.' He poured the last of the dessert wine. 'So what you're thinking is, you might give up your nice little job, sell your nice little house, have your nice little baby, bring it back to Denmark and give it to nice Sven Peterson. And all live happily ever after in Goltrup Vicarage.'

'Sven? Oh, you couldn't be wronger. For one thing he looks too much like Thomas. For another thing he doesn't interest me in that way at all.'

'In that way, huh?'

'And for another thing, I believe he's spoken for. And for another thing—'

'There's another thing?'

'The last thing on earth—'

'Oh, the last thing on earth is the other thing?'

'Yes. The last thing on earth I want—and it's all in the future anyway, I have to go back home, I have to wait and see—but whatever happens—' I drained my glass to the dregs and placed it firmly on the table '—the last thing on earth I want is a husband,' I said.